PRISM

Volume 2

Brandon Cruz
Illustration by Mici Villalpando

Printed in the United States of America

ISBN 978-1-7331362-5-9

First Printing, 2023

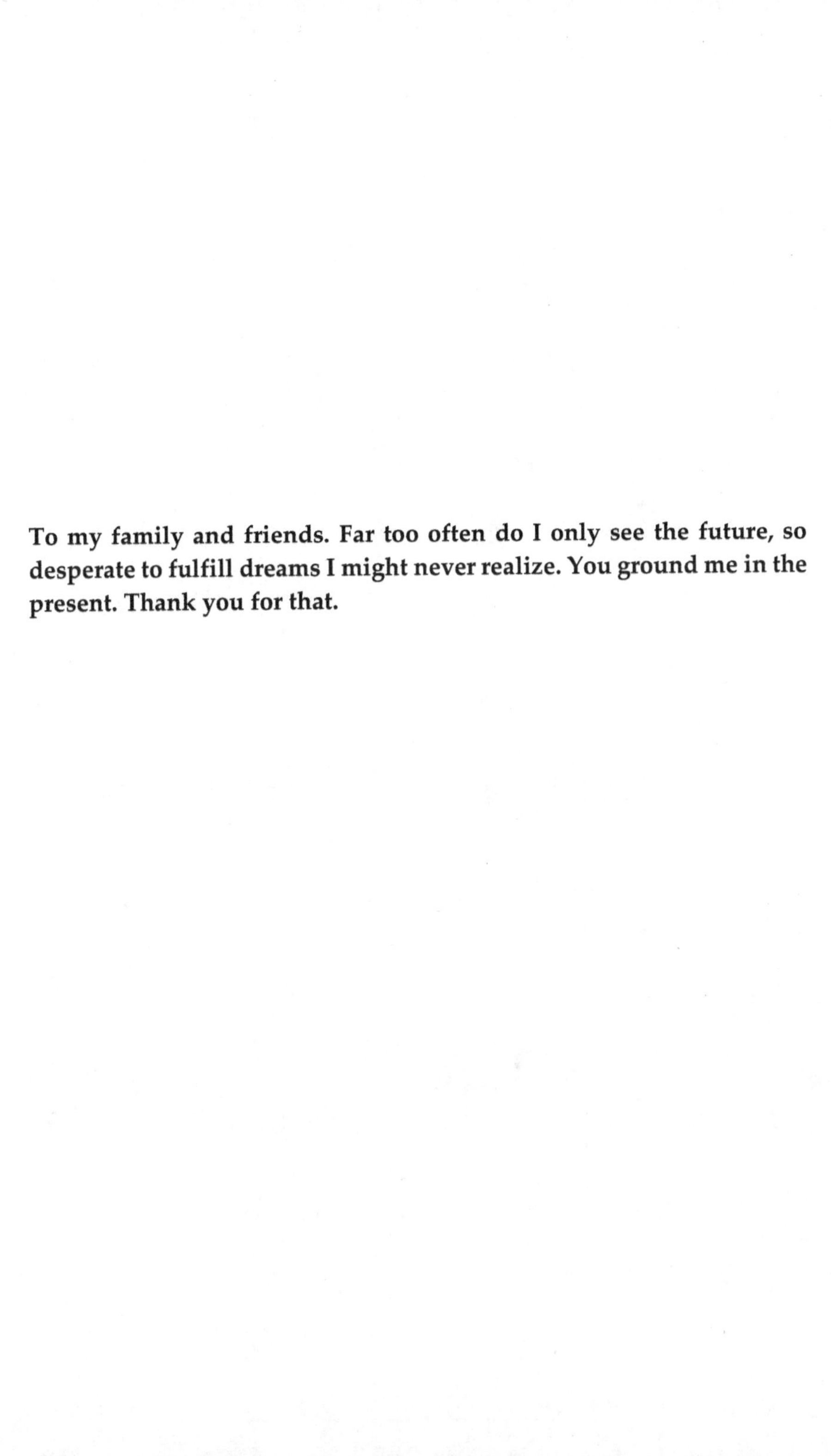

To my family and friends. Far too often do I only see the future, so desperate to fulfill dreams I might never realize. You ground me in the present. Thank you for that.

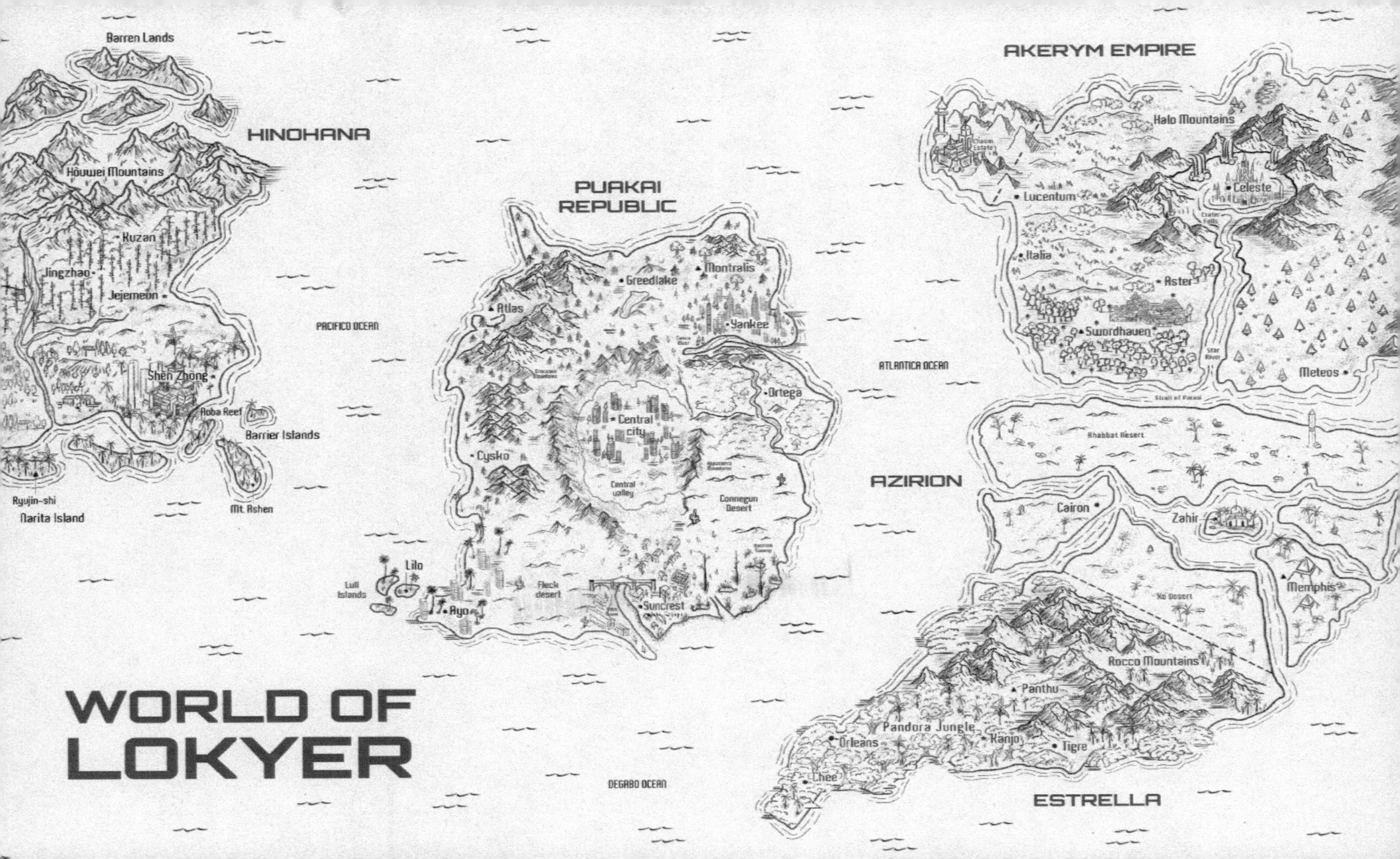
WORLD OF
LOKYER
HINOHANA
Barren Lands
Houwei Mountains
Kuzan
Jingzhao
Jejemeon
Shen Zhong
Aoba Reef
Barrier Islands
Mt. Ashen
Ryujin-shi
Narita Island
PACIFICO OCEAN
PUAKAI
REPUBLIC
Atlas
Greedlake
Montralis
Yankee
Ortega
Central
city
Central
valley
Cysko
Connegun
Desert
Fleck
desert
Suncrest
Ayo
Lilo
Luli
Islands
DEGABO OCEAN
ATLANTICA OCEAN
AKERYM EMPIRE
Halo Mountains
Lucentum
Celeste
Italia
Aster
Swordhaven
Star
River
Meteos
Strait of Paraoi
Khabbat Desert
AZIRION
Cairon
Zahir
Memphis
Xo Desert
Rocco Mountains
Panthu
Pandora Jungle
Orleans
Kanjo
Tigre
Chee
ESTRELLA

Prologue: Discord

An arrow of fire whizzed past Dalton's face as he barreled through the sand. He spun around a pillar of water that erupted from the calm ocean water to his left, and jumped over a crescent of strong wind from his right.

I'm feeling good today! Dalton thought.

****

The team just finished the final exam and enjoyed each other's company in a shawarma shop at Dalton's request when the Dean barged in and announced they'd all be living together in a new dorm.

"Huh?" they all asked.

"That's right, this spring semester I want you all to act like normal high school students and stop getting into trouble! I understand that's somehow hard for you all, but I'm sure you'll manage."

"Wait, why is this happening all of a sudden?" Monty asked.

"Because of you and Dalton at first," the Dean answered. "But now all of you are on Penumbra's radar, so I'd rather you be somewhere more accessible to me."

"I... guess that makes sense actually," Paige sighed.

"Oh, and to make sure you all turn into more normal high school students, you will be required to participate in this year's Azure Festival. Atlas is a coastal city after all!"

That got tired looks from the group except for Amy, who looked relieved.

"Oh, come on! The Azure Festival is so much fun! You get prom, carnival games, student skits and activities, a parade, the whole city is lit up during the Azure Festival! Anyway, you don't have a choice. Just enjoy your youth! It'll go by in a flash!"

****

Present Day...

And so, a month after their final exam and living together in the dorm, they were given their next assignment. It was seven o'clock in the morning in a nearly empty Tran-Zip station. Their sleep schedules in shambles, slumped in their chairs, they shivered, waiting for their teacher to arrive.

"I h-h-hate you…" Clara cursed. "I hate you b-b-both…"

The girls hugged themselves, huddling in their hoodies while Paige was turtling in his parka. Meanwhile, Monty and Dalton stood comfortably, dressed in t-shirts and boardshorts. Sagittarius told them they were going to the beach, but an Atlas morning is still cold.

"We all went on the same mission last month, right?" Monty asked. "You guys should be used to the cold by now."

"I hate the cold…" Clara muttered. "Fire and ice magic isn't fair…"

"Monty… give me some of your coffee," Amy groaned.

Monty walked around with a thermos and poured coffee into cups.

"Ah, thank gods, you are good for something," Clara said.

"Thank you, but… why didn't you pour this out sooner?" Elizabeth asked.

Monty smiled innocently with a sparkle in his eyes, "I wanted to see how long you guys would suffer before asking for some."

"You're such a meanie!" Amy pouted.

"Look at you, all huddled together like penguin-seals," Sagittarius laughed. "Good morning, everybody!"

"Morning," they all replied half-heartedly.

"Damn! You all seem tired! It's only seven!"

The students all groaned and rolled their eyes.

"Aw, boohoo! Let's get going, or we're going to miss our Tran-Zip. Once you get the Ayo sun on your skin, you'll wake up!"

They traveled to a beautiful beach with golden sand, tide pools, and adjacent to a thirty-meter headland bluff. Not so far away was a small island that, with the low tide, can be walked to from the shore. The weather was finally warm enough to shed their hoodies and not freeze to death.

"Today's goal is just practice at teamwork in a combat scenario. Your goal today is to get past my helpers and get me to move my feet."

"Helpers?" Elizabeth asked.

Sagittarius pointed with his chin and they turned around.

They looked out at the ocean to a double-hulled canoe with two people on it: a young man and a girl. The man looked to be in his early twenties with short, black, sun-bleached hair, a lean physique, defined muscles, and dark brown skin. "What's up, Sagi?!" the young man smiled as their canoe hit land, and his sharktooth Maui's hook necklace bounced against his black tank-top as he hopped off. The water made a splash as the man's yellow crocs hit the sand.

"Students, I want you to meet Pisces!" Sagittarius said.

An aquamarine oval opened up beside them, and another young man walked through. He had messy blonde hair, aquamarine eyes, a short-sleeved gray hoodie, and board shorts with skater shoes.

"Oh, and Aquarius."

"Sorry I'm late," Aquarius chuckled.

"Looks like your brother is rubbing off on you a little bit," the girl teased.

"Please don't say that again…" Aquarius sighed.

"Name's Nimbus!" the young man introduced.

"I'm Cloud! It's nice to meet you all," the girl smiled.

"And I'm Jiro. You may have met my older brother he uh… I think he subbed for Sagittarius at one point?"

A lightbulb went off in Dalton's head. "You're Taro's little bro!"

Jiro shivered at the title.

"Hey, you guys may have gotten casual with me, but they deserve your utmost respect. Zodiacs are the highest echelon of the Celestian Order! Get used to listening to us, cause even when you become Prestiges, we have higher authority than you."

"You can just call us by our names though," Jiro laughed.

"Especially us and Gemini," Cloud added. "It gets confusing when we just hear our Zodiac title."

"Wait, so like, do you guys just share a Relic or something?" Dalton asked.

"So, usually there's a single Relic that chooses who can wield it, but in the case of Gemini and Pisces, there are actually two Relics. The Pisces Relics are liberal with who they choose, while Gemini's Relics always choose siblings. In our case…" Cloud said.

Cloud shook her Oar, and Nimbus took off his necklace. With a lapis glow, the Maui's hook grew and transformed into a khopesh.

"I have my Oar, and he has his Hook. The Pisces before us were a couple before they were chosen. We just happen to be siblings."

"You see that small island just about fifty meters away?" Sagittarius pointed with his chin. "I will be standing there firing down arrows on you. Your goal is to make it past the Zodiacs, to that island, and make me move my feet. You can incapacitate them by making them move as well. They are not allowed to attack you if they're not in their initial position. Oh, and don't worry, they aren't allowed to use Amplification, but I wouldn't underestimate them. These three have known each other for most of their lives. I should know, I helped train them."

****

While team Prism huddled together, Sagittarius talked with Pisces and Aquarius. "Thank you guys for coming out, especially you, Jiro."

"Of course! There isn't much going on in Lull right now, so we're fine," Cloud said.

"No, it's fine, really," Jiro chuckled. "It's been a while since I've done something fun."

Meanwhile, Prism planned their attack. They watched as the Zodiacs got into position: Nimbus stood atop the headland to the right, Jiro stood among the tidepools to the left, Sagittarius stood in the center of the island, and Cloud stood on their canoe, anchored between the headland and the island.

"Okay, Pisces' specialty is the ocean and the wind," Paige explained. "So we can expect them to have some form of water or wind magic. Aquarius, I have no clue, but if he's like his brother, he'll have some teleportation ability that is useless here."

Paige strategized for a moment before continuing. "Okay, this isn't like the Sprawling Forest Mission. We want to prioritize offense over utility here. Monty and Dalton will go straight for the island to make Sagittarius move his feet. Me and Elizabeth will be with you for as long as she can stop time to give us that head start. From there, Dalton will make a staircase to the tide pools and the headland. Clara and Amy, you'll go right and take care of Pisces. Elizabeth, you got Aquarius. Keep them from helping Sagittarius."

Paige opened a pouch in his belt and took out a variety of talismans. He primed speed talismans with a piece of his aura, making the intricate drawings on the paper glow blue, and placed them on everyone's legs. He repeated the process with strength talismans on their backs, jump talismans on their lower backs, and finally shield talismans on their middle backs.

"Aight, everybody's all buffed out," Paige said. "Let's get ready to go."

"Everybody ready?!" Sagittarius boomed.

They all gave a thumbs up.

"Goooo!!!"

Elizabeth stopped time with Monty and Dalton holding her hands and Paige with a hand on her shoulder. Thanks to the speed talisman, they rushed forward and made it halfway to the island. The shallow water only reached slightly above their knees.

"Oh, what the heck? Did they teleport?" Nimbus wondered.

"Eh, well it was a nice try," Jiro thought aloud.

He extended a hand and visualized a portal in front of them. An aquamarine oval appeared in front and he opened another portal back to the beach. The four ran too fast to stop and rammed into Clara and Amy on the beach. All six fell down.

"Well..." Clara puffed the hair out of her eyes. "So much for his teleportation ability being useless."

"Yeh, yeh, change of plans," Paige groaned as he got up. "We need to take care of Jiro first."

Of course it couldn't be that easy, Paige cursed.

"Elizabeth, focus on getting Clara to Jiro while Monty, Dalton, and I keep going through the middle. He's gonna have to choose. Amy, keep your distance and keep prodding Nimbus and Cloud to use their magic."

"Sounds like a plan," Elizabeth said.

Okay, Paige, we got this. Don't stress out, just don't stress out. We did fine during the final exam... Paige thought.

"Aight! Round two people, let's get it!" Paige exclaimed and they ran forward.

Amy poured a little aura into her legs and jumped, the jump talisman letting her soar to the headland. She fired a barrage of feathers at Nimbus. Nimbus slashed with his khopesh and a gust of wind blew apart the feathers.

Amy turned to her team and shouted, "Nimbus uses wind magic!"

"That's not exactly correct!" Nimbus exclaimed.

Amy turned back and a gust of wind from a slash from his khopesh crashed against her. She grew wings and shielded herself. Caught off guard by the strength of the gale, she used a little more aura to create talons of shadow and rooted herself in place.

Meanwhile, Sagittarius opened fire and sent volley after volley of arrows at the students. Dalton created clones that sprinted ahead and made walls of ice that served as cover. Dalton created extra clones to help Clara and Elizabeth and Amy.

As the clones created staircases to their teammates, geysers of water erupted from the ground and caught them, turning them to slush.

"Looks like Cloud uses water magic!" Paige shouted.

Amy kept shielding herself from the strong gusts being thrown at her. One got through and slashed her shin, and then another, and another.

Just bear with it until he stops! At least he's not using it on them, Amy figured.

The wind suddenly stopped.

I gotta keep him occupied! Amy thought.

She dashed forward with all her might to try and catch him off guard, but this time, the speed talisman backfired on her. In front of her was a giant sea turtle made of clear water, coral, and rock with orange eyes. It was upright, balancing on the end of its shell which was being used as a shield. She nearly ran into it, but was able to react, jump, and flip over it.

Nimbus smiled and a tiny spark of yellow lightning flickered as he made a fist.

"Sorry in advance!"

Nimbus threw his punch and Amy went to block it. Her wings were obliterated and his knuckles drove into her forearms. She was blown backwards and sent flying off the other side of the headland and into the water. Her aura shield survived thanks to the shield talisman, but as she washed up onto a rock, her talismans fell off.

She pounded the rock in frustration. *Really?! No, I still have my aura shield, I can still do something!*

A portal of deep azure water surrounded by orange tribal sigils opened up underneath the giant turtle and it plunged into it before the portal closed.

Nimbus used a hand to shield his eyes from the sun as he watched for Amy. Once he saw she washed up on a rock, he let out a sigh of relief.

"I think I went a *little* bit too far..."

Dalton bobbed and weaved between pillars of water, crescents of wind and raining arrows with grace. Monty did his best to avoid using magic, but sometimes he couldn't help it, it was instinct. He'd occasionally create a small explosion in his hands to destroy incoming projectiles or to reposition himself to dodge.

I need to be careful, Monty cautioned himself, his right shoulder the only thing on his mind.

They were almost at the island thanks to Clara and Elizabeth keeping Jiro occupied. He used his portals to keep them running across the same space over and over again until Elizabeth stopped time and got them closer before he could react.

Elizabeth stopped time once more and threw Clara off the side of the tide pools. Time resumed and Clara threw a spear of lightning at Jiro, hoping to catch him off guard. He was able to react, and opened two portals: one to catch the projectile and the other to send it into the ocean.

"Whew! That was close!" Jiro said.

Uh-oh, Clara thought.

The lightning bolt hit the ocean and the electricity raced through the water and shocked all three of the boys. Clara plunged into the water with them.

"Cloud! Stop going easy on them!" Sagittarius shouted.

"Okay!"

Cloud extended more of her aura into the water and pushed it into the cove, unleashing a huge torrent. Dalton and the others were still recovering from the electric shock when the waves swept them up and spat them out back at their starting point. Elizabeth was soon to join them as Jiro forced her through a portal and sent her back to her team. Next, Cloud picked Amy up in a tube of water that carried her over the headland and plopped her on her feet next to her team. All of their talismans lost their glow and fell off their bodies.

Paige got back up and saw that the calm, shallow water that separated the beach from the island had transformed into a raging surf zone full of riptides.

Okay, that didn't work... Paige thought. *At least I know all of their magic now.*

"Okay, check this: boys go for Jiro and girls go for Cloud and Nimbus and then we meet on the island because going straight there ain't an option anymore," Paige said as he dispersed new talismans to everybody.

"Yeah, sure, good plan Paige," Dalton said. "But uh, I think I'll pass this time."

"Dalton," Paige shook his head. "Don't pull a you right now."

"Oh, I'm pulling a *me*," Dalton smiled.

Time to show these people that they need me, Dalton thought.

"Dalton, you can't take on three Zodiacs by yourself. I don't care if you think you're hot shit," Paige insisted.

"Paige, just let him," Elizabeth sighed.

"You know what? I hope you all brought some popcorn because the Dalton Show is about to begin."

"Pfft," Monty snickered.

Dalton took that as his starting pistol and ran forward with no talismans. The others followed suit, sticking to Paige's plan. As Clara raced forward, memories of the Sprawling Forest flashed through her mind.

I wasn't even able to fight to the end... I need to—no, I can do more! she thought.

As they approached Nimbus, they were confronted with tentacles of water that came up from the sides of the headland. Clara zapped them into steam while Elizabeth and Amy fired bolts and feathers at Nimbus.

Nimbus dropped his khopesh into a portal formed at his feet. He yanked upward and the turtle returned with the khopesh in its mouth. Its shell blocked all of the projectiles and Amy clicked her tongue.

If I could just use light magic I could obliterate that shell! she cursed. *No, I can do it with just my shadows!*

Amy rushed forward and went for a high-speed drop kick, her legs wrapped in her shadow and spun like a drill. She drilled into the shell for a couple of seconds to no avail.

Just how tough is this thing?!

Amy jumped off and the turtle began to move. Nimbus heaved the turtle around like a wrecking ball and Elizabeth stopped time, knowing his intention.

She touched Clara, who threw a spear of lightning at Nimbus. Time resumed and it was a direct hit, but Nimbus tanked it and followed through with his swing, batting Amy away and hurling the turtle at Elizabeth and Clara.

Not again! Amy cursed.

She created wings of shadow and started to glide back when she was blindsided by a tentacle of water and sent flying into the ocean.

Oh, come on!

Enough of this, I got it! Clara thought.

She quickly pulled an arcade coin out of her pocket and tossed it up in the air as she and Elizabeth jumped over the creature. Clara was able to fire her Railgun before her limbs were captured by the tentacles of water, holding her suspended in air.

"Woah!" Nimbus exclaimed before the shot hit him in the gut and sent him flying into the water.

Cloud turned her focus to her brother, releasing Elizabeth from her constraints in order to catch Nimbus and create a strong current to send him back up onto the headland. Clara wasn't having any of it. She zapped apart her constraints and sprinted over to the edge with a fist and slammed Nimbus in the head, sending him back down.

"Now how do we get over?" Clara wondered.

Between them and the island was a raging ocean with tentacles of water ready to catch them. Suddenly, a wall of ice erupted in front of them, providing a pathway to the island. They both looked over at Dalton, who was slowly making his way across the waves, creating platforms of ice under his feet as he stepped and freezing the waves temporarily. He gave them a thumbs up and a wink.

Don't feed his ego, they thought tiredly and continued on with no reaction.

Seriously, am I just losing my touch or something? Dalton wondered. *I'm telling you that I'm reliable!*

On the other side, Paige and Monty made their way across the tidepools and once he was within distance, Monty activated his Eye and put Jiro into an illusion. His right shoulder pulsed with pain and he nearly collapsed, his Eye instantly deactivating.

"Monty, you good?" Paige asked, catching him before he fell.

"Yeah, I just slipped," Monty chuckled. "He's in an illusion, don't touch him."

They continued forward and Monty's attention was even more focused on his right shoulder. *It's worse than I thought, but I can't let Amy find out! I need to show her I'm fine!*

Cloud finally grew tired of controlling such large amounts of water and fell on her butt, panting. *I'm done. It was fun, but I'm done.*

Monty and Paige continued across the tide pools when they were met by a volley of arrows. Monty incinerated them with an arc of fire, but Paige had nothing to protect himself with. A group of white arrows froze him in a cocoon of ice.

I could break out of this, but only if I sacrifice my arms… Paige thought. *This is a practice at the end of the day.*

"Go!" he shouted to Monty.

Monty, Dalton, Clara, and Elizabeth all finally landed on the island with Sagittarius, which was flat for the most part with vegetation sprouting across it. They flanked him, each of them blasting him with everything they had.

Their hearts sank when a portal opened in front of them. Jiro had broken out of his illusion thanks to Nimbus slapping him hard in the shoulder to see if he was okay.

Elizabeth was presented with two options as she stopped time: she could make Sagittarius move or she could use it to save Clara from taking the full brunt of their attacks. Dalton was in a slightly better position to save Clara, but…

He won't make it, Elizabeth thought. *Plus, he's probably just thinking about taking all of the glory of making Sagittarius move.*

Elizabeth chose to save Clara and pushed her out of the way. She braced herself to take the attack, but there was Dalton, blocking it with a shield of ice. Her eyes went wide with surprise while Dalton's were filled with dismay.

"I had it…" he muttered.

Clara meanwhile, jumped out from the cover of the shield with a spear of lightning readied, but was met with an arrow made of red light and flames.

Surely Lava Brain can get him, right? she thought.

She looked past Sagittarius and saw Monty falling to the ground, his face contorted with pain and his hand on his right shoulder.

Clara hurled a tomahawk of lightning as she was blown back by the arrow to her stomach. As she fell to the ground, she watched her tomahawk sail slightly off mark, and dissipate in the distance.

"Cloud! Stop being lazy!" Sagittarius angrily shouted.

A moment later, a large wave washed over the island and spat them back onto the beach. Sagittarius came over on the canoe with the rest of the Zodiacs.

Uh oh, he's pissed, Cloud thought.

"What was that?!" Sagittarius snapped. "This should have been *way* easier than the final exam! So what happened?!"

The six were silent. They had no response.

It's not my fault, Dalton thought. Although, he knew if he said that he'd get yelled at.

"It's my fault," Amy said. "I totally could've done more but... I... I just need to train more." She was too afraid to look up from the ground.

"No, it's my fault," Paige said. "I'm the leader, I didn't lead. I failed us."

I can't use magic, so I need to make up for it with brains. If I don't have those, I'm even less than nothing! Paige thought. *I guess the final exam was just a fluke...*

"Maybe if Dalton followed the plan..." Clara muttered.

"No!" Paige snapped before anyone could retort. "I lost his respect as the leader. That's my fault, not his."

No one but Paige thought it was his fault.

I could've done more... Even if Lava Brain choked at the end, I had to get saved again! Clara thought. *Never again...*

Monty just looked at his right hand, which was still trembling from the pain. Just how dire his situation sunk in. *Just how long can I keep this up?*

Sagittarius saw the defeated look on his students' faces. "Really? That's it?" He clicked his tongue. "Mozaveen! Take over before I bust an arrow in somebody's ass!" he roared as he stormed away.

They followed him with their eyes to their Dean, who was watching a distance away.

"Dean Mozaveen, what're you doing here?" Elizabeth asked.

"Well, I came to see my favorite students," he smiled. "Aquarius, Pisces, please calm Sagittarius down."

"It's fine, we were going to go eat anyway," Nimbus assured.

"Hey, I mean, I had fun," Jiro said as they walked away.

"There can be no victories without defeat," the Dean said. "Reflect on this moment. The answer to this dilemma must be found on your own. If we spell it out, you would just brush it off."

They sat on that, letting the sentence roll around in their heads for a minute before tossing it away like the Dean said they would.

****

Henry walked down the broken pathway, surrounded by the stars and the green alpines of the Croconoa Mountain range. He came into contact with a worn-out metal fence, and he knew he was close. Squirrelmunks scrambled around him, diving into bushes or going up trees.

About a kilometer away was a manor, the scheduled meeting place. It used to be owned by the Bernardino Asterium Company, but it was now taken over by overgrowth and signum. The paint was beginning to chip, and the vines grew past their trellises.

Henry walked up the steps and entered through the giant hole in the wall next to the large double doors. The inside was vacant and dusty.

"You're late," a deep voice growled. "Everyone is late."

"No, you're early Mark," Henry insisted. "The First told us to meet here at precisely one o'clock a.m. pacifico standard time."

The man emerged from the shadows and into the moonlight. He looked like a silhouette with his lean build, long legs, and dark skin. He checked his watch.

"Shit," he cursed. "I was still on Yankee time..." He scratched his short and scraggly hair.

"That's a shame," Henry shrugged.

"Hello boys," a girl's voice said.

The two looked up and saw the Seventh drop down from the ceiling. She wore a jean jacket, high-top sneakers, and her frizzy brown hair was tied back into a ponytail with a neon green tie. She wore a black coughing mask with neon Dia de los Muertos designs on it. Filters were on each side of the mask.

More footsteps were heard behind them as the rest of the Mafia Wings came in. All except the First, the Second, and of course, the Eighth.

"Let's hurry this up shall we?" the Fourth yawned. "I'm very tired."

It was true. Paired with his puffy black bedhead and his patchy beard, he looked like a phantom. He even wore a purple jacket to go with the whole outfit.

"It's quite rare for the First to assemble all of us in person," Henry remarked.

"It's obviously about you and your father's failure Henry," the Fifth said.

"Still reading minds are we?" Henry smiled. *Piece of shit...*

"You can drop dead for all I care," the Fifth replied calmly, having heard Henry's thoughts.

They moved to the dining room and gathered around the table.

"Thank you all for coming on such short notice," a voice emanated from the dark.

The rest of the Wings turned their heads to see the First's eyes, peering through the darkness. They glowed green, full of life that wasn't his.

“Where is Damian?” the Fifth asked. “He hasn’t been in touch for a year now.”

“The Second is currently with the Aragami in Hinohana, he is not needed tonight. I gathered you here regarding our friend, Daniel, the Eighth. Henry, he’s *your* father, what’s your plan?”

Henry gave a wicked smile. “It’ll go a little something like this…”

1: Normal School

The new dorm was two stories tall and stood near a park surrounding a large pond in Northwest Atlas and a five minute dash from Sagittarius' house. The bottom floor consisted of a common area, equipped with a study, a kitchen, a living room, two bathrooms—one for the boys and one for the girls, and a recreational room with ping pong, billiards, and exercise equipment. On the second floor were six rooms, with the girls' rooms on one side of the dorm and the boys' on the other half.

With their spring semester starting tomorrow, Sagittarius visited the dorm, and the students sat around him in their pajamas, ready to listen.

"Alright, school's starting back up tomorrow, so we're going over you're guys' classes," Sagittarius said.

"Wait, what about the classes we chose?" Dalton asked.

"Sorry Dalton, but those easy classes you picked aren't gonna fly."

"Huh? Why not?"

"Your aura is like a muscle. The more you use it, the stronger it gets. By training and using powerful attacks over and over again, your body gets used to it and can use aura more efficiently. Those with bigger aura reservoirs often have a harder time being more efficient than those with smaller ones. By doing this, you can strengthen both your magic attacks and the boosts to your physical attacks with aura.

"However, strength alone is not going to work against stronger opponents. You need to be able to maximize the utility of your magic. Clara is a perfect balance. She's studied the physics of her magic, and now she can blast people with coins launched at Mach speed. It is only because she studied Lorentz forces and applied them correctly. It took a lot of practice and hard work I assume?"

Clara chuckled nervously, "Yeah."

"My point is: you can strengthen your attacks by just practicing. But to truly utilize magic to help you in different situations, you need to understand it. Any questions?"

The six shook their heads.

Sagittarius gave a nod. "Good. Starting tomorrow you're all being enrolled in college-level classes. Dalton, your classes will be focusing on mechanical engineering, thermodynamics, and physiology."

That caught Dalton's attention. "Wait? What? Why?!"

"Ugh, do you have a brain in that skull of yours?" Monty groaned.

"Huh? Run that by me again?!"

"Oh, wait, I'm sorry! You don't, do you?" Monty gasped sarcastically.

Paige sighed. "Dalton, if you understand how something is built or understand how an organism works, your creations become stronger, and you can build more with your ice. Got it?"

"There's no backing out of this, Dalton. Just do your best," Sagittarius chuckled.

Dalton sank back in his seat, horrified upon hearing that his schedule would be loaded.

"Monty, you'll be taking pyrotechnics and thermodynamics classes. Amy, you'll be in an optics class," Sagittarius continued to explain. "Clara, Elizabeth, and Paige, because you've either taken proficient steps to utilize your magic or because of the unique nature of your magic, I trust you will schedule your classes effectively. I want you all to take at least one college-level class. Aight, that's it. Get some sleep tonight."

****

The boys decided to play some billiards when their conversation began that night.

"So," Dalton began. "We need to address the giraffellant in the room." He fired a shot and broke.

"What?" Paige asked as Dalton put a ball in.

"The Azure Festival is in two months, and there's no way in hell I'm going single. Before we begin our plot to woo the girls into being our dates, we need to make sure there's no love triangles. I, personally, like Elizabeth."

"Pfft," Monty scoffed. "You mean you like Elizabeth's *looks*."

"No! That's not it, although that is a big part of it," Dalton stuttered. "Look, she's not the most open woman, and I want to get to know her better. In fact, I daresay she's the most closed-off one in the group. You've been getting better, I've noticed."

"I don't feel like I've been becoming more open," Monty shrugged before missing a shot.

"Yeah, sure," Dalton laughed. He looked over at Paige, and they shared a nod.

"It's not a bad thing, Monty," Paige noted. "In fact, it's a lot healthier than just bottling everything up." *Hypocrite,* Paige thought to himself. *I still can't tell them that I feel inferior... They wouldn't understand anyway.*

"Anyway," Dalton said as he casually put another ball in.

"Damn it, stop being good," Paige cursed.

Dalton giggled mischievously. "*Anyway,* Monty, who do you like?"

"I—"

"Before you say, 'I don't like anyone.' I'd like to guess: it's Clara."

Monty gave a sharp glare to Dalton's face, which had a huge grin on it. He gave up. "Yeah, I like Clara."

"Boom. Easy. Paige that leaves you with Amy because, let's face it buddy, it's been pretty obvious for a couple years now."

Paige was lining up a shot when Dalton said this and scratched so bad he nearly ripped the matting on the table. "Allah-Buddha-Jesus!" he cursed, massaging the part he nearly wrecked.

"Bingo?" Dalton smiled.

Paige looked over at Monty, who had a blank expression on his face. "N-no. I don't like Amy. I just see her as a friend," he chuckled nervously.

"Paige, it's fine if you like Amy," Monty chuckled.

"Huh?"

"You're not like Dalton. You're very nice and intelligent and dependable."

"Hey! I'm those things!"

"You mean flirtatious and lucky?" Monty countered. "Plus, I know Paige isn't the kind of man to lay a hand on my little sister, right?" Monty smiled and placed a hand on Paige's shoulder.

"Mhm!" Paige nodded. *Scary!*

"Then it's settled!" Dalton said. "We'll help each other with our respective crushes so that we all have a date to prom and girlfriends by the end of the year! We can all relate to each other, what with our shitty pasts and all. Nothing like shared trauma to connect two people, right?"

"I guess so," Paige agreed.

"Great!" Monty cheered half-heartedly. "We can all get rejected together!"

****

Amy woke up to the smell of food downstairs. She yawned and stretched. She was in a different room than usual, with none of her drawings hanging on the wall, none of her papers and clothes scattered across the floor. But the aroma of breakfast was the same.

Monty? she thought.

Amy opened her door and slid down the railing of the stairs. She did a little skip and entered the kitchen. The table was already set for six. Steaming hot bacon, scrambled eggs, sausages, spam, and fruit rested on each plate. Coffee was brewing in the pot, and tea was on the stove.

Monty watched the TV set up in the corner of the room near the ceiling. Dark circles surrounded his eyes. He wore his spring school uniform, which consisted of the usual slacks with a white polo t-shirt with the school insignia on the left sleeve. The pink apron Amy gave him as a birthday present was over it.

"Monty? You cooked all of this?" Amy asked.

Monty didn't look away from the TV. "Nope, you cooked it. You woke me up in the middle of the night with all the noise you made. I found you in here cooking..." Monty yawned. "In your sleep. Maybe it has something to do with your shadow?"

He's hiding something... Amy thought solemnly.

Monty got up from his seat and walked over to the coffee pot. "I'm joking, of course. Wake the others please, the food isn't going to stay warm forever."

Amy ran up the steps and called out for the others. "Hey guys, stop snoozing your alarms! Breakfast is ready! Hurry up, we gotta get to school!"

Elizabeth walked out already in uniform. Amy noticed her new piece of headwear.

"Elizabeth, is that a new beanie?" Amy asked with a smile. "It's cute."

She looked surprised, but only for an instant. As quick as it came, her expression reverted back to a smile. She stopped and said, "Why, thank you."

"Isn't it getting kinda hot for beanies, though?"

Elizabeth started walking again. "Not really. The heat doesn't bother me too much."

Elizabeth entered the kitchen and saw breakfast was already ready. "Monty, did you cook all of this?"

"Yeah, I made lunch for everyone too," he said.

"Oh, you don't have to do all of that yourself! I could have helped. I'm actually a pretty good cook!"

"No, it's okay. I don't doubt your cooking abilities, but I can handle it on my own. You don't need to waste your time with it."

"But it's not a waste of time. I insist!"

"Elizabeth!" Monty narrowed his eyes and then gave a smile. "It's fine."

"O-okay..." Elizabeth replied and took her seat.

The next was Paige. He wore his uniform, but his tie was loose, and the top of his shirt was unbuttoned. He was cleaning his glasses as he walked down the steps.

"Morning, Paige!"

"Morning, Amy. Aren't *you* energetic?"

Paige tripped on a step, and Amy caught him. Their faces were close, and both did their best to not blush. Paige was still blind and couldn't really make out Amy's face, but he could tell it was too close for comfort. After a second's pause, Amy helped Paige regain his balance.

"And aren't *you* clumsy?"

Paige chuckled out of embarrassment. "Nice catch."

Eventually all six sat down and got themselves comfortable. "Thanks for the food!" They chowed down while the news played in the background.

"More Wanari immigrants continue to flood into Suncrest City," the female anchor reported. "These families carry nothing but the clothes on their backs and hope for a better future in Puakai. More and more families flee the harsh conditions they face in the Akerymic colony in Estrella. Years of hard work and labor for a ferry across the Degabo Ocean."

The camera switched from the newsroom to clips of citizens of Suncrest City. "We need to put a quota," one man said. "Too many of these Wanari people are comin' in and takin' all the jobs around here. It's sad with what they have to go through, but if this keeps up, it's not just gon' be hard for them, it's gon' be hard for everybody."

It switched back to another man. "We need better border security. We don't know these peoples' backgrounds! They could be criminals, for all we know! Hell, aren't they supposed to be the bad guys? And now we're expected to help them? Well, which is it?"

Back to the anchor. "So far, Baron Fernando has refuted the claims of maltreatment."

Elizabeth stabbed her eggs hard with her fork. "Why don't they interview a Wanari?"

"What? You a Wanari sympathizer, Liz?" Dalton asked with his mouth full. He was wolfing his food down.

"Yeah, so what if I am?"

Dalton swallowed. "Nothing. Just curious."

The news switched to a clip of them interviewing a young man. His name was Thomas Bernardino. "Yes, we're currently reaching an agreement with Preston Shipping Co. Negotiations are still underway, but we expect to see a mutual agreement in the next month while we plan out something that can benefit both companies and, of course, the customer."

Clara clicked her tongue.

"With an asterium deposit having been recovered in recent efforts of the Magistracy and Chasm, the two companies hope to mine, refine, and ship the material in the coming years."

Clara pointed a finger and zapped the TV, turning it off. "Traitor," Clara grumbled.

"Hey, don't break the TV."

****

Monty and Dalton were late. Again.

They ran out of their new dorm and booked it to the nearest bus station. Dalton looked out his window at the river of cyclists next to them. Four lanes were designated for bicycles, which the students took full advantage of. Bike lockers were everywhere, and cars were few and far between.

"I shouldn't have waited for you," Monty grumbled.

"We're gonna be fine!" Dalton said as they ran. "I've been in these circumstances before. Besides, the teacher isn't gonna care if we're a couple of minutes late. I mean, it's the first day. We're probably just going over a syllabus."

Dalton said this while looking over his shoulder and didn't see he was stepping out into the street. A car's tires screeched, and Dalton quickly turned and shielded himself with his arms. Ice shot from his feet and created a wall in front of him. *SMASH!*

Dalton stood frozen for a second, taking everything in before turning to Monty, who was standing safely on the sidewalk. "Dude! You want to tell me when I'm stepping out into the street next time?!"

Monty blankly said, "I thought you would notice eventually."

"Eventually?! What if I got blindsided and my legs got taken out?"

Monty tilted his head with a confused look. "You're half-demon, aren't you? Don't you have faster healing abilities?"

"It still hurts!"

"Hey!" a boy shouted.

Monty and Dalton turned to a handsome man. He stepped out of his broken, fancy car. He scratched his blonde, wavy hair with anger. He wore the student uniform like everyone else did in the city.

"What were you thinking?" he asked. His voice had a cut-glass accent, signifying he was probably from Akerym.

"I was crossing the street. What did it look like?" Dalton said.

"What are you going to do about this?" he motioned to the smashed car and wall of ice.

"Nothing? Pedestrians have the right of way, don't they?" Dalton chuckled.

"Not when the light is red you imbecile!" he shook his head disapprovingly. "We're going to have to exchange Chirp IDs."

"Huh? Why?"

"You're going to pay for the damage to my car!"

"No, no, no, no. I don't got that kind of money man. If you're rich enough to afford a car, you're rich enough to repair it."

"That logic is absurd! Listen you *mole,* it was your fault for stepping out into the street unaware! It's your fault for ruining my car!"

"Who you calling mole? Frickin' *posh.*"

"The Puakian in front of me, who else?" the young man chuckled smugly.

The man was just a tad bit taller than Dalton, forcing him to look up slightly and it was pissing him off.

Dalton clicked his tongue. He took a deep breath. *If I let my emotions get the best of me, I'll end up transforming by accident. Plus, getting pissed is more of Monty's forte.*

"Mole or not, you still owe me," the young man said, walking up to Dalton and prodding his chest with a finger.

Dalton slapped the young man's hand away. "Fine, deal," Dalton grumbled. *Asshole…*

"Shake on it."

The two firmly shook hands and exchanged Chirp IDs. Afterward, the young man pulled his hand back and wiped it on his pants before putting it in his pocket. "I'll be contacting you later, Dalton."

"Come on Dalton, we're gonna be late!" Monty urged.

"Yeah, let's go."

****

Amy, Paige, Clara, and Elizabeth sat in the classroom, waiting for the teacher to show up while Monty and Dalton hurried through the crowded streets, passing several cafes, restaurants, barbershops, offices, all of which had mostly student employees.

The two hundred schools in Atlas were organized in location by their focus of study and by how new the buildings were. High school-level classes were the lowest level of education in the city and were located mostly in the Southwest District. Dalton passed by high school after high school until he found Franklin High.

The school looked like a tech business complex with a courtyard right outside the front gates. Large, tinted-glass windows made up a large portion of the outer walls.

Dalton and Monty finally reached the perimeter of the school with their indoor shoes in hand. The gate was similar to the rotating pegs you'd find at a Tran-Zip station. They simply walked up to it, and their Omnicards communicated to the machine that they had student IDs and were permitted inside with a flash of green.

Why isn't the Prestige Building this flashy? Dalton wondered.

Dalton prepared to make a staircase of ice leading up to the classroom's window. He took out his Omnicard and called Amy.

"Hiya, Dalton! Where are you guys? Class is about to start!"

"Open the window!"

"Huh?"

"Just do it!"

Dalton created a staircase and the two ran up and over the fence of the school until they reached the second story. Dalton saw Amy with her fingers underneath, about to open the window.

Awesome! Full speed ahead! he thought.

He continued forward and expected her to open the window, but instead of finding himself in the classroom, he found himself crashing into the glass and bouncing off the window. He held a hand to his head and fell to the ground with a thud. He lost his grip on his Omnicard and it clattered to the ground beside him. He could hear laughter from it.

"Oh, by the way, those windows don't open," Monty warned, clearly amused by what transpired.

"Yeah, a little late with the warning," Dalton groaned and got up to his feet. "Why the hell don't they?"

They barged through the school doors and into the front lobby, which held shoe lockers and umbrella racks. Dalton frantically searched for his. Once he found it, he hurled his shoes in and quickly threw on the slip-on indoor shoes. He jumped up the stairs by three until he reached the floor his classroom was on. Monty was right behind him.

Dalton rounded the corner and nearly tripped over a small droid. It was about the size of a pillow, and it scurried atop floors, keeping them clean. He managed to jump over it and skidded to a halt in front of their classroom. He swung the door open and noticed a seat next to Clara, a seat in the middle next to the wall, or one in the back corner. Monty made Dalton's decision easier as he went for the one next to Clara.

I'll take the back corner so I can take naps, he strategized within a second and plopped in his seat. He put his feet up, his hands behind his head, and closed his eyes.

The bell chimed and students returned to their seats from their conversations. The teacher came fast-walking in and pulled out an Omnislate. "Okay, everyone in your seats, please! You probably noticed that we have some new students today! If you could please stand," she asked with a smile.

The six stood up and introduced themselves. After, they sat back down.

"Now, we do have one more new student today." She looked toward the door. "You may come in now."

Monty leaned his face on his fist over his desk while Dalton twirled his pencil between his fingers. Until they saw that the new student was the guy who nearly hit Dalton with his car this morning.

"Hello, everyone," he smiled. "My name is Henry Preston. I transferred from Swordhaven. My hometown is Lucentum, and I'm really into soccer and music. Pleasure to meet you all."

Dalton flung his pencil and it scattered across the ground to Elizabeth, who was just as stunned as he was. Monty's left eye twitched, and smoke began to billow from his head.

What the hell is going on? Who is this guy? Paige thought, utterly confused at his friends' reactions.

"Henry?" Clara asked with a nervous expression on her face.

Henry saw Clara and he smiled. He walked over to Clara's desk. Monty followed his movement by turning his head like a rusty machine, smoke still billowing from his head.

Why is everyone freaking out?! Paige kept wondering.

"Ah, Clara darling, I've missed you so much!" Henry exclaimed. He picked up her hand and kissed the back of it.

Clara simply looked on with a sad expression.

"Henry, just what do you think you're doing in front of everybody like this?" Elizabeth asked angrily.

Nervous whispers and giggles were being passed across the classroom.

"What? Can't a man flirt with his betrothed?"

"Huh?!" the class exclaimed.

Monty's eye twitched one last time and he snapped. His head swung down and slammed into his desk. The desk blew apart, breaking in half. Monty collapsed to the ground, unconscious, with blood leaking from his head. His paper-thin aura shield shattered easily.

"Monty?!" Clara exclaimed, nearly jumping with the rest of the class.

"Um, Monterey?" the teacher asked.

"I'll take him," Paige chuckled nervously as he raised his hand.

"Th-thank you, Paige."

Paige got up from his seat and walked over to Monty. He grabbed Monty's right wrist and dragged him out of the room. "Come on, let's get you to the nurse's office. So embarrassing..."

A trail of smoke followed Paige as he closed the door behind him. The class simply watched in awe.

"Why did I have to get the Prestige students?" the teacher lamented.

"What illness do you think that would be diagnosed as?" Henry chuckled. "Sure hope he's okay."

"Just shut up and sit down Henry," Clara said tiredly. She refused to meet Henry's eyes.

Henry's expression dropped. "As you wish..." He solemnly walked over to the last open desk and took his seat.

When you look sad like that, just what am I supposed to do?

Paige dragged Monty through the halls, nodding with a smile nervously at passing students. He looked down at his unconscious friend and something caught his eye. Something black on Monty's right shoulder.

What is that? Paige pushed Monty's sleeve back.

Blight. It was like a swirling, black ink. Paige inspected further and saw that it was starting to go toward his shoulder blade.

"Jesus, Monty," Paige murmured.

****

Monty woke up in the infirmary after a half-hour nap. Paige waited beside him, reading a book. He looked up from the text when he noticed Monty move.

"How you feeling?" Paige asked.

Monty groaned as he sat up and held his head.

"What happened?"

"A transfer student named Henry came in and you started to smoke from your head. Then you slammed your head into your desk so hard that it split in half after you found out he and Clara are engaged."

He buried his face into his hands. "What do I do now?"

I don't know! Paige snapped in his head. "Monty, I happened to see your shoulder when I dragged you over here."

Monty's face shot out of his hands and he looked at Paige with a half-guilty, half-irritated scowl. "I didn't mean for anyone to see that."

"Yeah, I figured," Paige scoffed. "Don't worry, the nurse doesn't know about it. Just me."

Monty relaxed a little bit. "Wait, do you think their marriage is arranged?"

Dude, chill with the romance! Paige shouted in his head. *I'm totally the wrong person to be talking with about this stuff! Also, I can clearly see you're trying to change the subject!*

"Doesn't Akerym still do that in their country?"

Paige sighed. "Yes, they have the CUPID Computer which calculates people suited for each other. Or something like that?"

"So I have a chance then! We're in Puakai, not Akerym after all!"

"Monty..."

"I know, I know. What do I even see in this girl? Well..."

"Cut the bullshit!" Paige snapped.

There was an awkward silence. Monty wasn't used to Paige being this aggressive. Finally, he solemnly asked, "Are you going to tell the others?"

"That would be the smart thing to do," Paige sighed. "But I have a feeling your dumbass is going to say differently. Convince me."

"I don't want anyone to worry."

"Worry?! Monty, you know what blight does to people! You need to come with me to my father's temple right away!"

"Keep your voice down!" Monty snapped in a hushed tone.

Paige flinched a little, but he didn't back down. "You can't go on any missions and we need to make sure that you're okay."

"Paige, if Amy were to find out, it would make Amy feel guilty, and I don't want that to happen. You like her don't you? Don't let her worry about trivial things."

"Trivial? You call this trivial?"

"Look, I'll get it treated and you can even oversee that. But my family has plenty of other things to worry about. The others should just focus on their studies and enjoy the Azure Festival. Please, for me Paige."

"Look, Monty," Paige began to whisper. "You know if Dalton finds out you're keeping a secret like this, he's gonna be pissed."

"All the more reason to not tell anybody. Just keep quiet about it," Monty shrugged.

"How are you gonna hide the—" Paige was interrupted by the door suddenly opening.

Dalton was standing at the door, worksheets in his hands. "What's up, guys? What were you talking about?"

The two looked at each other before looking back at Dalton. "Nothing," they both said in unison.

Dalton gripped the worksheets a little tighter.

"I was told to come over and give these handouts to you guys. Our class is doing a skit parodying the story of Syd Alyad."

The two went silent. Dalton passed them their worksheets.

"Syd Alyad? Like, the dude who brought the second wave of signum to Lokyer?" Monty asked.

"Yup."

"Like, the guy who threw chunks of a moon at people?" Paige asked.

"Mhm."

"The guy who betrayed everyone and tried to erase all mages?"

"What don't you guys get?"

"How are we going to parody him?!"

"I don't know. Henry proposed the idea and the class liked it. Including Amy."

"Of course she did," Monty chuckled and shook his head.

"Oh, and we're the stars of the show. Team Prism I mean."

"Why?"

"Henry's idea. Class loves the posh bastard. Apparently, he's the heir to a shipping company."

Acting in front of the whole school?! Paige worried. *That sucks!*

Monty got out of bed. "Anyway, I'm feeling better now. Thank you two for checking up on me."

"Anytime," Paige smiled.

Dalton threw his arm around Monty's shoulder as they walked out. "We can grab something to eat after school today."

"Why? What's the occasion?" Monty asked.

"Because you got swooped," Dalton said in a comforting tone. "But it's okay, with my charisma and Paige's intelligence, I'm sure we can come up with something." Dalton turned back to look at Paige and winked. "Right?"

Why do they keep asking **me** *for advice?!* Paige wondered.

"Thanks guys, but I have to get to culinary class," Monty said.

"Oh, maybe I'll come with," Dalton said and began to walk toward Monty when Paige stopped him with a hand on his shoulder.

He tightened his grip and with a menacing tone asked, "Where do you think you're going?"

Dalton chuckled nervously. The next thing he knew Paige dragged him away by his shirt collar. "No! I don't wanna! Mechanical engineering sucks!"

"You have to Dalton! Come on, it's really not that bad!"

"Ugh!"

****

Dalton decided to take a trip to the large sports complex at the back of the school, complete with a swimming pool, a soccer field, baseball fields, and two gymnasiums. Dalton was at one end of the court, alone. The rain outside filled his ears with a zen, white noise.

He used an actual ball this time and nailed three-pointer after three-pointer. Paige and Monty's secretive whispers plagued Dalton's mind.

What were they talking about? Dalton thought.

Swish. Again.

They were talking about me, huh?

Swish. Again.

Monty was probably talking shit about how he helped me.

Swish. Again.

I didn't need his help! I didn't need Teach's help! I had everything under control! They still need me!

Swish. Again.

I'm not losing my touch! Dalton laughed in his head.

Swish. Again.

A memory flashed in Dalton's head. He was in an old cinema in Yankee. Sweat covered his body, his hands stung, and knives were scattered about him. He lifted his hands from his knees and saw they were covered in bloody cuts.

"Not good enough Dalton!" His mentor's voice shouted. "Again! And don't cry on me this time! You don't want your hands to hurt? Do it properly! Guess the people at the orphanage were right about you!"

Swish. Again.

I haven't lost my touch!

Another memory. Now, he stood atop a snowy rooftop in Yankee. He passed his mentor several bags of money. "Good work, Dalton."

"I could do so much more though…"

"There's no need to flaunt so much power so suddenly."

Swish. Again.

They still need me!

Brick. Dalton didn't bother chasing it. *I don't care what they're hiding.* He heard the door open and turned to see Henry standing there with an umbrella.

"What do you want?" Dalton asked.

"I just wondered if you wanted a ride back to your dorm?"

Dalton raised a brow. "I thought I busted your car."

"Oh, I just bought myself a new one," Henry laughed as if that was the obvious thing to do.

I hate this guy, Dalton thought to himself.

"Would I owe you more?"

Henry chuckled. "No. Actually, I'd like to explain myself."

2: The Transfer Student

The pitter-patter of the rain hitting the windshield and the purring of the engine filled the silence inside the car. It was a luxurious vehicle; cars are already expensive as is, but luxury sports cars? That was on a whole other level. Dalton typed the dorm's address into the built-in navigation on the dashboard.

And this posh has two of them? Dalton thought to himself.

"Dalton, sorry for being rude earlier," Henry apologized.

"Uh, dude I mean I'd get pissed if my car was wrecked. But you didn't have to be a douche about it."

Henry chuckled, "Yes, sorry for bringing up the whole nationality thing earlier. It's just back in Akerym, order is a large part of our priorities..."

That's right, Dalton remembered. *This guy is engaged to Clara. I can get some info for Monty!*

"I don't know, I don't really like people telling me what to do."

"How Yankee of you," Henry smirked. "Truly, democracy has cursed this country."

"Huh?" Dalton exclaimed, irritated enough to forget his initial plan for a second. "One dude bossing people around? I don't know how you Akerymians stand it."

Henry simply shook his head. Dalton noticed Henry's grip on the wheel got tighter. "You're missing my point," Henry chuckled, irritated. "Let me try a different method. Dalton, tell me today's date."

"Today's March second, five-hundred and one U," Dalton said, not sure where Henry was going with this.

"And do you know what the 'U' stands for?"

"Unification?"

"Correct. It has been five hundred and one years since our wondrous world of Lokyer overcame the Second Astral War and defeated the scourge Syd Alyad. It was the day where we agreed to prevent any future wars from happening by banding together. One people. One culture. One language—hence it is called Ul for Universal Language, one religion, the world religion: Ur, and one government. Look around! Does that look like the world today?"

"Nope, can't say it does."

"That's because it isn't! The Azure Festival is a prime example! Only coastal cities celebrate… whatever it is they're celebrating! Different countries are even beginning to put their lesser gods on a higher pedestal than Celestia herself! Sure, Christ and Buddha and Mohammed are almighty figures, but they are no comparison to her Heavenly Grace!" Henry laughed and leaned back in his seat exasperated.

"Sheesh, no wonder Clara hates Akerym…" Dalton chuckled. "You guys got your panties in a wad."

The mention of Clara's name seemed to calm Henry down. "Clara… Is much like her mother—much like you lot. She values individuality, independence, and is stubborn. Ever since she returned from the forest, she became stoic, thinking she could do anything. She broke away from the status quo, and as a result, was ostracized and reprimanded."

Okay, so far so good, Dalton thought to himself. "Must suck being engaged to a girl like that, huh?"

"No not at all," Henry replied matter of factly. "In fact, it is the reason why I love her."

"Huh?!"

"The way she defies all orders! She's like a paper tiger in the face of a thunderstorm! The way she struggles and perseveres against all odds is truly a thing of beauty!" Henry explained proudly.

"Oh, that's um… So you like the underdog, huh? I can see the appeal… I would of phrased what you said a little less creepily, but I get it," Dalton chuckled nervously.

"Though, that exact behavior is what makes her hate me…" Henry said solemnly. "CUPID, the artificial intelligence system which pairs couples together by calculating their resources, the potential their relationship has and takes in the potential of their offspring into account, matched me and her because it believes our union would benefit the country. Me, the heir to a shipping company, and her, the heiress to an asterium company. Clara's mother spearheaded the movement which is making people refuse their calculated partners."

"Can't say I'd support this CUPID thing."

"No, it is probably a good thing for someone to choose who they wed."

Only probably? Dalton thought.

"But I don't mind it since I was in love with Clara anyway…" Henry's expression dropped to one of longing and sadness. A little glint in his eyes, however, kept Dalton uneasy.

Henry pulled to a stop in front of Prism's dorm.

"Well, Henry," Dalton said. "Thank you for the ride. And as for your whole shpiel, well, I guess we have to agree to disagree."

"I suppose we must," Henry smiled. "Sorry for being so rude earlier, I should've just explained myself more calmly. I'm usually more composed. As thanks for listening to me babble, you don't need to pay for the damages to my old car."

Dalton's eyes sparkled. "Wait, really?!"

"Yes," Henry laughed. "Really."

"Hey man um, I can be kind of a jerk sometimes, but I'm no liar. So trust me when I say this, but I'm real sorry about your whole predicament with Clara and the car bit. Mostly just the car bit, I'm kinda rooting for my friend in the whole Clara thing."

"Oh, but of course," Henry said. "But I hope this put us back on the right path to getting to know each other as classmates." Henry held out a hand.

"Yeah, sure." Dalton smiled back and shook Henry's hand. "Sorry again." He waved goodbye and got out of the car, closing the door behind him.

Henry watched him leave. A mustard glow came from the hand Dalton shook. A card formed in his palm, and on it was a photo of what appeared to be two children, as well as the runic symbol for "regret" on the back. One was a boy wearing a white hood that covered his face, and the other was a girl wearing a black jacket and black ink circling her eyes. Henry thought she looked familiar with her frizzy brown hair, and then he recognized her. He couldn't stop himself from bawling out in laughter. "I guess he really isn't a liar!"

Henry looked out his window and watched Dalton walk inside. He spotted Monty in the upstairs window. He thought about Clara, and it felt as though strings wrapped around his heart and tightened.

****

Henry had a crush on his classmate, Clara Bernardino, in the fifth grade. So when he learned of her disappearance, his grief was heavy. However, in sixth grade, she made a miraculous return, but something was different. She was quiet, conserved, there was nothing really notable about her. But after a couple of months, she began to talk back to her superiors, she became defiant, steadfast, and proud.

How cute, he would think whenever he saw her standing up for herself. *But the long hair was better…*

One day, Henry was playing by the banks of a river by his school with a couple of his friends. They decided to play a game of "who can stand deepest in the river?"

"This is easy," Henry had bragged. He strolled out to the middle of the river and took a bow.

He put on a nonchalant air about him, but in reality, he struggled to stand against the current. With his friends cheering, he decided it was enough and took a step back to the shore. His foot slipped on the wet rocks beneath and he tripped, being swept away by the current.

"Help!" Henry shouted. "I can't swim!"

He spun and flailed, struggling to stay afloat. He thrashed the water around him so loudly, he didn't hear Clara diving after him. Clara wrapped her arms around him and tugged on the rope which was wrapped around her waist. Elizabeth and Henry's friends reeled them in.

"Th-thank you," Henry said between breaths. *She's going to ask for something I know it…* Henry thought. *They're all looking for something to gain!*

"Just stop being a dumbass. I'm not gonna be here to save yours every time you decide to show off to your lackeys," Clara replied bluntly, wringing the water out of her shirt.

"Huh? What, you're not going to ask me for something in return? Money or a favor or what have you?" Henry chuckled in disbelief.

Clara slapped him in the face. "Don't you dare put me in the same boat as the others! I don't help people because I think I'll benefit! I do it because I want to!"

Henry held his throbbing cheek, stunned. He would spend his next years trying to win Clara's favor. Studying hard to remain in honors classes with her, attending parties and banquets the Bernardino family hosted, practicing violin so he could one day, stand on the stage with her and play.

Throughout their middle school years, Henry would see Clara struggle, and at times would see her falter. But never once did the flame she carry burn out. She was driven by something, and Henry wanted to know what kept her so defiant to this society.

Towards the end of their eighth grade, he found out they had been calculated as a couple by CUPID, Henry was ecstatic. But when he looked over at Clara, she had a surprised and horrified look on her face. *Why doesn't she like me? What can I do?* Clara transferred from Swordhaven to Constellation in a heartbeat.

I never even got the chance to talk it out with her… Henry thought angrily.

****

Monty hummed a little tune as he cooked. The smell of smoke caught his attention.

"Ah! The spinach!" He turned the heat off and shoveled the spinach into a bowl with a spoon.

Dalton and Clara were still out and about, but Amy and Paige watched from afar. Paige expected Amy to giggle at something silly like that, but she didn't look pleased.

"Monty's…" she trailed off. "Different. Isn't he?"

"Huh?"

"He looks… happier," she smiled for a second but went back to a worried look. "But tired. Really tired."

"Yeah, he does…" Paige agreed.

"Has he… said anything to you?"

Paige regretted shifting his gaze at Amy. Something was troubling her, he could see it in her eyes. She knew something was off, more than just a mood or personality change or… whatever Monty goes through. No, she knew there was something more.

Paige did something that would have made Dalton gag: he lied. "No, he hasn't said anything." Paige leaned back in his chair and glued his eyes to Monty. "He's been his usual self–closed off and all that."

Paige could feel Amy's gaze on him like a searchlight. He held in the urge to gulp. He was afraid he'd start sweating and she'd notice… So he froze. He sat completely still. For five long seconds, he forgot how to breathe, how to blink, how to function.

"Is that so? Well, I guess no news is… well, actually no news can be a good or a bad thing," Amy giggled.

Paige finally relaxed.

"Come on, dinner is almost ready. Help me set the table."

While Paige's nervousness was put to ease, Elizabeth, on the other hand, was still anxious. She watched Henry drop Dalton off. Henry spotted her with her arms crossed, looking at him coldly. He smiled and pulled up to her.

"Well, if it isn't Clara's little knight?" Henry greeted. "Cold out here, isn't it?"

"What're you doing here?" Elizabeth snapped.

"Haha! Oh, Elizabeth Baker, so distrusting," he chuckled.

Elizabeth walked closer to the window and leaned forward, pointing at Henry with a glare. "I'm watching you. If you do anything suspicious–"

Henry rolled his eyes and snatched Elizabeth's hand. Elizabeth yanked it free and pulled out her pistol. Henry laughed and put his hands up.

"—I will not hesitate."

Henry sighed and shook his head. "Two things: One, you have no position to threaten me at all. And two, you're hesitating right now."

With a smile, he snapped his fingers. Within a split second, the space around them distorted and warped into a castle.

The grass turned into a ballroom floor. The moonlight strained into thin, tall windows. A waterfall rumbled in the distance. A central staircase was across the room from a large door, and above them were glowing runestones that dangled from intricate chandeliers.

Elizabeth looked down at her clothes, which had been replaced with a maid outfit. Her hands instinctively went to her beanie but found only a bow in its place.

"Wha-where are we?!" Elizabeth shouted. Her voice trembled. *How does he know?!*

Henry stepped out of his car, which was invisible to Elizabeth, and ambled around the room, admiring it. There was something familiar about the place. "This place… Why do I feel like I've seen it before?"

"Stop ignoring me!" Elizabeth went to fire a warning shot, but her pistol had been turned into a scroll, *the* Scroll. "What?"

Silhouettes of invisible people danced along the walls. Elizabeth blinked and before her was a full gala of faceless phantoms.

"No…" Elizabeth murmured. She started to back away and was making her way up the stairs now. Her heart pounded against her chest.

"Seriously woman, what's got you so…" It dawned on Henry where he was. "Oh… Oh! Oh!" He bent over, laughing. "There's no way! You were *here*?!" He took a deep breath and composed himself. He wiped a tear from his eye. "Oh, this changes things a little! This makes things sooo much easier!"

Elizabeth's eyes darted to the clock. She remembered the time of that night vividly. The time she got her magic: 11:54:18 exactly. The clock showed 11:53:12.

"Make this stop!" Elizabeth pleaded.

"Listen here!" Henry boomed. "I'm here to make a deal with you! You see..." Henry yanked his collar down to show off his chest. On his right pectoral was a tattoo of a crow on a skull.

"I am Henry Preston! The Third Wing of Penumbra!" A wild look was in his eye and he had his arms up and spread as if basking in applause.

As he revealed his identity, a flood of icy wind burst through the doors behind him. Henry disappeared in the white fog and Vayne emerged from it. Elizabeth was grabbed by her wrist from behind and she turned to see a maid. The woman's eyes had circles under them from never getting a moment's rest, and a pair of black cat ears poked out from her curly hair.

Mom?!

This isn't real, it can't be real! Elizabeth tried to assure herself.

"Come on, Elizabeth!" her mother said.

Vayne rushed forward after them, pushing and clawing past the crowd before him, freezing all that stood in his path. He chased them up the staircase, bringing back a large broadsword of black ice and slashing at them. Elizabeth and her mother ducked, and the blade cleaved the wall behind them. A cyan ball of light whined in Vayne's palm and with a thrust, a beam shot from his hand and encased the entire staircase in ice. Elizabeth's mother hugged her daughter and dove out onto the balcony, frost biting at her ankle.

Elizabeth got to her feet first while her mother winced from the ice around her ankle.

No, no, no, no! Elizabeth started to hyperventilate.

"Take this scroll!" Elizabeth's mother grabbed her daughter's hand with the Scroll and pressed it against her daughter's chest. "Keep it safe! Trust it with no one! May its contents protect you!"

"No! I don't want it!" Elizabeth cried. She tried to push it away, but it felt like she was pushing against a boulder, and couldn't distance herself from it.

"I love you, sweetie. Remember that these are *your* powers too!"

Elizabeth remembered those words from the first time she heard them. She knew what would happen next. "Mom!"

A blade of ice shot from her mother's chest and blood splashed on Elizabeth's face. Her mother coughed blood that spilled at Elizabeth's feet. She sat, stunned, back to the railing as she watched in horror as her mother was hoisted into the air. Vayne held the sword in his hand, and behind him, Elizabeth could see the frozen ballroom. Vayne's helmet melted, revealing Henry's face.

"The Frostflame Massacre," Henry said. "A gathering of royalty went horribly wrong when Vayne came and froze everyone to death. It was here that the scroll containing all of the Asteria family's sword techniques was lost." He sounded like a boring teacher–his voice was monotone and dull. "It's your fault there's talk of a revolution now. Now that the Asteria no longer have their sword techniques, the ingrates are getting ahead of themselves."

Elizabeth's fear turned to anger. "You bastard!" She leaped at Henry and was met with a back slap across the face. She was sent flying over the railing of the balcony, and below her, she could see the raging rapids she was forced to jump into as a child.

Before she fell, she was caught by her throat over the railing. She flailed and kicked and growled but Henry's now black-armored hand didn't budge.

"Don't worry! This is all an illusion! There must be a lot of things going through your head, but listen up!" Henry took a moment to admire Elizabeth's face, which was full of rage and confusion. She was choking, dying for air. Henry laughed. "I'm sure you're worried about Clara, but I'm here to tell you that no, her father didn't send me. I was sent here because you and your friends keep messing with my organization! I'm only here for reconnaissance really, but I know where you guys go to school, where you live, where your families live–we have all of that info! So if you don't want me to call the other seven Wings, speak nothing of this conversation and I won't do anything to harm you and your friends! Do we have a deal?"

Elizabeth wanted to spit in his face. But she saw no better alternative, and she was close to blacking out.

"Good! Let's shake on it!" They shook and Elizabeth was sent into free fall.

Elizabeth still couldn't breathe, it felt like water was filling her lungs as she gasped for air while she fell. She hit the water with a splash. She swam to the surface but soon realized she was in front of her dorm, close to the shore, in the pond. She coughed, trying to regain her breath while looking for Henry. He and his car were nowhere in sight. The Scroll was gone, and her pistol too.

"Elizabeth?" Clara's voice asked.

Elizabeth's eyes followed the sound to her friend, who jogged toward her. Elizabeth heard the faint sound of music coming from Clara's earbuds. She splashed water as she ran up and helped Elizabeth to her feet.

"What were you doing in the pond? Those are hardly the kind of clothes you wear to go swimming," Clara chuckled.

What was the point in even telling me he was a Wing? Elizabeth wondered. *Has he some way to tell if I do reveal his identity? What was his magic? How does it work? Was it really all an illusion? It felt so real!* Elizabeth gingerly touched her neck with two fingers and quickly found out she was still tender where Henry's hand had been. *What just happened?*

"Lizzy? Are you okay?"

"I'm fine. I was just looking for you and tripped was all."

"Oh… well I'm glad you're not hurt. Come on, I hear Lava Brain is making dinner."

By the time they got back, spinach puffs and salmon fillets were on the table. Everyone greeted them back.

"I'm going to go change and I'll come back down," Elizabeth said.

"Same here," Clara added.

"We'll wait for you then," Monty said as he took a seat at the table.

"Oh, there's no need," Elizabeth said as she and Clara walked up the stairs.

"Just eat!" Clara insisted with a wave of her hand.

"But–" Amy started, but Monty interrupted her with a hand.

"Fine. Have a nice shower you two," Monty smiled.

When they came back down, the other four were sitting at the table. The food had not been touched. They had waited.

"Hey, I thought you said you weren't going to wait!" Clara moaned.

"That was a lie of course," Monty chuckled and began to pass the food around.

The six quickly found out their food had gotten cold and a line formed at the microwave before they were all finally seated at the table with warm food.

Monty noticed Clara had been wolfing down her food, particularly the spinach puffs. There was only one left, and Monty had calculated for Dalton's large appetite.

"Oh? Are you enjoying my food?" Monty snickered.

Clara's eyes widened and she swallowed her bite. "Yeah. It's actually pretty goo–"

Dalton swiped the last spinach puff.

"–Ah! Give that back! I was gonna eat that!" She exclaimed and grabbed the collar of Dalton's shirt like she was about to mug him.

"What're you talking about?! You've already had a bunch!" Dalton protested, once again, with a mouth full of food.

Dalton gulped down the food he had in his mouth, picked up the spinach puff, and devoured it in two bites before swallowing.

"Ah! You bastard!"

"I only got to eat one…" Amy pouted.

Elizabeth gave Amy one of hers. Amy responded by hugging her, much to Elizabeth's discomfort. *Honestly, these people…* Elizabeth chuckled. *It really makes my worries go away when we're together like this.*

****

Clara walked down the stairs to make some cookies. She was about halfway down until she heard Monty on the phone where she stopped around the corner.

"Yes, I'm doing fine Monica. Amy and I both," he said.

"What about you? You're not overworking yourself are you?"

There was a pause.

"Good. Yeah, no, we've been forced to do normal school stuff now so don't worry."

Another pause.

"We're doing a satire skit on the Story of Syd apparently, for the Azure Festival," Monty chuckled.

Yet another pause.

"Yeah, I don't know how we're gonna do it either. We're deciding more stuff on what's going to happen next week."

Clara grew impatient and just went downstairs. She passed Monty who was lounging on the living room couch, which was across from the kitchen. Monty watched her pass.

"Yeah, I'm excited to see you too… Okay, love you… Bye." Monty hung up and followed Clara into the kitchen. "What're you up to?"

"What?" Clara asked. She didn't turn around and instead started looking in the fridge.

"I don't want you blowing up the kitchen is all," Monty smirked. "I saw you in culinary class today. That poor, poor stir fry..."

"Well, don't worry because I'm baking some cookies," Clara said. "I may not be the best chef by any means, but I can bake."

"Alright, I'll be your sous chef then," Monty offered.

"None needed, thank you," Clara said, her head still in the fridge. She waved a hand behind her, shooing Monty away.

Monty frowned but gave a defeated sigh. "I know there's no point in arguing with you, so how about I make some coffee instead?"

"Sure," Clara said as she took out milk, eggs, and butter from the fridge.

Monty poured the beans into the grinder as Clara got more ingredients from the pantry.

"I'm surprised you actually bought the ingredients for chocolate chip cookies," Clara remarked.

Monty shrugged. "They're pretty ubiquitous ingredients for the most part. And plus Amy loves cookies."

"I know," Clara smiled. "She's a sweetheart."

And so are you at times, Monty said in his head. *Yeah, as if!* The beans were done grinding.

"Who were you talking with on the phone?" Clara asked.

"My older sister Monica. She's actually graduating this semester from Montralis."

"Oh, good for her! With what degree?"

"Nursing."

"Wow. That's crazy."

"Yeah," Monty chuckled. "She's always been pretty brilliant."

And so are you at times–okay stop! Monty thought and shook his head.

Clara put the cookies in the oven and they waited.

"Hey um," Monty began.

"What?"

Monty frowned. *I want to ask about Henry, but wouldn't that signal that I like her?*

"Come on, spill it," Clara chuckled and playfully punched Monty in the arm. His right arm.

Monty's whole body shook with pain and his knees nearly buckled. *That was a kiddy punch from her!* Monty knew. *Sure it's stronger than your average playful punch, but still! Is my arm that tender?*

Clara noticed Monty cringe. "Hey? Seriously, what? You look like you're about to cry."

"You know what? It's nothing actually. A stupid question," Monty laughed. The oven beeped. *Oh, thank gods.*

Clara gave a suspicious look. *Okay…* she thought before going to take her cookies out of the oven.

Monty went to do the pour-over and he noticed that his left arm shook and wobbled as he poured the boiling water over the coffee grounds. *My left arm is being affected too?!*

"Is the coffee ready?" Clara asked.

"Yeah, almost." Monty turned around and saw that Clara had chipped a small fragment off one of Elizabeth or Paige's arctic runestones.

Clara channeled a little bit of aura into it to react with the asterium inside and a cold explosion went off in her hand. Clara flailed her hand a little bit, "That's cold!" Snowflakes went over the cookies and quickened the cooling process.

"Taking shortcuts are we?" Monty laughed.

"Well, duh! Amy's waiting for me! We're watching a show together." She started breathing into her hand to warm it up.

Monty smiled and walked over. "Here, give me your hand."

Clara held her hand out and Monty took it. With his hand, he was able to struggle and muster some aura into his palm to heat it up slightly.

It's harder to control the flow of my aura now. Weird, that's not a symptom of blight though…

"Thanks," Clara chuckled.

"No problem," Monty said blankly. "This is why we don't explode runestones in our hands."

"Yeah, yeah," Clara said as she rolled her eyes and pulled her hand away.

"Well… goodnight," Clara farewelled and walked at a brisk pace back upstairs.

Monty watched her go with a disappointed look on his face. "Goodnight."

Clara turned and knocked on Amy's door. Amy opened it and let her in and they started watching a new show they picked up: *Stranger Things*. Dalton was waiting for everyone to finish season one before continuing.

Monty went back up to his room and locked the door behind him. He took his shirt off and looked in the mirror. The blight had started spreading from his right shoulder to his upper back and shoulder blades.

"Damn... It's gotten worse. I really do need treatment." Monty sighed and put his shirt back on. He plopped onto his bed and stared at his hand. He tried pouring aura into his palm and he could get a couple of sparks, but nothing more.

He gave a "tsk" and turned over on his side. *Just... get some sleep...*

He felt like his eyelids had sandbags tied to them, and drifted off into a slumber. He felt like he was only asleep for a minute when he woke up to the sound of a *"BOOM"* followed by the howling of a cold wind.

He could see the man covered in shadow break through a wall in the manor and cold winds swept through the room. The sight of the shadow man raking his mother across the chest with a blade of darkness was still vivid in his mind. He was standing right next to his mother when it happened too. He could feel her splattered blood lose its warmth on his face. He remembered her wiping off the droplets with a shaky hand and a smile. That was when she gave him her red scarf. He remembered her whispering with her last breath, "I love you."

He was stunned, as paralyzed as her mother's lifeless body. Raphael's shouts were muffled to him. He couldn't take his eyes off her corpse. His body felt frozen. His chest began to tighten, he started hyperventilating, his vision narrowed.

Raphael finally shook him to his senses just in time for Monty to see Kaze's eyes get slashed by a crescent of moonlight. "Get a grip!" Raphael shouted. "Get somewhere safe, *now*!"

How could I have been so useless? Monty thought. *All those practice sessions with Raph and what? When it actually comes to it I can't move?*

He had no idea where Monica or Amy was. Raphael turned back around and clashed blades with the shadow man. The shadow man quickly pushed Raphael off and blasted him back. Kaze threw a punch, and a gust of wind went off and completely missed the shadow man. The man created a guzheng of moonlight and strummed the strings. A flurry of crescents burst forth and ripped apart Kaze's chest. He flew back and crashed through a wall into the next room.

He loomed over Monty with the moon behind him. He could remember his sharp, yellow eyes. They were cold. They lacked malice. They seemed empty, filled with no emotion.

Do something! Monty shouted in his head.

Monty finally got control over his body again. He tackled the man's leg, but it did nothing. The man reached down and grabbed Monty by the throat. The air left Monty's body. He squirmed and thrashed, but the shadow man was unphased.

Damn it, Damn it, damn it! Monty cursed. Tears began to stream down his face.

The man pulled back a spear of shadow and was prepared to thrust it into Monty when a gold flash wooshed past. Monty dropped to the ground and pried the fingers around his neck open. He saw that the shadow man's arm had been cut off. The piece that still clung to Monty lost its black armor, revealing a tattoo showing a crow on a skull. He was a Penumbra Wing.

Monty looked to his left and saw Raphael's blade lodged into the wall. When he looked back in the direction it came from, Raphael appeared in a gust of wind in front of him. In the air, he spun and kicked the shadow man in the head and sent him flying.

He ran over to the wall and yanked the blade free. He whirled it back into a keychain and took a knee next to Monty. His left eye had changed. The iris was a deep blue and his pupil had turned into a white crescent and star.

"Look Monty, you need to get out of here okay?" Raphael said. "Everything is going to be fine, you, Monica, Amethyst, and Kaze are gonna get through this."

"What about you?" Monty cried.

"I'll be fine too," Raphael smiled, but Monty could hear the worry shake his voice. "Go upstairs, help Amy, and get to the car. Run!"

Raphael's eyes widened. He grabbed Monty and jumped to the side. A strum of guzheng strings and a barrage of spinning crescents of moonlight flew past where they once were. "Go, now!" Raphael shouted.

Monty sprinted toward the stairs, but was halted halfway up. He turned around and saw the shadow man's arm had grown back and from it, a band of shadow extended and wrapped around Monty. Raphael was pinned down by a bear of shadow. Monty was yanked through the air back toward the shadow man.

"Monty!" Raphael cried.

This time it was different. Monty felt something build inside of him. A burning desire to hurt the shadow man. He *hated* him. He needed to suffer for what he did.

Let me handle it, a voice exactly like his echoed in his head.

Monty did just that. He let his rage erupt with a roar. He turned and whirled his blade to life in the air and sliced the arm apart. His momentum carried him toward the shadow man and he used it to slice through his torso. He tumbled through the hole in the wall the shadow man had created. Monty turned and faced his aggressor to see that his attack did minimal damage. He couldn't cut all the way through. The small gash that was there was already starting to be sewn together by shadow.

The man opened his hand and a giant axe of shadow formed in his palm. At his feet, a wolf of shadow jumped to life and snarled its teeth. The wolf pounced on Monty. He went to stab the beast, but with a gust of wind, Raphael was in front of him. He kneed the wolf with such strength that it dissipated on the spot. He caught Monty's blade with his hand and blood seeped from it. In his other hand, he created a strong gale of winds and blew away the shadow man once more.

He turned to Monty and smiled, "Leave this to me buddy. I'll come find you. Just stay put, I know where you're gonna be." He struck the top of Monty's head with a light karate chop and winked. "I love you. Take care of the family for me."

As if an invisible tsunami erupted from behind Raphael, Monty was blown away by a force of wind so great it carried him through the hole in the wall and into the dark wilderness. He flailed in the air, trying to stop and run back to his family, but he could do nothing but watch through his watery vision as his cabin disappeared from view behind the howling winds.

Monty finally landed in the snow and was able to make his way to a nearby cave. In his solitude, his anxiety and confusion crushed him. His heart sank to his stomach and he bawled himself to sleep.

I'm so weak! I can't do anything! I'm sorry Raph! I'm so sorry Mom! I'm sorry Uncle Kaze! Monty cried in his head. "I'm sorry…" he sobbed.

Monty awoke in a cold sweat and quickly sat up. He looked at himself in his mirror and saw that his left Eye had activated, the deep blue iris and pupil like the moon staring back at him.

I'm such a sack of shit! Monty cursed. *I can barely light a candle now, much less help people! I'm a curse! Everyone I love gets hurt!*

His right shoulder had a sharp pain and he grimaced. He took a deep breath. He calmed down his breathing and took a minute to deactivate his eye before getting out of bed.

Take it easy Monty. That's the blight talking. Although…

Monty looked for that deep, burning desire for revenge like he used to. But he felt no ambition. What was once a forest fire was now a torch, ready to be snuffed out.

I have a lot to rethink…

He looked at the time on his Omnicard: 4:00 a.m. He had gone to bed at midnight.

"No sleeping tonight either, huh?" Monty chuckled. He put on his headphones and quietly opened his door.

Guided by the light emanating from his Omnicard's screen, he went down to the kitchen and began to cook. *If I cook everyone's lunches now, maybe I can squeeze in a cat nap before breakfast.*

3: Freedom & Expectations

Monty and Kaze sat on two beach chairs along the banks of a river in a large park in northwest Cysko. Monty and Raphael often came here to fish and train, surrounded by trees and wildlife. Now, it was Kaze who accompanied Monty twice a month. They remained silent, just taking in the sounds of the birds and the squirrelmunks rummaging around with the flowing water.

"Uncle…" Monty finally said.

"Yes, Monty?"

"I…" Monty's chest swelled, reluctant to release the worries. "I… I am so lost. Everything I've done, I've done to avenge the family I've lost and protect the ones who I still have. The hatred which fueled me is subsiding, leaving only sorrow in its wake."

"Hatred, guilt, these are but synonyms for 'obstruction,'" Kaze said. "They cloud your vision of what's most important to you. They make you a prisoner and chain you to the past. Only through forgiveness is your path made clear. By not forgiving, the very hateful flame which fueled you burns the very bridge you need to cross."

"But how can you forgive them?!" Monty insisted. His chest contorted, and tears filled his eyes. "I can't stop thinking about them, uncle," he croaked. "I see them in my dreams, in my nightmares. I can't help but think of how useless I was. I—"

"Monty," Kaze interrupted. "I was not talking about Penumbra. A moment of patience may ward off great disaster, but a moment of impatience may ruin a whole life. Their time will come, but we must not chase ruin. Chasing ruin is like chasing a storm; the closer we get, the more danger we bring to ourselves, and our family and friends don't deserve that. I am so proud of you for trying to make this change. But the key to forgiving them is by forgiving yourself."

"Huh?"

"You despise them for taking something dear, so do I. But you *act* in response to the hate you feel for yourself—your guilt. 'I could have done more. I hate my weakness.' You seek vengeance, for only then do you believe that you have permission to be happy. 'For how can I live my life when it's my fault my family can't live theirs?'"

Monty looked at his reflection in the river, and staring back at him through watery vision was his brother. Kaze put a firm hand on Monty's shoulder.

"You don't need permission to live your life, Monty… I have cast such thoughts to the wind, and now I am just as free. Learn to let go. Let go of the hatred and sorrow so you may open yourself to the love of the family you have now," Kaze said. "My head was also clouded by vengeance, but I had no time, for what was important was right before me: you and your sisters. I am not telling you to forgive Penumbra, for even I cannot. I am telling you to forgive yourself, so you may see the opportunity to live the full life you've been given and *seize it*."

Kaze hugged his nephew, and Monty began to sob, trying his best to stop the tears as they soaked into Kaze's shirt. "I miss them so much…"

"I do too," Kaze said. "I do too…"

When they were heading home, Kaze left Monty with two last pieces of advice: "Self-forgiveness won't come instantly. It will be like rebuilding that bridge piece by piece. Go see your friend Melody; I'm sure she misses you more than she blames you for what happened. Also, see Taro, for he is on the same journey as you…"

****

A sweet, summer sun blessed Taro's skin. It was a time before Taro was ever the captain of Flow. He was but a boy. He was half asleep, his limbs woven around the outside of the rigging of the ship. His black hair was longer in the front, his bangs almost covering his eyes. He wore a red bandana to signify that he was a part of Yankee's Liberation Force. He was what they called: a Red.

He recently came back from his coronation. He was officially the Zodiac Guardian Aquarius. It had a nice ring to it. His coronation wasn't like most, though. Taro was never formally recognized as Aquarius. He refused the responsibilities that came with being a Zodiac, so they refused to give him his Relic.

Each Zodiac had a Relic, and the Relic chose who could wield it. The way Taro saw it, it was his right to wield Aquarius' Goblet. It chose *him* after all. Who were other people to tell him no, when the real authority had already spoken? So he took what was his.

He looked at the Goblet now, raising it to the sky. He examined it like a cat playing with a ball of yarn. The gold cup had a band of diamonds around the lip and a large pearl in the neck. When he held it in his hands, it was strange but... he felt whole.

"Hey, Starboy!" a crew member shouted. "Get back up in the nest! We're expecting company!"

That snapped Taro out of his daze. He hooked the Goblet to his belt and quickly scrambled up to the nest.

He earned the nickname when he accidentally teleported onto their ship, and they confused him for a stowaway. They beat him until he "saw stars," hence the nickname.

But as of right now, he found himself helping a revolution. The crew he was a part of were privateers by Yankee's Archon, and their job was to ransack any reinforcements Akerym might send. They got a large commission for every convoy they stole from and every base they raided.

Taro clambered into the crow's nest where his cutlass, runestone bandolier, and pair of pistols lay. He willed to his hands *Constellation's Cradle*. An ancient magic object that he claimed as his first treasure after pillaging a Wanari temple occupied by Chasm. He had decided to name it *Cat's Cradle*.

The strings shined a light, almost white blue. Along the strings were a couple of celestial blue dots. He spread his fingers until the strings were taut. Around him, a replica of the shape he made expanded, almost like a hologram. He scanned the horizon. By changing the pattern in the string he made with his fingers, he could change how far out he could see. The more he stretched the strings apart, the further he could see, but the lesser his field of vision.

He spotted the sails of a Chasm naval vessel. He changed his pattern again, sacrificing what was visible on the y-axis for expanding the x-axis. It was like peeking between floorboards from below. He was able to see the moving water and the hulls of an entire fleet.

With just seeing a little of the sail or a little of the hull, blue dots appeared, connected by white lines like a constellation. Taro saw the outlines of the frigates through the fog. Next to the blue dots, pieces of information began to pop up, like what the ship was made of, how tall it was, etc.

His *Cradle* informed him of two espadons: medium-sized ships with twenty-four broadside cannons, two cannons on the bow, and a machine gun at the stern. The other ship was a mano: bigger than the espadon with hang-glider sails at the stern and a sampan rig on the main deck with fifty-six broadside cannons and more on the bow and stern. Both models were meant for low-altitude and naval warfare.

"A convoy spotted to the southwest!" Taro shouted. "Four ships in total! Two espadons, a large freighter, and a mano!"

The captain stepped out of his cabin with a wild grin on his face. "They're starting to take us a little more seriously, boys!"

The crew cheered and laughed triumphantly. They were using an espadon airship themselves.

"Soon, they'll start needing Prestiges to protect their sorry asses. We should be honored!" he said sarcastically.

The crew fell into uproarious laughter.

"Alright, enough standing around you dogs! Man the cannons! Prepare for takeoff! Take us to low altitude!"

The crew started barking orders and scrambling, preparing for combat. Taro sent *Cat's Cradle* away, clipped his cutlass and pistols, and put on his bandolier.

"Starboy!" The captain roared.

Taro instinctively froze and directed all of his attention to him.

"Beautiful weather we have, don't we?!"

Taro smiled. "Aye, aye, Cap!" He took his Goblet and thrust it to the sky.

Dark clouds rumbled and billowed, swirling above in a tumult until a drizzle showered the area. Taro felt invigorated. The Goblet's rain put aura into his veins where it surged like the rage of the sea. The crew felt it too, and they cheered and hollered in excitement.

Taro climbed down and hung onto the rigging. The wind in his face, the rain dropping on his skin to wash away the sticky humidity, there was no better feeling. He brandished his sword and felt the ship lurch as they began to gain altitude.

****

Taro's story was interrupted by a buzz from his Omnicard. He looked and saw a text from his brother that read, "Remember, this afternoon, 5:00."

Aw crap, I lost track of time, Taro cursed. *I should get some jobs in before I go.*

"Sorry Honey, but I got to go," Taro apologized.

He was in Monica's apartment in Montralis. He finally found a break to visit her and was telling her a story from his swashbuckling days to go with her coffee. She was laying on her bed while Taro was standing as he liked to put body language and charades into his stories.

"Aw, come on! Just five more minutes! It was finally starting to get good!" Monica pleaded.

"My brother needs me this evening, so I gotta cram some jobs in before then. Sorry," Taro chuckled nervously.

Taro gave Monica a smooch on the lips before he teleported away.

****

The clock dialed back by three hours and the early morning breeze struck Taro like a slap to the face once he teleported to Cysko. He stumbled over and needed to regain his balance from teleporting over such a considerable distance. He caught his breath and summoned his hoverboard to his hand: the *SunSkate* or the *Zoomy Marty,* as he called it. It was black with mint green arrows across the deck. He hopped on it and began zooming above the cars and bikers in the city.

His first job was on a food and drink run for a company. He saw no need to teleport and just used his *Zoomy Marty* to grab the food and deliver it. His next job was helping an elderly couple clean their house. Next was walking someone's dog. He decided to multitask and took the dog with him to his next job, where he helped an understaffed barbershop.

"Are you the guy?" the woman asked.

"Yep, I'm Taro," he greeted. Taro summoned his cosmetology license to his hand and handed it to her. After she gave a nod of approval, he took it back and sent it away.

Taro cut people's hair for hours, making conversation and going on about his days traveling across the world.

"That's dope, bro. You're like an *actual* pirate!"

"Thanks!" Taro smiled. "But I'm not much of one anymore."

"So you're not wanted or anything?"

"Not anymore. The Archon of Yankee granted everybody pardons after the city's liberation. Honestly, he was a pretty cool dude. The other guy right now is a tool, though."

"Are Prestiges really all *that?*" another customer asked. "I mean, Chasm are the ones doing the heavy lifting and finishing off the signum while you guys do… what exactly?"

"It depends on the person," Taro shrugged. "Prestiges just grab any job posted by the Magistracy that's available to them. But I'd say once every two months, we're given a required mission by the Magistracy. So even a guy like me who just does odd jobs has to be prepared to take down rogue Prestiges or help the Celestian Order with their efforts."

After finishing the job, Taro got his commission from the Magistracy and gave a sigh of relief as he took the dog back to its home. "I'm so glad they only take five percent of the pay on low-priced ones like these..."

Taro performed four more jobs that day before teleported back to Pioneer Square and took a pitstop at Alright Guys, where he got his usual: cola and rum.

"Long day?" Memphis asked.

"Yeah," Taro sighed before taking a swig. "And still got a lot of work to do. How's business today?"

"It's starting to ramp up. It's almost dinner after all."

"Yeah, I—" Taro's eyes widened, and he checked his Omnicard for the time. "Oh crap, I'm late!" Taro downed his drink and vanished in a white flash.

Memphis stared at the empty seat for a second and sighed. "I'll just put that on your tab."

****

Jiro rechecked his Omnicard. It was 5:15 p.m. The setting sun painted the sky hues of orange as it dipped below the horizon. Fishing boats came, in reeling their catches. Jiro stood on a grassy field. A five-minute walk to his left would bring him to Pier 48, which featured booths, shops, a farmer's market, and restaurants. A thirty-second walk would bring him to Glass Beach, where the wet sand reflected the sunset like a mirror.

The sound of an "oof!" and the rustling of palm leaves behind him caught his attention. He turned and looked up at the slightly bent trunk supporting Taro's weight.

"Ugh..." Taro groaned. "I didn't quite stick the landing this time."

Taro rolled off the palm tree and summoned *Cat's Cradle*. He spread it out and raised his arms. The holographic constellation projected above Taro's head, and it acted as a parachute, letting him down to the ground gently. He tumbled as he landed and sent his string back to his island. He laid on the emerald bed of grass with his limbs spread out for a while.

"Sorry, I lost track of time doing some jobs," Taro apologized.

"Of course you did..." Jiro sighed.

Taro sat up as a gust of wind blew past, bringing with it the smell and saltiness of the ocean. The sound of squawking turtlegulls, floating and bobbing along the low, rolling waves added to the sensation.

"It never gets old, does it?" Taro sighed, a soft smile spreading across his face.

"No, it doesn't…" Jiro sighed. But no smile could be seen on his face, only an expression of longing and disappointment.

"Every time I go traveling, I always love coming back here."

Jiro followed his brother's wistful gaze to the Lull archipelago, about eighty kilometers west from the Ayo Marina. He remembered when he was first taken there. Jiro could remember Taro proudly wearing his bandana on his head, representing his pirate crew, Flow, after Yankee's liberation from Akyerm. A rolling wave, their insignia, was being brandished instead of being tucked away in the folds as it was presently.

****

Ayo's port was full of life in the early morning, a refreshing sight for Taro to see.

He was with his little brother, Jiro, who asked, "Taro, where are we going?"

Taro knelt and smiled. "We're going to Lull, buddy. You'll meet Nimbus and Cloud there. I'm sure you three will make great friends."

Gossip surrounded their departure. "Is that who I think it is?"

"Yup, that's Aquarius."

"Is he ever around?"

"Nope, not much of a guardian, is he? Ever since the Goblet reacted to his brother, he's been trying to push all of the responsibility onto him. See that bandana of his? He's a pirate."

"*Really*? What a good-for-nothing!"

"I know. Why would the Goblet ever choose *him*?"

Taro sighed and got up on his feet. "Come on, Jiro. Let's get you to where you need to go."

They set sail, and Taro forgot all that was said about him. The salty sea breeze, the morning sun, the sound of the wind flapping in the sails, and the shanties sung by his crew, nothing could beat it.

Jiro thought the same. A big smile ran across his face. "Hey Taro…" he peeped.

"Wassup?"

"When will I see you again?"

Taro chuckled, "I'll stop by to visit on occasion. Don't worry." He ruffled his brother's hair with a smile on his face.

The next time Jiro would see his brother would be when he became a Prestige four years later. Jiro spent his days with Nimbus and Cloud, getting lessons from Sagittarius and the Pisces at the time. His mind always drifted to the open ocean.

****

Taro's magic manifested in response to an unquenchable thirst for adventure. He was daydreaming of being a pirate one day, and he suddenly found himself on the deck of a Yankee Liberation ship.

I wanted that same adventure. I'd always hear the stories, Jiro thought. *When Taro's magic manifested, he could teleport to anywhere in the world. When my magic manifested, I was able to open a portal to only places I could see.*

"Yeah," Jiro scoffed with a reminiscent scowl. "Always so happy to leave too."

Taro watched him march ahead with a frown full of remorse. "Yeah…" His brother looked tired. *He's so tough to be able to go into it headfirst when he's only fifteen…*

"Follow me," Jiro said. "I purposely told you to meet at an earlier time, so if you were late, we'd still be early. We have an arms deal to get to."

Taro summoned *Zoomy Marty* beneath him and sat cross-legged on it, hovering next to Jiro as they passed through the lively streets of Ayo. Thumping bass and bright lights greeted its residents as the sun dipped further below the horizon.

They entered Hinatown in downtown Ayo. The smells of dumplings, ramen, fresh fish, and bulgogi hung in the air. Many of the shopkeepers and chefs of the noodle bars waved hello, and old aunts in sandals walking their dogs waved and greeted him.

"How are you so well known here?" Jiro asked.

"I've been hired by most of these people at some point," Taro explained. "Prestiges usually go for missions that pay well, and selfless missions often coincide with that. Small, local businesses don't often have a lot of money to spend on a Prestige. I'm one of the very few that take the jobs that help the little man. 'A friendly, neighborhood Prestige' as I call it," Taro smiled. "Plus, it's cool to hear people's stories."

Jiro scoffed. *If you're still helping people, why not just be Aquarius?*

They entered an empty restaurant, and Taro recognized the owner. "Doc Tao!"

The old Hinohanan man turned and smiled upon seeing Taro, who was finally standing. "Taro! It's so good to see you!" They hugged. "Have a seat at that table over there. The others should be arriving shortly."

Jiro and Taro took their seats. Jiro leaned over and whispered: "How do you know that guy?"

"He used to be a mob doctor back in Yankee," Taro whispered. "I guess he's in the food business now."

"Hello, Aquarius?" a woman's voice asked.

Taro and Jiro looked to the front door. Standing there was a woman and a young man followed by a group of Wanari with swords at their hips. The woman had orange irises, blonde hair, and a lion's tail poked out from behind and wrapped around her waist. The young man's dark skin contrasted with brilliant sapphire eyes. Poking out of his black, wavy hair were two small deer antlers with decorative strings wrapped around them. He was missing his left arm and had a katana at his hip.

"The leaders of the Stella Lumine?! Taro whispered. "You planned a meeting with Wanari civil rights activists?"

"Indeed," Jiro sighed.

"Ms. Sierra and Mr. Amahara, this is my brother, Taro; he will be joining us this evening. He is a capable Prestige," Jiro greeted.

"Pleasure to meet you, Taro," the woman greeted with a silky, elegant voice. "My name is Carmen Sierra. Please just call me Carmen."

"Aoba is fine for me," the teenager said with a firm handshake.

"These two have agreed to help with Penumbra's activity in the Wanari communities," Jiro explained. Penumbra's presence has increased as of late. The Stella Lumine have volunteered to pose as gangsters in a sting operation to buy weapons from Penumbra."

"They're bringing drugs and guns into my community," Carmen said sternly. "I grew up in the housing projects here in Ayo. I will ensure that my home doesn't become a warzone."

Aoba walked up to both of them. "I disagree with working with humans. Wanari problems should be solved by Wanari. I don't care if you're a Prestige and a Zodiac. We're still putting lives at risk for *humans*."

"Aoba!" Carmen snapped.

Aoba ignored her. "My kindred's lives come first. If things go south, I'm taking the situation into my own hands. Got it?"

Jiro gulped. "As you wish."

Aoba and his men exited the room and returned to the van they arrived in. Carmen walked up to the two brothers. "I apologize. Aoba has... experienced more hate than love in his life. I appreciate your help, Jiro."

"Of course," Jiro said. "Let's get a move on."

****

"I'll go over the plan once more," Jiro said as they drove to their destination. "Carmen, Aoba, Taro, and I will remain in the van with a couple of others. Once the deal gets going, I'll open a portal behind the Mafia members, and we trap them in a pincer attack. Got it?"

Everyone nodded in agreement.

The cracked sidewalks and identical townhouses of the Torchlight and Surgelight neighborhoods rolled past Jiro's window. Terramancers constructed most of the low-income housing, each one following the same simple blueprint.

"Did you know dad helped build these neighborhoods?" Taro asked.

"Yeah," Jiro replied. "I know."

They stopped the van, and the Stella Lumine men stepped out with the bags of money and traded their swords for the pistols Jiro brought them. Jiro and the others watched from the van as the others walked down the alley. Minutes later, a car pulled in and Mafia members got out, wearing their usual suits. Three more people poured out of the vehicle.

One was a young man wearing a mask covering his mouth and nose. He wore black Hinohanan clothing with a katana on his back and a pistol under his arm. The second was a Wanari man with a coyote tail, and the third was a teenage girl with frizzy brown hair in a ponytail poking out of a snapback with a Dia de Los Muertos mask covering her mouth and nose.

Taro recognized the girl instantly. *Riley!*

Aoba gripped his blade tighter as he watched.

"Hello, gentlemen," the coyote man said. "You were interested in buying some new armaments?"

He snapped his fingers, and two grunts brought a case and opened it, revealing a bundle of magic rifles. The Wanari examined them.

Only Chasm has magic rifles like that! Jiro thought.

"Where's the money?" the coyote man asked.

The man with the sword, Akio Furuidate (the Fifth), was suspicious. He read the minds of their customers. He leaned close to Riley.

"Aquarius and a couple of others are waiting to ambush us in that van over there," Akio whispered to Riley.

"Thata fact?" Riley snickered. *I'm going to drop a veil of smoke. You book it. Trust the other guy to follow.*

Akio read Riley's mind and gave a subtle nod. Riley fished out two handfuls of smoke pellets and chucked them into the ground, unleashing a large cloud of smoke.

"Scatter!" Akio barked at his grunts. "They have a Zodiac and a Prestige in the van! Forget the weapons and drugs!"

Riley took a deep breath as she entered the smoke, turning invisible within the cloud. She primed four smoke runestones and chucked them in different directions, creating four rivers of smoke for her to swim away in. The coyote Wanari also turned into smoke, and they dispersed.

Jiro immediately opened a large portal beneath the boxes containing the weapons and drugs and opened another portal in the van. The boxes landed in the car with a *clang*. Aoba was about to leap out of the van, but Carmen gripped his wrist. Taro teleported out and kicked a grunt in the face, turned, and summoned his revolvers *Butter* and *I Can't Believe It's Not Butter!* to his hands. Their chambers rotated to shock isotope, and he fired two quick shots, stunning two of the grunts.

The other grunts ran for their car, firing blindly at the smoke. Jiro opened two portals: one in front of him and one above his head, redirecting the gunfire to the sky. Taro stunned the remaining stragglers and the smoke cleared. Akio, Riley, and the coyote man escaped.

"Is everyone alright?" Taro asked.

The Wanari unanimously replied: "Yeah."

"We got what we wanted," Jiro said. "Let's get out of here."

****

Jiro thanked the Stella Lumine for their help, and he and his brother walked back to his yacht.

"You saw that coyote dude, right?" Jiro asked. "He also used smoke magic."

"It might've been Envy, but we don't know for sure," Taro said.

"I don't want to keep using the Stella Lumine," Jiro sighed. "But they want as minimal Chasm and police activity as possible. I'll have to see what I can do on my own..."

"H-hey Jiro," Taro said. "If you ever need any help, just let me know, okay? I know how tough and scary being a Zodiac can be, and our lowest point is when we need others the most, so... Uh... What I'm trying to say is..." Taro was interrupted by the buzzing of his Omnicard.

"It's fine, Taro. I get it," Jiro smiled. "Go."

Taro nodded and answered the call, "Monty? Yeah, I'll be there soon." He teleported away.

Jiro sighed and kept walking back to his yacht. *I can never be mad at him for too long...* Jiro considered himself tired, but he could see it in his brother's eyes that he was in the same boat. *Just how many jobs does he take a day?*

Jiro sat down at his desk and heaved a sigh. He held the Goblet in his hand, its weight filled with the expectations that spilled over its brim. *I never wanted to be a Zodiac...* Jiro thought. He could see himself going on adventures with Cloud and Nimbus, sailing across the open sea like his brother. A false future, a present never meant to be.

I don't have the same drive to help people like you do... Just take the Goblet back, you lazy bum... Jiro buried his head in his arms and laid across his desk, the fatigue of the day finally getting to him. His nap was interrupted by the sound of something slamming onto the deck. Jiro opened his door and saw a familiar face.

The man wore a heavy, black winter coat with white fur around the hood. His arms were free of the sleeves, and the coat's torn bottom swayed in the breeze. His eyes were sharp like a hawk's, and his black spikey hair had frosted tips.

"About time you showed up, Jiro!" he said with impatience in his voice.

"Masamune?"

The young man gave a smile. "I have business with your brother. Where is he?"

****

Taro teleported to the Cysko Hospital and landed in the courtyard near the front entrance with his face on the ground and his butt in the air. Monty looked at him for a good couple of seconds before punting his butt. Taro flipped over and was now on his back, stunned on the ground. People walked past, giving them confused looks.

"Why?" Taro asked sleepily.

"Sorry," Monty apologized with an innocent and dry voice. "You were wide open. I couldn't help myself."

Taro felt his Omnicard buzz again, and he fished it out of his pocket. It was a text from Jiro:

Jiro Takahara: Masamune just showed up on the yacht looking for you. He's heading toward the Runeseekers.

Taro sat up and reread the text. *Is he here because of the Mafia too? Did the Dean get a hold of him somehow?* He heaved a sigh and put his Omnicard back in his pocket. *I need to lay off taking jobs for a while… I can't keep this up.*

Monty stood next to him with a bouquet of azaleas in his hand.

"Oh hey, those flowers for me?" Taro asked.

"Of course not. They're for a friend," Monty said. "What's with the hair?"

Monty referred to Taro's new haircut: the top was a little shorter than usual with the same part on his forehead. The sides were buzzed before his ear lobe. Past it, his hair was present but still on the short side. The hair in the back was tied in a ponytail that went slightly past his shoulders.

"Just trying something new," Taro shrugged.

Monty averted his gaze and fell silent.

"I talked with Kaze this morning. He told me to talk to you."

Taro titled his head. "About what?"

"H-how did you change yourself? How did you find something else to motivate you?" Monty struggled to ask. "Kaze said you're on the same path as me when it comes to uh… self-forgiveness."

Taro looked up at the night sky. "Wow, that's... um... that's a toughie." *No it isn't,* Taro scoffed in his mind. "I uh… Uncle Kaze and a couple of other people still found value in me when I didn't value myself. I'm a bad person like you, and everyone else thinks Monty. I was chosen to be Aquarius. I didn't want the responsibility so much that my magic manifested, and I teleported onto a pirate ship with the Goblet in hand. I shoved my burdens onto my younger brother and all to just lead my pirate crew to their deaths and become a deadbeat drunk in Yankee… I'm the worst."

Monty's expression softened.

"The reason I take so many jobs is just… I feel like I'm atoning in some way. I don't know… I used to only think about myself, so it's only right that I do whatever I can to help others now."

Monty knelt and smiled. He patted Taro on the head patronizingly. However, he spoke with an understanding tone: "You know… I uh…" Monty gulped. "I may be treating you too harshly."

Taro's eyes widened, and his lips pursed out of surprise.

Monty averted his gaze. "You seem to be making Monica happy, and that is something I cannot do as well as you can, apparently." Monty smiled. "So thank you. You're not such a bum after all."

Taro wasn't so convinced yet. "Thanks," he chuckled before teleporting away.

Monty continued to the physical therapy area. He stopped and peered through a window at a studio on the other side of the wall.

Melody was between two mounted parallel bars, slowly making her way to the end. A nurse was beside her the whole time, closely monitoring her movements. She looked like she was about to fall, but she always caught her balance without the help of the bar. When she finally made it to the end with no assistance needed, she collapsed to the ground, tired, soaking in sweat with a victorious fist raised to the sky. Nurses and her parents rushed to her side to help her up with tears and smiles on their faces.

I'm done running… Monty thought to himself. He looked at the looming curtain of guilt between him and Melody. *It's about time I faced my guilt properly…*

4: Masamune Lands

Henry was watching the Runeseekers headquarters, sitting bored in his car.

"How are things going down in Ayo?" Henry asked.

Riley, Akio, and the coyote man were in an apartment in Ayo. "The Stella Lumine are cooperating with Aquarius to impede our efforts," Akio said.

"So they're resorting to working with wild dogs now?" Henry chuckled. "That's fine. In fact, it's really good. The more we spread their attention across Ayo and Cysko, the better. Envy, if you're going to replenish your aura, do it in Cysko. Make them bounce back and forth."

The coyote man's skin warped into the black miasma that made Envy's body. The shape of his glowing yellow eyes was the only thing conveying emotion. "Doesn't matter to me. Humans taste the same everywhere," he crowed.

"I'll focus on tearing Prism apart," Henry said.

"You're sure having fun," Riley scoffed.

"They locked up my father," Henry said. "It's only fair I get to make them suffer for it. Keep me updated."

"Henry," Riley said. "Dalton is off-limits…"

Henry hung up. *Elizabeth cares too much for Clara that she won't risk endangering her. Clara is too stubborn and will want to settle things with me herself. I just need to find a way to separate them…*

It was then that Henry saw a black dragon come down from the sky and land on the rooftop of the building in a magnificent display of purple light and rippling shadows. He dropped his joint in awe as he saw a man jump down from the roof and land in front of the entrance.

No way… is that?! Henry thought, pulling out his Omnicard and using its magnifying feature. *It's Masamune Asteria! Oh, this just made my job a whole lot easier!* He put his Omnicard back in his pocket and held in a laugh.

****

Masamune entered the headquarters and the bell chimed as the door opened. "Yo, it's been a while."

"Ah, Masamune!" Kaze exclaimed. "We were just about to have some tea! Would you like some?"

"No, I'm not in the mood right now," Masamune replied.

"Hey, Spiky Hair!" Taro greeted with a salute. "How was the weather on Mt. Ashen?"

"Shut up," Masamune growled and shifted his gaze to Taro. He noticed his hair and began laughing, "And you can't say anything about my hair."

"Agh, screw it!" Taro cursed. "My hair is fine, thank you very much."

"In any case," Masamune said as he composed himself. "I'm sorry to say that I'm not here for a cute little reunion with you lot. I'm on official business."

"With who? You're usually not one to listen to somebody," Sol asked.

"Leo hired me to look into some reports of ice monsters in the area. We think Vayne might be active around here," Masamune explained. "But first, food! Where can we eat something? I'm sure you know a place."

Well, that lines up perfectly… Taro thought.

****

Taro took them to Alright Guys, which by the time they arrived, was already closed. Taro knocked on the door and Luke came and answered.

"What're you doing here so late?" he grumbled.

"We're here to drink and eat of course!" Taro cheered. "Besides, as part of our agreement, I get to come and eat here whenever I want."

"I know, I know," Luke said as he let them in. "Doesn't mean I can't whine about it though."

They sat down at the bar and Masamune exclaimed, "We'll have burgers and stouts!" He laughed with a cheerful smile.

As they were served their drinks and food, Nathan came down from his office. He paused for a split second upon seeing Masamune before continuing his descent.

"Taro, what brings you here so late at night?"

"Nathan, this is Masamune Asteria. Masamune, this is Nathan," Taro introduced after suppressing a burp.

"I know who this man is," Nathan said with a smile. "Sir Asteria, it's a pleasure to meet you."

"And it's a pleasure to eat your food," Masamune replied.

"Nathan, if it's fine with you, Masamune has some questions about Vayne. A common enemy between the two of you."

"Oh, is that so?" Nathan asked.

"Yeah, so hurry and take a seat," Masamune snapped. "I recognized your foulness the moment I entered the restaurant, demon."

"Oh-ho!" Nathan exclaimed. "So you were able to recognize me, eh?"

"Ha! How could I forget the leader of the group of demons trying to kill Vayne?"

Sol and Kaze looked over at Taro, confused.

"What? They seemed like alright guys. Hence the title! Even if they are demons, they haven't killed a single person since opening up their restaurant!" Taro explained.

"So, what is it that you need?" Nathan asked, taking a seat beside Masamune.

"Tell me everything you know. Especially about how Vayne is able to teleport somehow. He never possessed such an ability in life."

Nathan gave a sigh. "Vayne is now part lich. He's still partly alive, so he can go back and forth between the Overworld (our dimension) and the Spirit World."

"It's possible to do that?" Masamune asked.

"Of course it is. If one can enter the Spirit World after dying, it stands to reason that one could exit it. However, it takes an immense amount of aura to traverse between dimensions."

"That would explain how Vayne was able to commit the Frostflame Massacre," Masamune muttered to himself. "So you're saying he can't do it too often?"

"No, he can't. And when he does, he's left with a fraction of his power. He uses quite a bit to open a rift and then pop back out here. So sometimes when he's had enough, he'll send the occasional monster after us just to keep us on our toes. When someone dies, they usually become a faint, weak spirit made of pure aura that can't be regenerated. So if they were to travel between dimensions, they wouldn't have enough aura to travel again. Vayne isn't totally dead, so he's still able to regenerate aura, hence why he is able to do it."

Masamune gave him a distrustful glare. "I'll accept your explanation until I have a better one myself. But as of right now, that's as close to a solid story as I've gotten."

"So what's the next step for you?" Kaze asked.

Masamune gobbled down a handful of fries. "I've already talked with Aquarius and it appears that Envy has joined forces with Penumbra. I have an interest in just how strong a Sin can be…" Masamune gave an eager smile, imagining the epic fight that would break out.

"Then you can help us with our investigation," Sol suggested. "Penumbra seems to have targeted some new members of ours. So we've moved them to a dorm in Atlas where they are closer to Sagittarius."

"New members?"

"Yeah, we got Monty Cruz, Amethyst Violet. They're relatives of Vega you know," Taro said.

"And my nephew and niece," Kaze chimed in.

"Is that so?" Masamune asked, his intrigue starting to build. "Who else?"

"Clara Bernardino, her last name needs no introduction. Dalton Drake, Paige Tovera, son of Miles…" Taro kept listing.

"My, this is quite the team," Masamune commented. "How did you all get in touch with them?"

"They're all a part of this Prestige Program that Atlas has pioneered. Apparently, other schools are starting to form their own programs. There's only so many capable mages out there, right? Why not scout them out?"

"I don't like the sound of it," Masamune grumbled. "Doesn't this just sound like a ripoff of Team Majestic?"

"I suppose it kind of does," Kaze laughed. "Man, those were the days."

"Oh, and there's this girl that can stop time right?" Taro asked.

Masamune was in the middle of a drink before he started to cough.

"Oh yeah!" Kaze exclaimed. "Elizabeth Baker! She came out of nowhere! She's a friend of Clara's apparently."

Masamune's tone suddenly got serious. "Where is this woman's house?"

"We don't know, somewhere in Atlas. They wanted to keep it confidential," Kaze explained.

"Useless!" Masamune snapped. He got up and briskly walked to the door.

"Where are you going?" Sol asked.

"I'm already full anyway," Masamune growled. "I'm taking a quick trip to Atlas. I need to find this Elizabeth girl."

"She's probably asleep!" Taro insisted. "Aw, wait, what do you care?" he grumbled. "Why don't I just call her to stop by headquarters tomorrow?"

"Nope," Masamune quickly replied. "I don't feel like waiting that long."

He walked out the door and turned the corner out of sight.

"What's up with him?" Taro asked.

"No one knows..." Kaze sighed. "Best to just let him be."

Masamune turned the corner and bumped into a teenager with his hood pulled over his eyes. It was Henry.

"Watch it," Masamune threatened.

After he got his bearings, Henry quickly said, "I might have something that interests you, Masamune Asteria."

"I don't care," Masamune scoffed. He loaded his legs, a tail of shadow sprouting from his hips and black wings growing from his shoulder blades. Eventually, they shifted down his back and formed into a complete dragon between his legs.

"It concerns the Scroll," Henry added as he got to his feet.

Masamune froze. "Speak or I obliterate you here and now."

"Now, now, no need to be so aggressive," Henry chuckled.

He held his Omnicard in his hand and shook it playfully. On the screen was a text conversation of Henry telling Elizabeth to go to Greedlake, posing as Masamune.

"Elizabeth Baker is heading toward Greedlake as we speak. I set up an appointment for you two. If you go now, you'll be able to catch up." Henry gave a sly smile.

"Bastard, you're making me go quite a long way," Masamune growled. "Who do you think you are?" Four spears of moonlight appeared above Henry's head, ready to be launched.

"You won't kill me. Because you can't."

Masamune grew tired of him and let the four spears loose, piercing Henry's head and shoulders. However, Henry's image shimmered and faded away.

Brat uses illusion magic... Masamune observed. *Whatever. I have more pressing matters to attend to.*

Henry watched him launch into the sky with a devilish smile on his face. *And there goes three of my biggest problems. I guess my father wasn't so useless after all. The Chirp addresses he gave me actually came in handy. Now, as for Monty and Clara...*

****

Dalton woke up on Sunday to expect a morning breakfast with his friends. How disappointed he was when found the building to be empty. Monty already cooked breakfast. Two plates, one with a humongous helping of bacon and turkey sausage and scrambled eggs and one with pancakes and bacon, and a fruit bowl remained. Each had a sticky note next to it, but Dalton could tell who they were cooked for by looking at the food. Dalton looked at the clock: 8:00 a.m.

Just how early does this guy wake up to cook? Dalton wondered. He heard shuffling and walked around the corner and looked down the hall. Monty and Paige were putting their shoes on, ready to go somewhere. "Hey, where you guys heading?" he asked.

Monty and Paige quickly shared a look. Monty was the first to speak. "Nowhere special."

"I'm heading to school to work on homework," Paige explained.

"Oh… Well, okay then. Monty, mind if I tag along?" Dalton asked with a nervous smile.

Monty could see Dalton was uncomfortable. *Damn Popsicle Prince. Wears his stupid heart on his sleeve.* "No, but where I'm going is pretty boring, so I don't want to do that to you. If you're looking for something to do, bother Elizabeth or hang out with Amy." Monty finished putting on his shoes and opened the door. "See you guys."

"See you guys later," Paige said with a smile and they closed the door behind them.

Dalton was left alone. And he hated it. *They're hiding something from me.* Being alone meant time to think, and when he had time to think, nothing good came of it. He went back to the kitchen and scarfed down his food. *The others must have already eaten. Strange, Amy is usually the first one up other than Monty…*

Dalton decided to take Monty's advice and went upstairs to check on Amy. He brought her food with him, freshly warmed up. *Maybe she's just in her room drawing?* Dalton hoped. He knocked. "Hey Amy, you up?"

There was shuffling and an aggressive, "Argh!" After seconds of silence, finally, she groaned a response steeping with disappointment: "Yeah, I'm up…"

"I got your breakfast right here. Monty made you pancakes."

"Just um… Just leave it at the door. I'm not really hungry right now."

"You sure?"

"Yeah."

"O-okay then." Dalton put down the platter next to the door. *Weird.* Dalton stood back up and leaned closer into the door, tempted to open it. "You doing alright?"

An inaudible murmur came from Amy.

"What was that?"

"I'm okay."

She's not okay, Dalton quickly determined. He wanted to kick down the door and get to the bottom of what she was thinking. He clenched his fists and gritted his teeth before clicking his tongue. "Alright then. If you need to talk to someone we're all here for you. Alright, my partner-in-crime?"

"Yeah... Thanks..." Amy chuckled.

Dalton walked away feeling defeated. *All of my life, I've been trained to read people's body language—guess their next moves and thoughts—why doesn't it work with these guys?*

"Dalton? What are you doing?" Elizabeth asked.

Dalton's heart fluttered and he turned around to see Elizabeth dressed in her armor, but she only had one pistol strapped. *Did she lose the other one?* However, much to Dalton's delight, she was still wearing high socks and a skirt that was a little on the short side. *Huh, that's weird...* He crossed his arms with a puzzled look on his face. "Hmm..."

"What?" Elizabeth asked, feeling a little violated. She took a step back.

Dalton sat back up. "It's just... I never understood why you girls wear skirts to battle. Like, are you wearing shorts under there or something?"

Elizabeth gave a sigh. "It's a battle skirt."

"A what now?"

"A battle skirt!" Elizabeth repeated and stomped her foot. "It's made so that you can be maneuverable while keeping what you want hidden, hidden."

"Huh, that's actually pretty cool!"

Elizabeth sighed and walked past him down the steps. "I don't have time for this. I was assigned a mission for Runeseekers and I need to get going."

"Oh, let me come with ya!" Dalton smiled, bouncing to his feet.

"I really don't need your help," Elizabeth insisted.

"Aw, come on! I like our little chats. Don't you? Besides, you can do more when you work together with your team!" Dalton justified with a finger in the air.

"If you follow me I'll shoot you."

"A little harsh don't you think?"

Elizabeth just glared at him and the next thing Dalton knew, she was already out the door. "Ah! You stopped time, that's not fair!" Dalton reached out to Elizabeth, but she closed the door behind her.

Dalton was alone again.

He heard the hum of Clara's car starting and he clenched his fists.

It's because you think I'm worthless, huh? I'll show you! I'll show you all how useful I can be! I've proven it so many times before and I can do it again! Watch me this time!

His eyes burst with yellow and he focused on Elizabeth's scent with his nose. A wispy trail of orange aura appeared in front of him. *I'm on the way!*

****

The Northern Rail was a prototype of the Tran-Zip and the only way to efficiently get to Greedlake without flying. Ninety percent of it was on the surface of Lokyer which left it prone to signum attacks. The train was soon abandoned and plans were made for the Tran-Zip that is used today. During its time of operation, it would run between Atlas and Montralis, refueling halfway at the Asterium mining town now known as Greedlake. The town is currently a ghost town, its people wiped out by signum in 245 U, hence there is no Tran-Zip route to Greedlake.

Pinecones, pine needles, and acorns from the trees accompanied the dirt that was strewn across the floor of the train station. Rust and vines covered the sides of all twenty of the empty train cars. Most were meant to carry cargo, but others were built for livestock and passengers. Elizabeth went to the locomotive at the front of the train. She pulled at the door handle, but the door didn't budge. She tried again, yanking harder; no use. She pulled out her pistol and fired an arcane bolt at the door hinges. The door dropped to the floor with a *clank* and it moaned as it tipped over and fell.

The engine was a simple asterium siphon. You would place a large block of whatever asterium in the cubby and it would be siphoned and used to power the engine.

How much asterium would it take though? Elizabeth wondered. She checked the cargo cars and found one with a convenient amount of bricks filled with asterium.

She carried it to the locomotive and stacked them until the cubby was filled. She pulled down on the lever, and the orange scorch isotope ore began to flow between the cracks of the bricks and into the engine. The train jerked and it began to move.

Well, that was simple...

By the time Dalton got to the station, the train had already left and the sun was low in the sky. He ran over to the tracks, sword in hand, and looked for the train.

It's powered by asterium so... Dalton thought and activated his demon eyes again. He looked far in the distance and saw a blob of asterium in a car-shaped space. It was about three football fields away and picking up speed. *Crap!*

Dalton sprinted toward the train. "Wait!"

He took a deep breath and slowly let it out. His breath was a chilled wind that whipped up in front of him to create three clones, each one further forward than the next. Like a baton pass, Dalton caught up with the first clone and it grabbed a hold of his wrist and hurled him forward. It gave a salute before turning into slush.

"I'm coming!" Dalton shouted with a smile as he sprinted toward the next clone.

Elizabeth took a seat in the passenger car and leaned against the wall. All of the seats had been removed and so she sat on the floor. It was moldy and a little damp and she could feel the water being displaced as she put her weight on it.

I've slept in worse places, Elizabeth chuckled to herself.

Her rest was short-lived.

"Liiiiiz!" Dalton's voice faintly shouted. "Liiiiz!"

Elizabeth's ears perked up and she checked outside. Dalton was sprinting alongside the train. His form was breaking and he was totally winded.

"Dalton?!" Elizabeth exclaimed.

When Dalton saw her, he threw his arms out. "I'm here to help you!"

"Dalton..." Elizabeth murmured. She blushed a little and smiled.

She's happy I'm here! Dalton thought giddily.

Elizabeth, with her blush and smile still on her face, quickly pulled out her pistol and shot Dalton in the chest.

Dalton was blown back and electricity surged through his body. "Oh, *come on*!" He tripped and tumbled across the ground until he came to a stop and began to spasm.

Elizabeth gave a nod of satisfaction and went back inside. She closed her eyes and let out a sigh of relief.

"Is that really your reaction when I come to help you?" Dalton's voice asked.

Elizabeth's eyes darted to the source of the voice: Dalton's head, which was upside-down, looking into the cabin. She fired a shock bolt and it grazed the top of the door frame. Dalton gave a "Woah!" And ducked out of sight.

"What are you doing here, Dalton?!" Elizabeth snapped.

"I could ask you the same thing," Dalton sighed as he came out of hiding and swung into the car. He brushed the dust off his clothes and smiled. "What's up with you running off like this? He leaned against the wall with his hands in his pockets. "You didn't even text in the group chat."

Elizabeth heaved a sigh and holstered her pistol. She slumped back down to the floor and pulled her beanie down over her eyebrows. "Ugh, it wasn't supposed to go this way."

Elizabeth buried her face in her hands and stared at the floor in front of her. Dalton felt bad and also a little irritated that the floor was getting more attention than he was seemingly.

"When's your birthday?" he asked.

"Huh?" Elizabeth responded, lifting her gaze from the floor.

"When's your birthday?"

"Why do you want to know?"

"I just want to know. Isn't that reason enough?" Dalton asked. He looked over at Elizabeth, and he could tell she was raising a brow. "My birthday is December eighth, four-hundred and eighty-four U. What's yours?"

Elizabeth finally gave in. "May tenth, four-hundred and eighty-three U."

Dalton counted on his fingers. "Wait a minute, you're a year older than me?!"

"Mhm," Elizabeth nodded, not impressed by it. She couldn't really see why Dalton would be impressed by it either.

"How? Why are you in our grade?" Dalton asked.

Elizabeth began to speak but held her tongue. After she thought about what she was going to say, she explained that "I started a year late."

"Oh? Is that so?" Dalton said. "Why?"

Elizabeth leaned forward, confused. "What's with these questions?"

"Who wouldn't want to get to know someone as gorgeous as you?" Dalton shrugged as if he were caught guilty.

"*Dalton,*" Elizabeth urged.

He regained his composure and looked out the window over Elizabeth's head. The moons were starting to become more visible. Dalton sighed. "Whenever I see someone like you or Monty try and do this stuff on your own, it pisses me off."

"I just don't want anyone to–"

"Worry? It doesn't work," Dalton tiredly interrupted. "It's easy for me to see most of us at Prism are wearing masks lately. Well, Monty I don't know. He's been in an upfront mood lately, it's kinda creepy."

"Oh? And what's my mask?"

"The fact that you always act like everything is under control when you're actually worried and uncertain," Dalton quickly explained. "Kinda like what you're doing with me right now."

Elizabeth went quiet.

"Please, tell me what's going on," Dalton pleaded. "Just trust me."

"I don't know..."

"Eh? Why?"

"Maybe it's because children like you aren't responsible enough to do adult things," Elizabeth mocked with her nose in the air all smug-like.

"Huh? But I'm only a year younger than you!"

"Making you?"

"Seventeen."

"And me?"

"Eighteen?"

"And which of those ages are considered to be an adult?"

"Now who's the one not being serious?"

Elizabeth giggled and smiled. After several seconds of contemplating and looking at an anxious Dalton, she decided, "I'm going to bed. Goodnight." And she laid down, turned onto her side, and closed her eyes.

Dalton decided to do the same and laid down next to her. Dalton had his eyes open, looking at the ceiling, hoping Elizabeth was just kidding and she'd open her eyes and start talking again. Minutes passed by, nothing.

"Hey…" Elizabeth finally turned onto her back. Dalton raised a brow. "Do you want to kiss?"

Silence filled the room like water trickling into a bucket. Once it was filled, Dalton was finally able to process the question and give a response. "You must have fun teasing me, huh? Well, it's only fair because I tease you too."

Elizabeth was still looking at the ceiling. "Aaaaand you lost your only chance. Goodnight for real this time. She turned so that she was on her side, looking away from Dalton.

"Huh?! Wait, you were serious?!" Dalton blurted out. He got up and tried to look at Elizabeth's face, but she wouldn't let him. "Let me try again!"

"Too late. Goodnight. You take the first watch. Wake me up later."

Dalton buried his face into his hands and laid back down. *I blew it!*

Elizabeth looked at her hands which were cupped together in front of her. Dalton was added to her list of uncertainties.

So I guess he isn't here to make a move on me… Elizabeth thought. *Further testing needed. There's no way he's here to just help me. He must have some ulterior motive. Everyone does!*

Hours passed and Elizabeth woke up to a small ray of sunlight that hit her eye. That and Dalton's heavy breathing.

"Hey, just what're you—?!" Elizabeth snapped and turned to look at Dalton.

He was asleep, but sweat dripped from his forehead and soaked his shirt. Then it hit her: *the train hasn't stopped.*

She quietly got up so as not to wake Dalton up and climbed up onto the roof. The morning sun's warmth was comforting in the brisk breeze as the train pushed forward through the alpines.

She walked up to the locomotive and swung inside. A Dalton clone was there. A block of ice filled with aura was in the cubby and the Dalton clone was constantly replenishing it with an icy wind from his palm.

Elizabeth landed loudly on purpose so it got the clone's attention. She crossed her arms and raised a brow.

The Dalton clone jumped and slowly looked over to where the noise came from. "Aw, crap. She found out!" he muttered under his breath. He stopped the frostflow from his hand and turned away.

"Okay, just act natural," he murmured to himself. He turned back around and leaned with one hand on the wall. He used the other to brush his hair back. "Hey, didn't see you there."

"What are you doing?" Elizabeth asked, her right foot tapping with impatience.

"Uh... I was stretching."

"Stretching? Are you sure? Cause it looks like you've been up all night powering the train."

"Pfft, what? Nooo," he chuckled with a wave of his hand. "I uh, was looking out for signum so the real me could sleep and the locomotive was–"

"Dalton, why are you here?" Elizabeth asked, exasperated.

The Dalton clone heaved a sigh. "Go wake the real me up, then we can talk." The clone placed his hand on the ice block and poured his remaining aura into it before turning into a normal pile of slush.

The train continued to barrel along the tracks. It's wheels clacking and creaking.

5: Cloak and Dagger

Dalton's back was against the wall, literally and figuratively. He shook his shoulders and took a deep breath.

Elizabeth was standing across the aisle, waiting for an explanation. When one didn't come, she sighed. "I'll ask again... why do you keep trying to concern yourself with me?"

"It's just like I said yesterday: whenever I see you or Monty do this whole solo act thing and try to take on all of these burdens and bottle them up, it hurts me too. Because I've been there, and it sucks."

Elizabeth said nothing, but Dalton could tell she wanted him to elaborate further. Her foot hadn't stopped tapping. She hunched her shoulders and crossed her arms. *She's not gonna give unless you give something first, Dalton,* he thought to himself.

"Do you recall hearing anything special about Yankee six years ago?" Dalton asked.

"It was the first time Puakai appealed to the World Council," Elizabeth answered. "Something about Penumbra growing stronger and a chain of robberies by some thieves. Why?"

"Well... I was one of those *vigilantes*. Not a thief."

An uncomfortable silence filled the car. "Wait," Elizabeth chuckled in disbelief. "You were a thief?"

Dalton pursed his lips a little and nodded his head, "Yeah, okay, sure I was a thief."

Dalton's being... humble? Elizabeth thought. *Usually, he'd keep fighting for that vigilante title...*

Elizabeth continued, "But you stole from—"

"Everyone," Dalton interjected. "You see, Akerym occupied Yankee from the Second Astral War until about 15 years ago or so? Well, the fat corporate cats—a.k.a the posh—still controlled many businesses and city-state government. People weren't too happy about that. Everyone was poor, and the press blamed it on 'low-productivity and alcohol and drugs,'" Dalton said sarcastically in air quotes. "So, people turned to gangs. It was survival of the fittest; we stole from Penumbra, rival gangs, and the posh living in their penthouses." He thought about it for a second. "I guess that's not technically *everyone*, but you get the point."

Elizabeth looked down at Dalton, bewilderment and disbelief written across her face. *Usually, he'd be upset that I'm looking down at him, or he'd be bragging.* Dalton's usual upright posture was weakened to a slight slouch.

"Honestly, you being a thief explains a lot," she finally said and took a seat.

Dalton could relax a little more, but he knew he still hadn't broken through Elizabeth's defenses. After all, he's done the majority of the talking. Dalton respected honesty, he lived and breathed transparency, always saying what was on his mind. *But this...* he thought, *this is hard to say.*

"I was an honorable thief at least," Dalton chuckled. He went silent and stared at the ceiling for a while before his eyes panned down to Elizabeth, who was waiting for more. "You know, it's not fair that I'm the one doing all the talking."

"No, please, continue. You were on a roll," Elizabeth insisted with a smile.

Wow, she really wants to be thorough, huh? Dalton thought.

"Fine," Dalton groaned. "Maybe after I tell you my story, you'll understand that doing things alone doesn't work that well."

He looked out the window and watched the blurry trees go past. They slowly morphed into buildings, the sunlight snuffed out, and snow began to flutter to the ground as his imagination kicked in. "When I was super young, I belonged to an orphanage. My mom had died shortly after giving birth to me, and my dad was M.I.A.

"I ran away like a child running from home with no destination in mind. Like an idiot because they were upset and didn't know what else to do. While the other kids did chores, focused on their studies, yada-yada, I wanted to play. I was, what? Ten? I didn't know any better. I was called useless, they told me there was no way I would succeed, so I said 'screw 'em' and ran away. The first couple of months were the toughest..."

****

"Hey! Get back here!" the baker shouted.

A young Dalton sprinted through the snowy, slippery, and windy streets of Yankee. A loaf of bread was in his hand and another in his mouth. He turned a corner into an alley, hoping to find a fire escape and use it to get on the rooftops. What he found was a dead end.

The baker cornered him and beat the crap out of him. Dalton crashed into a pile of garbage, his stomach aching, his head throbbing, and his skin freezing.

"That's what you get, you little runt! Try and steal from me again, I dare you!" The baker spat, and it hit Dalton in the face.

Happy birthday, Dalton! He got up and wiped his bloody nose with the back of his wrist. *Stupid! Stupid! Stupid!* He repeatedly kicked the dumpster until someone interrupted him.

"You're wasting your energy, kid."

Dalton looked up, and there he was, dressed in dirty and worn-out wool clothes. A green sweater with a brown overcoat and fingerless gloves, bushy brown hair. A girl about Dalton's age wore a similar outfit with a scarf covering her mouth. She had messy brown hair that was let free to go wherever it chose. Some of it was sticking up, other parts were matted, and others went downward.

"Name's Simon," the teenager introduced himself. "And this is my kid sister, Riley." He pointed at the girl with his thumb. "What's yours?"

Dalton still didn't know whether to trust them. "Dalton," he peeped.

"You look a little rough, Dalton," Simon said. "You need some help?"

"I don't need charity," Dalton spat. He instantly regretted those words. *Crap, I provoked him.* He immediately prepared to sprint away if need be.

Simon laughed. "I can see you're finally getting the hang of the flight or fight thing, huh? You must be new to the streets. You didn't have much of that a couple of seconds ago." He smiled and said, "a rule of thievery: only steal things you know you can get away with. Stealing it is one thing, actually keeping it and getting away is another."

He tossed something down to Dalton. Dalton couldn't make out what it was, so he cautiously stepped forward, keeping one eye on Simon and Riley at all times. He recognized that it was a piece of bread. He inched closer, still looking at Simon, who was watching over it, squatting on the ledge of the roof like a hawk. Dalton reached a hand out when he heard a quiet, nearly inaudible whistling in the air. He tumbled to his right and looked at where he once stood. Simon had thrown a knife at him.

Simon laughed, "Nice awareness and reaction! You passed the test. The bread is all yours!"

Dalton slowly crept forward like an animal. He snatched the bread and ducked for cover. He gorged on it, wolfing it down in a couple of bites and nearly choking.

"Easy now!" Simon chuckled. "Tastes good, doesn't it? Do you want more?"

Dalton raised a brow, waiting for the catch. "What's the catch?" *There's always a catch.*

"We're trying to change Yankee!" Simon declared, full of hunger and ambition. "What do you say? You'd be a good addition to the team!"

"Nah, I'm better alone!" Dalton chuckled. "I could give a rat's ass about the people of this city!"

"And that's where you're mistaken!" Simon snapped. "Working in a team is the only way to live in this town. And you, with your snappy tongue, would be great in ours. Nothing better than helping people with food in your belly, right?"

****

"After that, I followed them to their hideout, an abandoned cinema. And so I met the rest of the Cinema Club–that's what they called themselves. The others aren't significant. Well, actually…"

Dalton thought about it for a second.

"There was this guy Oz, he was alright, but all you need to know about is Riley and Simon." Dalton adjusted himself to get more comfortable. "So, to get into the Cinema Club officially, I had to do an initiation of sorts. I had to steal something with them."

****

Dalton, Riley, and Simon hid around a street corner. Across the street and down the way was a restaurant with shining lights. Fancy cars pulled up and were valeted to a parking garage somewhere in the area.

"Okay, our goal is to raid that kitchen," Simon explained. "I'll be here for backup in case you two need it."

"Hey, wait, then what are we doing?" Dalton snapped.

"Just shut up and follow me," Riley sighed and dashed across the street.

Dalton scrambled after her, almost slipping on the icy pavement. They hid behind a dumpster in the back alley.

"What're we doing?" Dalton asked.

"Waiting for someone to go on a smoke break," Riley said as if the answer were obvious.

After ten minutes of waiting, the door swung open, and a young waiter stepped outside.

"Bingo," Riley snickered.

The waiter lit a cigarette and puffed out a cloud of smoke. Riley began twiddling her fingers, and the smoke began to swirl. It wrapped around the waiter's neck and began to strangle him. It flowed back into his lungs, and he coughed and wheezed until he passed out.

"You can use magic?!" Dalton exclaimed.

"Ssh!" Riley snapped, her hair slapping Dalton across the face as she pivoted around. "Yes, I can. Now come on!" she urged in a hushed voice.

Kind of a jerk, isn't she? Dalton thought to himself as they took the waiter's keys and crept to the door.

"Wait. This leads right to the kitchen. We'll need a distraction first," Dalton said.

"*Or* I could roll the cigarette under the door, use the smoke coming out of it to get across without anybody seeing me," Riley smiled at Dalton like he was a dumbass.

"Then what do I do?" Dalton grumbled.

"*You* will be the lookout, and you can help me carry the food."

"Magic is stupid. Why do you get to have it?"

"Stop being a baby."

Riley creaked open the door and saw the pantry down the hall. She took a puff of the cigarette and began to cough—this was obviously her first time using one—and then rolled it into the restaurant and under the pantry door. Her body began to melt into smoke, and she was able to travel along the small trail of smoke that the cigarette left behind.

She came back empty. "Damn!" she cursed.

"Where's the food?" Dalton asked.

"For some reason, the food won't turn into smoke with me!"

"Wow, and you were acting like hot stuff earlier too," Dalton jeered.

"Shut up! I've never had to steal food using smoke magic before."

"You suck."

"Well, it's not like you have any better ideas!"

"I do, actually. I'll distract them. And you steal the food. Simon is there to help. He and the others need food, too, right? So they can help you carry it."

"What's the distraction going to be?" Riley asked suspiciously.

"You'll know it when it comes. Running away is my specialty, after all."

"Says the person who got cornered in an alley and had the crap beat out of 'em."

"That's in the past! Watch, I'll even steal some stuff while I'm at it."

Dalton grabbed the knife out of Riley's pocket and cut the sleeves off of the knocked-out waiter. He did the same with his pants, shortening them, so they at least stopped at his ankles, even though they looked like parachute pants on Dalton. It was passable, and it would buy Dalton at least a couple of seconds, which was all he needed.

It was Dalton's turn to enter the building. He waited until a couple pulled up to the front and trailed them in. He loitered around, watching the couple, and saw they took their coats and put them on a rack. The rack spat out two tickets with numbers. Their coats took up the last two hooks, and the stand whirred to life. It shot up and ran along some rails that moved the coats high above people's heads. A new, empty frame took its place.

Good! It looks like they have a clothing thing super far away from the kitchen. I'll make a mess and steal some shit while Riley steals food!

Dalton followed the moving rack into a room full of coats. Adjacent was a booth where someone watched the outgoing and ingoing racks.

Dalton strolled up to the window and knocked. The man jumped and turned. When he saw a child with messy hair, he became suspicious.

"What's the matter?" he asked.

"I think the coat thing at the front is stuck," Dalton said innocently. He tried to act like he wasn't sure what was going on or why he had been sent. "My mom and dad put their coats on it, but it won't give them the ticket things. It just stays put, even though it's full."

The man clicked his teeth. "Great." He got out of his seat and opened the door, storming off in frustration.

Dalton caught the door with his foot before it closed and snuck inside the room. It was an array of racks with serial numbers displayed on a screen on their shafts. Dalton quickly began grabbing as many expensive coats as he could.

I don't have much time before they come back!

After grabbing all he could carry, he went to leave the room, but a coat in the corner caught his eye. It was black and appeared to be made of wool. A roaring white lion with a mane of flame was printed on the back.

It called to Dalton. His vision tunneled. His feet felt like they were hovering across the ground as if a gravitational force pulled him toward the coat.

He feared to touch it, but his hand lurched forward and gingerly grazed the sleeve. His senses returned, and everything else popped back into existence. The color of the coat began to change to a shade of beige, and the texture of the material changed.

"Huh?" Dalton peeped. He tried to pull away, but his hand was glued on.

The coat began flapping sporadically like a flag in the wind. It detached from its perch and hovered in place for a second before blasting off with Dalton along with it.

"Woaaaaah!" Dalton yelled in surprise as they flew past people at high speed.

Dalton closed his eyes and hung on for dear life. He felt his body being whipped around a corner as people gasped and spouted other exclamations. Then suddenly, he stopped.

Dalton slowly opened his eyes and saw that he was still hanging onto the coat. However, he was now in the dining area, held up by a tall man. Everyone's eyes were focused on him.

The man was holding his coat with a look on his face that showed confusion and discontent. He had short, brown hair and the beginnings of a beard. He had striking blue eyes and had a tall, masculine build.

At the table was a teenager with black spikey hair and frosted tips. He was wearing a yellow t-shirt and black jeans that didn't reach his ankles. Definitely not formal attire. He had a look of amusement on his face, and his sharp eyes gleamed with interest. But he wasn't looking at Dalton. He was looking at the coat, which was now half beige.

"Let go, boy," the man with the whisker beard said nicely. It was bizarre. He had a bright expression, and his tone was lighthearted, but something about his voice commanded respect.

Dalton's whole body instantly reacted, and he dropped to the floor. Whispers and murmurs filled the room.

"Who's that hanging onto Leo's Mane?" a man asked.

"So he *is* Leo," a woman gasped, referring to the bearded man.

"Who's the one with them?" another wondered.

Leo. The name rang in Dalton's head. While he thought his caretakers were stupid, they did teach them about the Zodiac Guardians. Leo was one of, if not the most, powerful of them.

He's a mage. Run! His body shook with fear and acted upon it. Dalton scrambled to his feet and sprinted away.

"Wait!" Leo boomed.

Dalton's body wanted to listen, but he shook the command out of his head.

Waiters and customers alike tried to stop him. The worst he had gotten was a beating. This time, he tarnished Leo's coat. *I'm so screwed if I'm caught!*

Dalton weaved between tables and waiters. He heard footsteps behind him and could imagine them reaching out their hands to grasp him.

Dalton snatched silverware from a plate and hurled it behind him. Leo was now wearing his coat and was walking toward Dalton. The projectiles glanced off Leo's coat and cluttered to the ground. Leo was now wearing his coat and was walking toward Dalton.

Dalton didn't stop running and jumped onto a table. He kicked the food and silverware off of it, making several of his pursuers hesitate. But not Leo. He kept walking forward as the silverware and food bounced off of him. Dalton's heart raced, and he took off toward the door. He shoved it open, pushing back a waiter who was getting a breath of fresh air. He kept sprinting, not daring to turn around. He could hear the hollering start to fade away.

Oh, thank the gods! He thought.

He finally turned around and saw that no more waiters were pursuing him. Only Leo was.

Dalton cursed to himself and kept running. Leo lost his patience and started running too.

All Dalton could think about was not getting caught. The cold wind stung his lungs as he gasped for air. He planted his foot firmly with each step, so he didn't slip in the snow. His shoes were wet, and his feet were cold. He was so cold. He turned down an alley and saw it was a dead end. He kept sprinting until he reached the end. He leaped to the wall, pushed off of it with his foot to the other wall, and pushed off again until he was able to grab the ledge and pull himself up to the roof. He didn't have time to marvel at what he had just done. He got up and kept running.

Surely he's gone now, right? Dalton thought. He turned around and saw that Leo was now in a dead sprint after him.

"Wait!" his voice boomed again.

Dalton began to panic. He could hear his heart pounding in his ears. His arm started to tingle. He grabbed a hailstone from the roof, making his hand cold. "Just. Leave. Me. Alone!" Dalton cried and hurled it behind him.

He didn't turn around still, but he had heard the crackling of ice, and he was suddenly so exhausted he felt like passing out. He endured and jumped down from the roof, intending to use a pile of trash bags as a cushion. He crossed his arms and closed his eyes, bracing himself for impact. Instead, he heard the crackling of ice again and felt himself sliding down something. He opened his eyes and saw he was on a slide of ice. He rode it to the ground and continued to flee.

It wasn't until after he disappeared into the crowds of people in downtown Yankee that he realized he was now able to use magic. He chuckled in amazement. *I was able to run away from a Zodiac!* News spread of a thief trying to steal Leo's artifact: his Mane. Dalton saw on the tv screens that he had created a giant wall of ice which was enough for Leo to lose sight of Dalton. Dalton found his way back to the abandoned cinema with his chest puffed.

"What's with the smug look?" Oz asked.

Simon, Riley, and Oz were sitting around a pile of food. They snatched it while Dalton was causing a ruckus in the dining hall.

Dalton said nothing and instead demonstrated by holding up his index finger. He brushed the air above it with his hand, and a white flurry of snow began to form until it made a spinning ball of ice on his finger. After it had reached the size of a baseball, Dalton tossed it and caught it before chucking it at Simon's head.

Simon tilted his head out of the way and the ball shattered against the wall behind him. A wide grin went across his face. "Welcome to the Cinema Club, Dalton. Good to have you."

"Good to be here."

****

"Over the next few months," Dalton explained, "Simon and Oz would train me and Riley. Riley would juggle regular knives while I used my magic to create my own and juggle those. I cut my hands countless times, and every time I let a blade hit the ground, Simon would express his frustration and disappointment. While Simon was teaching me how to fight, Oz was the one who taught me how to act and to use misdirection to steal things.

"We decided the dynamic we used to steal the food was effective enough: I would be dramatic, cause distractions, and steal whatever I could while Riley stole what we wanted. I was the decoy. We stole money from rival gangs, the posh, banks, anywhere where there was money. Simon and Oz would act as ambassadors and the sons of barons, which we could pull off since Oz was originally from Akerym, and we could use his documents and family name. They found out where the money was going, and me and Riley would steal it."

"So you and this Riley girl were Cloak and Dagger?" Elizabeth asked.

Dalton nodded his head. Elizabeth chuckled in disbelief.

"Our impact was huge. And while Simon was tough on me, us four were like family. He was a symbol of strength for me. I was blinded by admiration so much that I didn't realize I had come to surpass him. As we started to grow bigger and bigger in infamy, I thought I could do more."

****

Dalton was dressed in his Dagger outfit: a white hoodie, black ripped jeans, and sneakers. The hood was large enough that he could hide the top half of his face. Riley was in her Cloak outfit: her frizzy hair was tied into a spiky ponytail, and she had a half mask on. She was wearing a dark-purple jean jacket and black jeans. Oz and Simon were waiting for them.

Their symbol was graffitied on the wall of the building they were on. It was a wavy black cloak being whipped around someone. Two sharp cartoon eyes peered out from the darkness behind the cloak, and a shiny white dagger was the smile.

Dalton and Riley dropped their bags of money. Dalton threw his hood back. "We could be getting more," he insisted.

"No, this is all we're capable of," Simon quickly replied and began counting how much they had.

"But it's not! We could get way more if we just started hitting more Penumbra depots!" Dalton whined.

"Dalton," Riley snapped and shook her head.

"Dalton, you're still just a kid. There's no way we're going against Penumbra. We're better off targeting posh treasuries. Besides, we don't want to start a war with them. Our gang has four members in it. They have hundreds. Besides, the World Council actually sent a Chasm legion here. We need to lie low for a while," Simon said.

"But they won't be expecting us to rob Penumbra! They'll be too busy protecting the posh!"

"No."

"I bet I could go in and steal it all by myself..." Dalton grumbled.

Simon got up in Dalton's face. "Don't get ahead of yourself! You're good at *running* away, not *fighting*! Don't ever think you're better than anyone here cause you're *not!* Without us, you're *nothing*. You're *worthless*! Get that through your thick skull already!"

Simon's fierce glare made Dalton want to cower, he wanted to cry the words stung so bad, but he stood his ground. *Not this time...* Dalton thought to himself. He turned away and started walking.

"Oi, where ya goin'?!" Oz asked.

"To improve!" Dalton shouted back.

"Dalton!" Riley called out.

Dalton kept moving forward and reached the roof's ledge, where he paused. He stared at the street beneath him and watched the snow flutter past.

Am I really bringing the team down that much? Am I really the weak link?!

Dalton stepped off, creating a slide as he fell. He curled it upward and shot off, soaring across a roof. He landed and tumbled before running off. He jumped and used the fire escape to slide down. He coated his palm in ice to not hurt it as he descended to the ground.

He walked among the crowd. The workday was finally over, and mothers and fathers were rushing home to their families. Children scurried about, trying to pick pockets and scavenge for any food they could find. A group of kids ran down the street with spray cans in their hands. They were about his age, each with their hoods up.

He followed the action to a plaza that was playing the news on a large hologram projected onto a skyscraper. Chasm Trailblazers were surrounding the perimeter of a large protest. People held signs and shouted insults. If they were a girl, they had their hair tied in a ponytail with a neon green band—Riley's signature look. If they were a guy, they had a hood up.

"Archon Wilkin spoke today about the rising tension in the city of Yankee," a news anchor reported. The screen switched to the city's archon at a podium in a press conference. "My fellow yanks, as a result of the recent chaos being ensued by Penumbra, Broncos, and Cinema Club, particularly the thieves calling themselves 'Cloak and Dagger,' I appealed to the World Council and received help. However, it seems even with Chasm's presence in our city, these criminals remain at large."

Dalton scoffed, "Wow, aren't we popular?"

"For the safety of the city of Yankee, and so that we may make our protectors' lives easier, I am temporarily banning the support of these criminals, and anyone wearing a white hoodie or a half-mask will be detained and questioned."

The protestors roared angrily, shouting insults and shaking their fists. The fervor was so intense that even the Chasm officers at their turrets started to sweat in the ice-cold weather.

"This policy will be in effect starting tomorrow. I pray you understand the situation we're in and that every measure must be taken to rid our city of the blight of gang violence and criminal activity. Thank you."

The screen switched off, and people's anger shifted toward the Chasm officers. They pelted the officers with snow and rocks.

"What're you protecting the damn posh for?! It's us that are in deep shit!"

"I bust my ass off every day, and what do I get? Nothing! Cloak and Dagger are the ones giving us what we deserve!"

They began rushing the Trailblazers and shaking them. "Get back!" the officers shouted, but no one listened. It was only until they began firing warning shots off into the sky that the people's anger turned to fear and the protest was dispersed.

Dalton used it to leave the area. *Just stay calm and blend in. They don't know what you look like. Just don't attract any attention to yourself.*

Then, Dalton spotted a flying rock. It struck an officer in the head and knocked him unconscious. Sirens blared and screams went out. The engine of a Trailblazer roared and people scrambled out of the way. Dalton spotted a group of people being chased by a squad of Chasm officers. Undoubtedly they were the ones who threw the rock. Dalton clicked his tongue and threw his hood up. He followed alongside them some distance away until they were isolated and held at gunpoint. Dalton jumped in, a shield of ice ready, and blocked the bolts. He bashed his shield into one officer and, in one motion, created a dagger in his hand and threw it at the other, making him flinch in pain. Dalton swept the officer's leg and froze him to the ground.

Dalton pressed his palm to the ground and created a wall of ice dividing the other officers from the protestors.

"Run!" Dalton shouted and they broke out of their daze.

Dalton heard the hum of an engine and jumped to the wall. He made himself a little ledge to spring off of and scale his wall. On the other side, he saw an Instigator. People were cornered by it and Chasm officers held them at gunpoint, slowly closing in on them.

He could hear Riley and Simon's voices clearly in his head: *"You're good at running, not at fighting." "You're too nice. Stop worrying about others, it's gonna get you killed."*

The Instigator behind them had four panels like feet that ejected purple flames, making the vehicle hover above the ground. It had gray, plated armor with arc runes written across like racing stripes that gave a white glow. A giant railgun was on a swivel. Oz had taught Dalton how to deal with these.

Dalton jumped down and landed on top of the vehicle. As the officers in front turned, he threw handfuls of daggers at their hands, disarming them. Meanwhile, he channeled aura into his feet, freezing the manhole shut. His next order of business was freezing the barrel shut so no projectiles could be fired. *Good, that should be enough to let the people and me get away,* he thought as he let out a foggy breath.

The protestors sprinted past, taking advantage of the Chasm officers' surprise to run away. Dalton created a flight of stairs to a rooftop and started to run up when... *BOOM!*

He turned around and saw a man had blown off the cover of the Instigator and a man climbed out. His hands were glowing purple, an indicator he could use arcana magic–aura in its purest form. He was a Prestige.

The man shot a purple energy beam from his hands and shattered the staircase. Dalton was high enough to the point where, as he fell, he was able to reach and grab onto the ledge of the roof. He pulled himself up and ran. Waiting for him were two men in exosuits.

"We got him," one radioed in.

You haven't got shit! Dalton retorted and swept the ground around him with his ankle. Ice frothed and shot up to make a spout. Dalton skated along the walls and was about to use the momentum to launch himself away when a purple glow welled up in the walls and the spout shattered. Dalton fell, but he was caught by a cable and pulled in.

"You're not going anywhere," the Prestige chuckled.

Damn! They're even bringing in Prestiges now?! Dalton cursed.

Relief washed over his body like a wave when he heard two pops and a fizzle. Smoke filled the area and the three men were choked out and unconscious within two minutes.

"Why are you here?" Dalton pouted, trying not to show that he was actually thankful.

"Because I know how stupid you are," Riley explained as she cut Dalton's bonds. "You really need to stop trying to save people."

"What do you mean? We're vigilantes!"

"We're *thieves*."

"Whatever."

"Come on. You were heading toward the pirate, right?"

****

"There was this guy, he subbed for our class once actually," Dalton chuckled. "Taro, he was always our source of information. He'd often join Simon and Oz for drinks after successful missions too. He told us about this really expensive gem Penumbra recently got from some sky castle. So me and Riley went there to steal it. I wanted to prove to Simon that I could do it without him. That they needed me." Dalton fell silent.

Elizabeth tilted her head to try and meet Dalton's eyes which were directed at the floor. "Then what happened?"

Dalton frowned. "We underestimated them. We found the gem, I was able to grab it, but we couldn't both escape." Dalton frowned. "Anyway, I of course blamed myself and knew I had to rescue Riley. There was no way I was going back to Simon and Oz, so I went to Taro."

****

"Taro! Taro!" Dalton called out.

Taro looked up and saw a beaten and bruised Dalton fall from a rooftop and land in a pile of garbage. "Dalton?!" Taro ran over and helped him to his feet.

Dalton stood for two seconds before plopping down in the snow. His breathing was hurried and his cheeks were red. "I messed up…" Dalton whined, tears running down his face.

"What's wrong? Where's Riley?" Taro asked.

Dalton shoved his hand in his pocket angrily and chucked something bright at the other wall of the alley. It bounced off and clattered to the ground beside Taro. It was the gem. From a distance, it had looked as if a small shard of the sky itself was lying on the ground.

"Woah!" Taro exclaimed and quickly picked up the gem and shoved it back in Dalton's pocket. "Keep that out of sight! What're you doing?!"

"The hell is the point of that thing? What makes it so special?" Dalton cried. "This keeps happening! No one believes in me and I go to show them they're wrong and I end up making them right!" he sobbed. "I really am worthless. A piece of street garbage!" To further emphasize the garbage bit, Dalton slowly leaned to his left until he tipped over and he used the trash bags as a pillow.

Taro sighed and gave a sympathetic look. He crouched down and just stared at Dalton for a while. "Come on. Stop sobbing into the garbage. It's disgusting."

Dalton sniffled and wiped his nose with his sleeve before getting up.

"Let me ask you a question, Dalton," Taro said. "When you put your hood on, you act like you're hot stuff, right? And then you do all of these amazing things and you call yourself Dagger, right?"

"Yeah, but that's all an act! I'm not actually that good! Simon does all of the planning! All I am is a decoy! Everyone else does all the work. I just run away!"

"Dalton, even if it is an act, people love you. You are a symbol of hope to them! You and Dagger are the same person! All of the amazing things Dagger has done, it was you!" Taro got up and held out a hand. "Look, if you don't think you're worth anything, keep faking. It's very convincing. So much so that maybe you'll see it as the truth one day."

Dalton looked at Taro's hand and grabbed it. Taro pulled him up and Dalton wiped his face with the back of his sleeve once again.

"Can you teleport me to their base?" Dalton asked.

"You aren't thinking of doing this alone are you?"

"Yup."

"Dalton, it's okay to rely on people. Simon might be an asshole, but he's right when he says we're stronger together than alone."

"I know, but this time… This one I gotta do myself," Dalton insisted. "What? You don't think I can do it? We're talking about *me* here!"

Taro looked at Dalton who had his chest puffed out and chuckled. "That's the spirit. But first, we got to patch you up."

"There's no time. We're going to save Riley now."

Taro gave a defeated sigh. "I'll be there when you need it. Just call my phone."

"With what exactly?"

"Oh, right." Taro teleported an Omnicard to his hand. "Here, you can keep this one. It's an older version, but it works."

"Thanks."

"Don't mention it. As soon as you make contact with Riley, call me, describe where you are as much as possible, and then I'll come get you two, okay?"

Dalton nodded and Taro teleported them to the compound. It was a skyscraper–a home for the offices of hundreds of jewelers. It had a casino on the bottom floor, and on the domed top floor was a restaurant called *Vertigo*. Below were drug labs, Penumbra offices, and parking garages.

"So, what now? The security is probably tighter this time around," Taro said.

"I don't know. Simon usually comes up with the plan. And if it isn't Simon it's Oz or Riley." Dalton shrugged. "I'll just have to do all of the roles at once."

Dalton closed his eyes and imagined a group of snowmen around him. He had remembered watching a movie in the Time Capsules where this ice lady was able to create a living snowman. He simply tried to recreate that. He felt aura flow down his arms and to the ground where it spread out like veins and gathered in puddles before spiraling upward. He opened his eyes and he was looking at himself. He had created three identical clones of himself.

"What's the plan?" one of them asked.

"Two of us should just create distractions up top while the others should look for Riley," another suggested.

"No, wait! Each of us make another clone," the real Dalton said.

They each did so and there were eight Daltons standing in a circle. *It's easier now!* Dalton observed.

"I have a better idea," the real Dalton said with a smirk. The others turned to him. "Let's just raid the base."

****

"That night, I learned how to create clones. And I also realized how they work," Dalton explained. "The more clones I create, the more I have to distribute my power. It gets easier to make clones after a certain point because of how little aura it takes. That night, I made the most clones I've ever made at once: one-hundred and twenty-eight. And each one held a one-hundred and twenty-eighth of my power. You could poke one and it would turn into a pile of snow."

****

"Alright, gentlemen!" the real Dalton boomed with crossed arms. He was standing on the ledge of the building, facing his new army of Daltons. "Tonight, we run into battle! To show that we can do things ourselves, together! And to save a friend…" He fell quiet to let his words soak a little. "Our mission is to find Riley! As soon as you do, you are to help her escape and alert us by dying! Die bravely, I will see you all again someday!"

"Die bravely!" they shouted back with fists in the air and threw on their hoods.

"Let's go cause some chaos!" Dalton cheered and the rest followed suit.

They jumped off the ledge, creating different slides to launch them at different angles. Some soared through the air while others tumbled as they landed and began to sprint alongside each other. Others bounced off other clones' backs to propel themselves higher in the air. A wave of Dalton clones were used as battering rams to break the glass windows, allowing the others to infiltrate the building. With each clone's death, the others felt the aura being redistributed and filling them with more power.

Dalton blended in with the wave that stormed the first floor. They threw a flurry of daggers at the oncoming guards, hitting their guns out of their hands. The wave behind them jumped on their shoulders and leap-frogged over to propel them forward. They began pummeling the security while the others began to run amuck. Alarms blared and people screamed as knives were thrown across the room over their heads.

Good, now to look for Riley, Dalton thought and ran for the staircase. *I got plenty looking upstairs, I should go downstairs.*

Dalton swung around the corner and saw four grunts on their way up. He tapped his foot and created a flow of ice that froze the steps. They slipped, falling atop one another down the steps. Dalton slid down, keeping his balance along the way. When he reached the grunts, who were trying to get back to their feet, he jumped, grabbed onto the railing, and swung himself over the next flight. He landed and his momentum caused him to crash into the wall. He stumbled and nearly fell to the ground. He held his dizzy head with one hand, his aura shield spared him from a concussion, but nothing more.

As a grunt pulled out his pistol, a wall of ice sprung up from Dalton's foot, blocking the bolts and effectively stopping any hope of pursuing him. Dalton shook his head and continued his descent until he reached the basement. He slowly cracked the door open and peeked inside. Grunts dressed in lab coats and oxygen masks were running around frantically, getting ready for intruders.

I need to get through, but there's no way I can fight off all of these guys with the amount of aura I have left… Dalton thought. *If I had Riley here, she could just slip past them.* Dalton shook his head. *No, no point in thinking about that. There's only me. Think, just be invisible, be… like air.*

Dalton closed his eyes and imagined a snowy plane with a twilight sky. He imagined himself being as fluid and as light as smoke, flowing through the air like Riley. He entered the room with that thinking and imagined a water droplet sending a wave across a calm pond. *Tranquil Snow…*

With the expanding ripple, a cold cyclone whipped up and surrounded Dalton and the guards. The realm Dalton was imagining came to life. The guards searched frantically for Dalton, but couldn't find him.

I'm invisible… Dalton thought with a smile. *It worked!*

The spell, however, was taxing, and he decided to avoid battling the guards and started running toward the door. Memories from the defeated clones started to fill Dalton's head, giving him information on the number of guards, what was on the different floors, and possible escape routes. A large number of the clones were eliminated by a man on the upper floors.

The man had dark skin, a lean build, and short, stubby hair. The skin on his arms turned silver and his fingers came together to form a spear. His arm extended and the blade pierced several clones, killing them instantly.

Of course there's some Wings here, Dalton thought as he finally ended his spell and went through the door.

Scorch bolts singed it as he closed it behind him and he put up a wall of ice to make sure no one could follow him. The door had led to a dimly lit corridor that stretched about a hundred meters. Dalton created another clone and sent it down the hall to check for traps. Nothing. It was safe. Tunnels split off everywhere. Dalton recognized that they probably were a part of the network of tunnels underneath the Burrow.

There were no guards, no personnel–nothing. Dalton kept following the ceiling lights until he came across prison cells.

"Riley?" Dalton called out.

No response.

Dalton knew he was running out of time. He could feel the number of his clones starting to fall faster and faster as the guards got their bearings and of course, the Wing decimated any squad of clones he came across instantly. He was sweeping every floor and was making his way downward.

"Riley?" he called out again.

"Over here, numbskull!" she finally hollered back.

Dalton ran to the source of the voice and found Riley sitting on the ground, back against the wall, in her cell. She looked unharmed apart from a black eye and a couple other bruises.

"Riley!" Dalton beamed.

"Hey," she said tiredly back with a smile. "You're dumb for coming back for me. Seriously, how do you plan to break out of here?"

Dalton pressed his thumb to the lock and filled it with ice. He gave it a little twist and unlocked the cage. He rushed over and helped Riley to her feet.

"Run. That's how."

They began running back to the surface, their hurried footsteps bounced off the walls and their breathing filled their ears.

"Taro is waiting for us. We just need to get to the surface and I can give him a call," Dalton said.

They bolted up the stairs and got to the door. A memory flashed in Dalton's head. His last clone was gone.

"Uh-oh," Dalton said.

"What?"

"We need to turn around."

"What?"

A white flash ran diagonally through the wall of ice and the top half slid off and hit the floor. Behind it was the Wing, and with him was a group of grunts with their pistols ready to fire. The Wing retracted his arm and it returned to normal. He held an Omnicard to his ear.

"Yeah, I got them. Don't bother making the trip," he said to the person on the other line.

Dalton wanted to run, to just be left alone. He tried to activate Tranquil Snow, but botched it. In a panic, he let loose his aura at full power to try and create a massive wall. The gem in his pocket hummed instead, the vibrations slowly getting stronger. Riley and the Wing saw it glow from his pocket and exchanged a glance. Riley went for a pistol and the Wing extended his arm into a blade to stop her.

"Just screw off already!" Dalton shouted angrily and a whirlwind erupted from his pocket. A lightning bolt fired from his chest and struck the Wing, sending him flying.

Riley gave a nod of appreciation, wide-eyed. Dalton didn't know what happened either, but that didn't stop them from running.

They found a ventilation shaft and Riley quickly shot off the cover before putting her pistol in her coat pocket. Dalton cupped his hands together and Riley used it as a step. She lifted her other foot off the ground and Dalton threw her upward. When she was in the vent, she spread out her arms and legs and used the walls to catch herself. She climbed further in and Dalton made a pillar of ice extend from his feet into the vent. He shattered their trail before continuing upward.

"Sorry for keeping you waiting. And a lot of other things…" Dalton chuckled.

"Don't sweat it. You came back for me, right? That's enough. No need for sorries. It grosses me out."

Dalton smiled, glad to see being held captive hadn't changed her attitude. "Thanks."

They reached the fortieth floor before exiting the vents. They took the grunts in their room by surprise and quickly subdued them before they could alert anyone else. Dalton made a baseball bat of ice and hurled it through a window, shattering it. Dalton created clone after clone, which passed them further away from the building until they were low enough to create a slide and land on a rooftop.

A storm was outside to meet them. The winds were high and moaning, and the rain was nearly falling sideways. The boom and crash of thunder echoed in the distance as lightning danced across the sky above them. The entire building was surrounded by Chasm Instigators and Trailblazers with their cannons ready to open fire.

"Get them! They're trying to escape!" a Chasm grunt shouted.

They landed on an adjacent rooftop and began sprinting away. Dalton called Taro. "Taro! I need you to pick us up!"

"Tell him to meet us at the drawbridge!" Riley said.

"Meet us at the drawbridge!" Dalton relayed.

"Got it! I haven't been there before, and I don't want to teleport myself to a random drawbridge. It'll take me a bit before I get there!"

"Hurry!"

Dalton hung up the Omnicard and put it in his pocket. There was an explosion behind him so close, it nearly knocked him off his feet. He created a squadron of clones and shuffled himself in between them, running back and forth among them so they couldn't tell which one was the real him.

Bolts whizzed past their heads and the icy rooftops threatened to make them slip and fall. Neither turned around. Riley fired blindly behind her and Dalton clones acted as shields to protect her. Ziplines and the sound of steam started to fill the air. Dalton clones would turn around and tackle the pursuers whenever they got too close.

Now even Chasm is after us?! Dalton cursed.

Aura buckshots knicked Dalton's heels and made him tumble over the edge of the roof he was on. He crashed through a window and landed in someone's apartment. They were watching the news which was covering the rioting of hundreds of hooded people in the city. Dalton created a clone that ran and jumped through the other window and crashed into another building. The real Dalton started running downstairs to the street. Once the clone reached the next apartment, it repeated the process, creating a clone and going downstairs to the street.

Soon, there was a group of sixteen Daltons weaving up and down from the rooftops and the street, using structures of ice to maneuver about. Four clones were always used to protect Riley from projectiles.

"You're slow!" Riley cursed at a clone near her. "And when did you get this trick up your sleeve?"

"Just tonight," the clone explained. "And it's not my fault! I've been running all night already!"

"Whatever. We can't bring the Mafia to the bridge, much less Chasm officers. Draw them away and we'll meet up."

"Sounds good," the clone agreed and saluted and turned to slush.

Dalton received the information and made his clones dissolve. He created a new squadron and sent them in different directions, pulling the Chasm officers away by taunting them.

The real Dalton had two on his tail as he peeled away from Riley. He saw that one still followed Riley before he turned and ran. He was starting to feel the fatigue hit him now. His heart pounded against his chest, his calves burned, and his lungs were on the verge of bursting.

Out of the corner of his eye, he saw his ticket out: the Tran-Zip. He used every ounce of energy to catch it, zig-zagging and dodging the aura buckshots that nipped at his heels like wolves.

Make it, make it, make it! Dalton chanted in his head before he leapt from the roof he was on toward the passing line of Tran-Zip cars. A shockwave of pain emanated from his back and right leg and he lost his balance. He crashed against the side of the Tran-Zip and desperately threw his hand up before he bounced too far away. He slapped the wall and clung on by using ice.

He created two clones on top of the roof and they helped him up. They carried him between the cars and when they entered the next car, they dissipated and Dalton fell to the floor breathless. He rolled onto his back and groaned. His aura shield was barely holding on, but he finally felt safe.

This sense of security vanished almost immediately when he heard the clunk of boots on the roof of his car. Dalton mustered the strength to get up and he finally took notice of the mass of people in the car. They were all wearing white hoods.

They looked at Dalton, trying to figure out if he was the real deal, if their champion really was a child. Dalton was wide-eyed, mesmerized like he was put under hypnosis. Under each hood he saw a different face, but the same bewildered eyes as his own. He took a deep breath.

Show them what they need to see, Dalton said to himself. *Show them that you're invincible.*

Dalton was able to manage a wink and smiled as he pulled his hood further over his face and limped past and was behind a group of people before the Chasm officers entered the car.

"Hey kid! Stop right there!" one shouted.

"Later, losers!" Dalton shouted before bolting away.

The Chasm officers followed, but the hooded passengers swarmed the officers, blocking their way and shouting insults.

Dalton couldn't help but chuckle. He ran through the doors and jumped, landing with a thud atop a nearby rooftop. He groaned and began the long journey back to the drawbridge.

When Dalton finally made it back, Riley was waiting there for him in the middle of the bridge on the sidewalk. The streets were full of stopped traffic.

She's safe! Dalton cheered in his head and relief washed over his body like a wave. He stopped next to her and put his hands on his knees.

"Where's Taro?" Riley asked.

"He should be here soon," Dalton said between breaths.

"Do you still have the stone?" Riley asked.

"Yeah... it's right here." Dalton reached into his back pocket. When his fingers touched it, he could feel a tingly hum of energy flow through his body. With a closer look, he saw storms surging inside. He pulled it out and showed it to Riley. "See?"

"Awesome!"

"There they are!" a man's voice rang out.

A cluster of Chasm officers were at the end of the bridge, running at them, weaving through traffic and sprinting down the sidewalk.

"Hey guys!" Taro's voice called out from the other end.

"Taro, hurry!" Dalton cried. He turned to Riley and smiled. "Come on, we're getting out of—"

Riley hugged Dalton and snatched the stone from Dalton's hand. "I'm sorry Dalton," she whispered. She pushed Dalton away and whipped out a pistol. With a sad and painful expression on her face, she pulled the trigger.

Bang. He heard it, but he didn't even feel it at first. All he could do was stare at the contortions in her face, her eyes nearly brought to tears. Everything was muffled, everything was numb.

Huh? Dalton wondered. *What just happened?*

Like a plume of ink in water, screaming pain started to stream out from Dalton's shoulder from the scorch bolt that burned his flesh, but his heart ached so much more. He lost balance and fell over the edge of the bridge, his aura shield shattered.

Through watery eyes he watched her turn away from the ledge. He closed his eyes and his tears fluttered upward as he plummeted. He felt someone grab him—

****

"—and the next thing I knew, I was in Pioneer Square in Cysko," Dalton explained. "With Taro passed out on the ground next to me. And that was the last time I saw her, or Yankee for that matter."

Elizabeth had a sympathetic look on her face, but Dalton wasn't a fan of it. That's when he realized he was tearing up.

How lame! he thought as he wiped his eyes.

“Come on,” he said. “We’re deep in the woods now. Someone’s gotta make sure we aren’t getting attacked by signum. Also, I’m starving. We need to hunt some food down.”

6: While They Were Gone

The Day Elizabeth and Dalton left...

Amy sat on her bed cross-legged with her eyes closed. The only light source was the sunbeams which showered her from an open window. Everything else was cast in shadow and thus was forgotten to her. She felt nothing but the warmness of the sun Plexis' glow and the air as it ebbed and flowed with her breaths. She heard nothing but the beating of her heart, and the calm wind fluttering into her room. She had her hands cupped as if shielding a blossom from the wind.

Come on! She urged. *Just do it like you did in the forest!*

Her breath left her body once more and she inhaled again.

Just start bubbling in my hand. Flow into it and surge... she told the sunlight softly. When she felt nothing, she grew frustrated. *Come on stupid light just form already!*

She felt a little tug on her hands that made her flinch. She was afraid to open her eyes, not sure if it was light or shadow in her clutches, and not sure if opening them would cause it to dissipate. She, very carefully, was able to pry them open to a squint where she was nearly blinded. After flinching once more, she let her eyes adjust and saw the little blip of golden light in her hands.

It was small to be sure–and dim, but it wasn't insignificant, at least not to her. A smile as wide as a valley went across her face in pure delight and her eyes sparkled like diamonds.

"Yes!" She cheered quietly. She pushed further, trying to make it brighter and bigger. *Come ooon!* She struggled and struggled, but the blip refused to transform. She put all of her focus and concentration into this tiny orb. Everything was but a dark void except for this tiny beacon of light that warmed her hands. It grew brighter ever so slightly until it reached the intensity to that of a glowstick. Amy concentrated even harder, but the light refused to glow any brighter. She forced herself to dive into an even deeper state of focus, but the light still wouldn't shine brighter. She focused harder and harder until...

A knock came from her door, and a muffled voice, Dalton's voice, broke through the silence: "Hey Amy, you up?"

Her environment slowly came back to her. First, it was her bed, and then the floor, and then the ceiling and walls until she was back in her room again. She lost concentration and the light faded away back into the sunlight. Her jaw dropped, and she remained frozen.

"Argh!" she cursed and flailed about her bed. She rolled onto the floor and looked up at the ceiling through her hair. She puffed it out of the way and replied with irritation and disappointment. "Yeah, I'm up..."

After her response, she began to lightly slap and bonk her face and head. *Stupid Dalton! Stupid Dalton! Ugh!*

"I got your breakfast right here. Monty made you pancakes."

Amy frowned. *Why is it so hard for me to be mad at people?* She sat up and heaved a sigh. *No... it's not entirely his fault. The light wasn't really listening to me anyway...*

"Just um... Just leave it at the door. I'm not really hungry right now."

"You sure?"

"Yeah."

"O-okay then." An awkward silence filled the room for a second. "You doing alright?"

"Just despising myself," Amy grumbled sarcastically.

"What was that?"

"I'm okay," Amy replied. *Yeah, keep telling yourself that.*

"Alright then. If you need to talk to someone, we're all here for you. Alright, my partner-in-crime?"

"Yeah... Thanks..." Amy chuckled and shook her head. *More like your sidekick...*

Dalton's footsteps grew quiet as he walked away from the door. Amy got to her feet and stretched her arms to the sky. *Whatever, just relax...*

She could feel a sluggishness creep along her body as if she were traversing through molasses.

Maybe some bass would help...

She tried that, plucking away at her strings to the punk rock in her headphones, but to no avail.

She threw off her headphones, plopped down on her bed, and found herself staring at the ceiling. The beam of light from her window hit her eyes. She growled and used a shadow to snap the blinds closed.

She yawned and turned on her side. She could feel her Omnicard vibrate. They were texts from Monty, telling her that breakfast was ready and asking if she was okay.

I'm fine! Leave me alone! Amy groaned in her head and tossed her Omnicard off her bed before drifting to a slumber.

****

Henry watched the whereabouts of the Prism dorm residents on an Omnislate. The screen was split into four quadrants, one for each signum mouse with a small camera mounted on its back. They scurried around the ventilation shafts and under furniture, capturing video and recording sound. He was in his apartment, lounging on his bed and Envy was leaning back in his chair across the room.

"Humans have such small aura reservoirs," Envy sighed, examining his black claws. "I've killed eight people already, and I'm nowhere near full. I need mages."

"We'll get you some," Henry said. "I need you as full as possible for the next part of this plan. You can even get yourself some mages amidst the chaos."

Henry watched Dalton rush out of the building with his sword in hand.

"Well, it seems Dalton and Elizabeth have left just as planned," Henry noted. "The only one in the dorm right now is Amy. Time for me and Clara to have a little chat," Henry chuckled. He pulled out his Omnicard and began typing away.

Envy let out a sigh.

"What?" Henry asked.

"Nothing, just don't let that stupid girl distract you," Envy warned. "Just be rid of her already. Killing her will be better for your health. Trust me, I knew a guy who dedicated his life to a girl? Didn't end well for him."

"I intend to give it one more shot at least," Henry sighed. "Unlike you, I'm human. I still have feelings, even if I kill people."

Envy simply replied with a guffaw and Henry scowled.

"What's so funny?"

"You just remind me of Syd. He had cute little dreams like you, always thinking about how he was dragged into the terrible situation he was in and making excuses for himself."

"Please don't compare me to a demon like Syd. And I guess you haven't been paying attention to us being in complete control of the situation?"

"No, no, no, that's not what I meant," Envy said, wagging a finger. "I meant your life situation."

Henry scoffed. "And what would you know about me?"

"I'm serious, I've seen it all before. Let's face it, this Clara girl you're after isn't going to want to follow you to whatever paradise you're dreaming of escaping to. All that's going to happen is more suffering for you if you keep hesitating to get the job done."

Henry crossed his arms and had wrinkles across his forehead from frowning.

He's so easily crossed. I love it! Envy thought.

"Look, my point is that you aren't thinking for yourself. You *think* you are, but you're not! You want this Monty fellow to suffer because he hurt your father and is trying to steal your girl, sure. But who wants him to suffer as well? The Mafia and your father," Envy said.

"I want the same thing as they do, but for different reasons. The sooner I help my father with his debt, the sooner I can get out."

"Ah, ha!" Envy exclaimed. "You just released a piece of info to me."

Henry clicked his tongue.

"You're telling me you're helping your *father* clear his debt? You're more of a fool than I thought!" Envy bawled. "You had a childhood crush on a girl who doesn't return the sentiment? And further, than that, you assumed part of your *father's* debt? This is rich!"

"We're family. Of course I'd help my family!"

"Oh, Henry my boy, you are so blind it is *hysterical.* You're letting these obligations and expectations get in the way of what matters. What. Do. *You.* Want. To. Do?" Envy had his arms spread out in an exasperated fashion, even though the black miasma held no expression other than the widening of his orange-yellow eyes.

Henry could picture him and Clara enjoying the Azure Festival. Visiting the booths and seeing laughter and happiness. The cold sting of the Atlas nighttime air would be relieved by Clara's arms wrapped around him. The color of fireworks reflected in her sky blue marble eyes.

No more Wings. No more Debt. No more killing... Just... normalcy...

But reality wasn't as kind. Henry shook the fantasy out of his head. "You don't know anything..."

Envy leaned back and crossed his right leg over his left. He had no visible mouth, but anyone could tell he was smirking.

****

Henry: We need to talk. Meet me at the cafe next to the library tonight at 9pm. I'm sure you have a lot of questions. I'm willing to answer them.

Clara rolled her eyes upon reading the text. She texted back: **I'll be there.**

She was antsy; she needed to do something to take her mind off of things. Too many questions lingered in her head, pounding against her skull relentlessly. *Why is Henry here? Did father send him? What's he planning on doing? As far as my father knows, I'm just doing regular studying. Gods, I hate Henry's dumb face, should I punch it?*

She had gone for a run to clear her head when it started raining halfway through. *Welcome to Atlas.*

However, she found running in the rain surprisingly soothing. The sound of the light drops pattering against her hood and feathering her skin was serene. With the drizzle, her footsteps, and the pounding of her heartbeat flooding her ears with their beats and melodies, everything else seemed to fade away except for the road in front of her. No direction existed except for forward. At the edge of her tunnel vision, a silhouette appeared. As she continued forward, more features slowly came into view.

Monty stood underneath a streetlight with an umbrella in his hand. He looked at her with an expression Clara couldn't pin down. A combination of nervousness and worry perhaps? Or was it happiness?

She slowed to a trot as she approached him until she came to a stop. He didn't say a word. "Why are you standing in the rain like an idiot?"

"You heading back?"

"Huh?

"Are you. Heading. Back?"

"Uh… yeah?"

"Then walk with me."

"O-okay…"

The two started to walk along the trail around the lake. Their dorm's lights could be seen a ways away down the road and Sagittarius' house was on the opposite end of the lake, equidistant to where they were. Clara's eyes were trained to the ground, not wanting to display any unneeded messages to her friend beside her.

We're sharing an umbrella! This is kind of cute! she thought, blushing a tiny bit. *Monty's probably too dense to know what he's doing though.*

Incorrect.

Monty knew exactly what he was doing. Unlike Clara who only thought it was "kind of" cute, he was actually really embarrassed, blushing slightly and trying to avoid touching her with his shoulder. His heartbeat filled his ears and disoriented his thoughts with an odd warmth.

"I-Is everything okay?" Monty asked.

"Yeah, of course," Clara chuckled. "Why wouldn't it be?"

"You've just been acting distant lately is all."

"I like to run. That's all it is."

"Okay… Well, you seem off recently."

Clara looked over, whole-heartedly expecting Monty to be looking at the ground like he usually does. But instead of the side of his head, she was greeted with eyes the color of autumn. It was a soft gaze. Cold chills didn't go through her body like they did in their fight with Floyd. She didn't feel the sting of the raging inferno they had when they first met in class. Now, all she felt from them was the warmth and comfort of a campfire.

"You also seem off."

Monty raised an eyebrow. "What do you mean?"

Clara tilted her head a little bit. "Don't think I haven't noticed that the malicious stench that once surrounded your body is gone."

"Did… did you just say I stink?"

Clara rolled her eyes. "You're helpless."

"What?!"

"I'm saying you're not emanating any bloodlust anymore. It used to annoy me so much, like that time on the cable car. Plus, you seem… tired."

Monty was about to speak, but he stopped himself. *She's changing the subject…* "And *I'm* saying you're not as boisterous as usual."

"I'm not boisterous!" she retorted.

Monty gave a tired look as if to say: "really?"

"I can be a little energetic at times, but that doesn't mean I can't also be calm and reserved."

"You think I'm pretty stupid, huh?" Monty chuckled.

"I *do* call you Lava Brain for a reason," Clara retorted with a smile.

"Well, then you can at least trust my eyesight, right? Everyone has a coping mechanism. Dalton shoots baskets, Paige buries himself in books, Amy doodles, Elizabeth pulls her beanie down, and you, well… you go running."

"My, aren't you the astute one? Well, I think you use cooking and cleaning as yours," Clara sneered.

"Maybe that's why I'm great at cooking, and you suck at it."

"Well, I haven't seen you training recently!"

Monty looked up at the sky and fell silent. "I've just been busy with school work."

"Sure."

He's trying to get me to open up, but he's definitely hiding something too. Well, if he's not going to open up, then why should I? Clara thought.

"Hey," Monty said. "Where did you get that scarf?"

"Oh, this thing? A friend gave it to me a long time ago. He uh..." she paused. She felt the weight of her stubbornness and pride hanging from her throat, preventing her from speaking. "It's a long story..."

"Well, we're still pretty far."

Clara became suspicious and noticed Monty's eyes were drilling into her scarf. It was as if he was looking at a ghost, his gaze so intense that it made her shudder.

"What?" she asked, taking a step back.

"N-nothing..." Monty said, looking away. An awkward silence fell between the two along with the constant drizzle.

Monty decided to give up getting her to talk. "Come on. Let's just get back."

Clara finally noticed that Monty's other shoulder was outside of the umbrella's protection and was consequently drenched. She playfully shoved Monty's shoulder with her own and it took all that he had to not scream in agony and crumple to the ground.

"Why?" Monty groaned.

"You've been acting like a wimp lately. I haven't even been hitting you hard."

"I feel like we have two different definitions of the word 'hard'."

"Okay, not as hard as I used to."

"By the way, do you want to start walking to culinary class together? You always speed off after homeroom."

Clara stepped a little closer to him so that her shoulder was feathering his. Only the most minuscule of blushes briefly blemished her cheeks before fading away.

"It's not like I'm avoiding you. Just walk faster, slowpoke."

Monty noticed the gesture, and a smile went across his face as he was able to fit his entire body underneath the umbrella. "Will do."

Cheerful, playful chatter pranced along with them while they walked. Monty's eyes kept glancing at the scarf. His heart's painful pounding against his chest allowed certainty to creep in, but his mind told him otherwise. *There's no way that's my mother's scarf, right? It's a one in a million chance! Even so, she's engaged to someone else...* The feeling entered his stomach. *I can't stand it. I have to ask.*

"So, uh, are you sure nothing's bothering you?"

"You know, your nosiness is starting to get on my nerves," Clara said.

"Not even that Henry guy?"

Clara stopped. She raised a brow and tilted her head. "Why the sudden curiosity?"

Monty frantically searched for the words to not give away his feelings. "We actually ran into him before the first day of class. Dalton ended up destroying his car at an intersection and he was furious with us."

Clara giggled. "I gotta thank Dalton when he gets back."

"So, you don't like Henry?"

"No, of course not! He's my fiancé, yes, but it wasn't *my* decision. It was that stupid CUPID computer that decided that. The dude's a total douche."

Monty let out a sigh of relief and relaxed his shoulders. "Oh thank gods."

"What?"

"I thought maybe you were gonna beat me up or something for hurting your friend." *That's a good lie,* Monty thought.

"What? No!" They both chuckled. Then, bashfully, Clara asked: "Are you that scared of me?"

"Kind of?"

"Well, you shouldn't be," Clara said as she got up. "I know we argue a lot but, it's kind of fun, right?"

"I'd say most of the time," Monty smiled.

They arrived at the dorm, and Monty opened the door for her. He bowed and motioned with his arm. Clara rolled her eyes and smiled.

"Thanks."

Monty followed her up a couple of steps before stopping. "Y-You know... I'm–I mean, *we're* always here for you."

Clara turned and chuckled. "See you later, Lava Brain."

"Later, Thunderhead."

****

The drizzle followed Monty all the way to Cysko. He walked through the halls up to Melody's room soaking wet. His feet were cold, and he could feel the water in his socks being displaced with every step, sloshing around like he had sponges for shoes. His skin was pale and his dark circles were nearly black around his eyes. He winced as pain surged through his left arm again.

He knocked on Melody's door. A second later he heard the pitter-patter of bare feet on the hard floor before Melody swung the door open and gave Monty a giant hug.

Monty gave an "oof" as the wind was knocked out of him and he nearly lost his balance. He smiled and patted Melody on the head. "Oi, did you even look when you hugged me? What if it wasn't me who knocked?"

Melody took a step back and gave a big smile at Monty. Her emerald eyes sparkled with almost the same vigor as they did before. "Well, the only people who ever visit me are people who I wouldn't mind hugging." She shrugged playfully. After a second or two, she rang her hoodie. "Also, you're wet."

Monty chuckled. "Congratulations on being able to walk again."

"I might need you to carry me back though. I haven't done any cardio for years," Melody smiled.

"Come on. Let's go eat."

****

After two bus rides, they finally found themselves within walking distance of Carmela's. Monty carried Melody on his back and sprinted through the rain, across the street, down two blocks, and into the restaurant.

"Welcome in! What can I–" Carmela greeted with her back turned. She stopped mid-sentence when she turned to face her customers and recognized a familiar face. "Oh my gods, Melody!" The two embraced. "I haven't seen you since you were a little chick! How have you been? Better obviously!"

"Yes! Much better," Melody beamed. "I'm finally able to walk on my own again."

Carmela leaned a little bit to the side to look at Monty. "And you! No injuries, I see!"

"Yeah," Monty chuckled. "I was wet earlier, but Melody made a great umbrella."

Melody turned around and pointed at her back, which was soaking. Her red hoodie and gray sweatpants had turned crimson and black, respectively.

Carmela laughed. "Have a seat, you two. I'll prep your usual?"

"You remember mine?" Melody asked gleefully.

"Of course I do, silly. I'll have them both out in a minute."

Monty and Melody took their seats: Monty with a cup of coffee and Melody with a cup of tea. "Anything interesting going on?" Melody asked.

"Not really," Monty said between sips. "We've been forced to go to normal school for the past two weeks. So it's been boring for the most part."

"Then do the talent show with me. Me as a violinist, you as a pianist!" Melody leaned in with a sparkle in her eyes that had become foreign to Monty at this point.

The spark was brilliant, so much so that Monty had to cower away from it, hunching his shoulders and leaning back awkwardly. Melody saw the action, and the shine left her eyes. She also retracted, embarrassed that she'd made him uncomfortable.

"S-sorry…"

"No, no, no, no…" Monty stammered.

He took a deep breath. His hands trembled at even the thought of playing piano. Before, he couldn't imagine playing it without her, but… There he was: playing a soft tune with a breeze that inched through an open window with golden sunbeams, making the translucent curtains flutter. And… surprisingly unsurprisingly, Clara was there beside him, humming and playing along with him.

It's different now. Melody wants this… he assured himself.

"Sure," Monty shrugged.

"Huh?"

"Yeah, I can do that. We can work on it whenever you're ready."

Melody was taken aback. She chuckled. "I expected more resistance."

"I've been doing a lot of thinking recently…" Monty chuckled before taking another sip. "I'm done running from my guilt, Melody… I haven't been fair to you. From now on, I'm gonna be here for you."

"You've always been here for me, silly." Melody giggled, but Monty knew the words stung her still. She leaned on him for a second before sitting back up again.

"I'm very rusty," Monty chuckled. "You'll need to give me some time to catch up to speed."

Melody watched Monty with a newfound fascination at his change in character, or at least his attempt at it. She thought aloud, "Your eyes were always glued to the ground. I nearly forgot what they looked like."

Monty was taken aback by the comment. He remembered Clara and the cove and chuckled. "Well, I promise you that you'll be seeing them a lot more from now on."

Their food finally arrived. It never tasted better.

****

The streets were empty that night in Atlas. Rain showered the pavement and the streetlights created tents of yellow light along the sidewalks. The cafe walls that faced the street had large windows that revealed the vacant interior of the establishment. A single barista worked at the counter while Henry sat alone at a table with two cups already prepared.

Clara swung the door open, and the smells of rain collided with the aromas of the coffee beans. The barista paid no attention as she sat down across from him and put her feet on the table with an assertive thud.

"My, aren't we spry this evening?" Henry chuckled as he took a sip of his tea. "I got you a cappuccino. I remember you love coffee."

"What do you want, Henry?" Clara sighed.

"My, my, why the attitude? See? Aren't I kind? I got you a drink even after you trash-talked me earlier this evening with uh… Lava Brain, was it?"

Clara gave a hostile glare, and an electric spark ran across her chest down to her toes. Henry noticed the tiniest quiver in her fingers on her arm.

Her bravado is so cute, Henry thought to himself. *She's racking her brain for ways I could know and she's nervous.*

Henry simply laughed. "Easy there. I'm not here to fight you. I'm here to talk."

"You're sure taking your time getting to the point…" Clara growled.

"Oh, you're no fun."

"This isn't fun."

"It is to me. It's just laughable how clueless you are. Little ignorant you, poor little Paper Tiger."

"Why are you here, Henry?"

Henry took another sip of his tea. "Not because of your father, I can assure you of that. I don't think he's the least bit upset that you transferred from Swordhaven to Constellation. No, I'm here for a different reason."

"You finally stoop so low as to stalk me now?" Clara scoffed. She got up to leave. "This is bullshit..."

Henry grabbed her wrist and held on tight. Clara went to punch him instinctively, but his words acted as a shield: "I know your little kitty cat's secret." Her fist stopped and her eyes widened.

"What secret?" Clara asked as she yanked her hand free from Henry's grasp.

"Oh, don't play dumb. You're harboring an enemy of the Empire. Just one little text to your father, and you'll have Chasm operatives breaking down your door."

It didn't matter how he found out. "You can't tell anyone!"

"Oh? And why shouldn't I?"

"Because... because..." She slumped her shoulders and sighed. "I'll... I'll go with the marriage..."

Henry froze for a second. And then a chuckle. And then a laugh. He wiped the tears from his eyes. "You're a little late to be offering that! You blew your last chance at that literally at the beginning of this conversation. No, I have a better idea." Another sip of tea, this time long and with a loud slurping noise to piss Clara off. It worked.

"Spit it out already!"

Clara looked at the barista in worry, but he was simply wiping mugs while humming a tune.

"No need to worry about him," Henry chuckled. "He can't see or hear us." He got up and leaned in. "Let's make a deal: you speak *nothing* of this conversation and of me to *anyone* and you treat the others like shit, *especially* Monty. And I'll know, like how I know about your conversation last night. I also have another method involving a little magic, of course."

Clara held in the temptation to punch him.

"I trust you'll be able to pull it off. Just in case, here's something to motivate you..." He whispered in Clara's ear: "If you do end up breaking our deal, I'll tell Chasm where she is, I'll tell your father you're in danger and need to be brought back, and I'll call for the other Wings to be here."

As he backed away, he relished in the shocked and fearful expression that Clara had. She was wide-eyed, realizing the amount of leverage Henry had against her and her friends.

"And if you're thinking about just beating me up here and now, I'm actually quite the mage myself. You remember those evolved signum in your little final exam? Hint: I'm responsible," Henry snickered.

For the first time in a while, he felt good, really good. He was right to take Envy's advice.

"Now that everything's cleared up, do we have a deal? Or an ultimatum rather?"

Clara came back to her senses and begrudgingly held out her hand. It trembled in the air and refused to hold still even as Henry grasped it. But it suddenly stopped, and she squeezed it with all her might and surged electricity through it. Henry went to his knees with a groan as Clara stood over him.

"Scum," she muttered, and she briskly walked away.

"Oh, and don't worry! I'm sure those two will turn up sometime! And take that hair tie off!" Henry laughed.

Clara stopped at the door. Worry made her heart beat faster, and she hurried to her car, where she hoped to calm herself down. Tears began to trickle down her eyes. Her fingers glazed over the hair tie and hesitated, remembering that night on the cove. But that was drowned out by her worries for Elizabeth. She pulled at the string, letting her hair loose, and shoved it in her pocket. *Lizzy, please be safe!*

Henry watched her go, sitting on the floor with a smile. He felt like he could jump and fly. He felt liberated. *We're almost at the tipping point now…*

****

Amy and Paige were back at the dorm, alone. Clara was out on another run, Monty was with Melody, and Elizabeth and Dalton were still M.I.A. With no cook, mac n' cheese was all that was on the menu tonight.

"My specialty," Amy giggled as she placed the two bowls and took her seat across from Paige.

They ate their food in silence. Rain pitter-pattered against the glass, and their spoons clinked against their bowls.

"This place is kinda…" Amy began.

"Empty?" Paige finished.

The door opened, and Monty stepped into the kitchen. "Sorry I didn't cook tonight," he apologized.

"Ay, don't worry about it, bro," Paige said. "Mac n' cheese is still shmack."

Monty chuckled. "Have you heard from Dalton or Elizabeth?"

Paige shook his head. "No, I'm pretty sure his Omnicard is dead, or he doesn't have any service."

"Elizabeth too," Amy sighed. "I'm worried about them."

Monty wished them goodnight and walked to his room, where he called Sagittarius.

"What is it, Monterey?" Sagittarius asked.

"Have you found out where Dalton and Elizabeth are? Everyone's worried about them."

"No, I haven't yet. The Dean and I are working on it. I'm sure they're fine. They're my students, after all."

"I'm sure, but that doesn't make me any less worried."

Sagittarius noticed no aggression in his tone. It was completely docile. He'd figured Monty was the type to go out on his own and find his own answers if others couldn't. "Just get some sleep, Monterey." Sagittarius was about to hang up when:

"And uh, hey, about what you said to me during the final exam..."

Sagittarius remained quiet as he brought the Omnicard back to his ear.

"My eyes are open now."

Sagittarius gave a silent chuckle. "You're a good kid Monterey. Now get some rest. That's an order."

"Okay," Monty chuckled. "Goodnight."

****

The next day, Clara bolted out of homeroom, and Monty played his game of catch up so they could walk together to culinary class.

"Hey, wait up!" Monty said, but she didn't slow down. In fact, she walked faster.

Monty started to run out of breath, and his arm ached, the blight stinging and constricting it. When he finally caught up, he asked, "Hey, Melody wants to do a song with me, but my piano skills are rusty. I know it's a bother, but I was wondering if you could help me out?"

Clara said nothing and kept increasing her pace.

"What's wrong?"

Clara wouldn't respond.

"Hello? Anyone home? What happened to walking to culinary class together?" Monty asked and went to jab Clara, but she parried it, and countered with a punch to his arm.

It roared with pain, and Monty nearly stumbled. His eyes widened, and his cheeks inflated like pufferfish, holding in an "Ow!" and watched Clara walk away.

"Don't talk to me," she threatened with a look.

Monty felt his body tremble all at once before he froze as if he had been turned to stone. Monty's arm ached, and so did his heart. It took all of his strength to keep from falling to his knees. He watched her walk away. "Did I do something wrong?"

7: Lokyer's Strongest

A day and a half passed since Dalton told Elizabeth his story. Dalton insisted on keeping the train going, and she didn't object. They each stood watch at opposite ends of the train, easily disposing of any pack of signum that tried to attack the train. Soon enough, the sun had set once again, and the two found themselves with nothing to do.

Elizabeth was sitting on the floor of a car with her legs dangling over the edge as she watched the passing scenery. She had the Scroll in her hand and gripped it tightly. *How am I going to deal with Masamune tomorrow?*

"Hey," Dalton greeted from the roof.

Elizabeth quickly put away the Scroll. "Hi."

"Mind if I sit next to you?"

"Sure."

Dalton eased himself down a little ways away and let out a long sigh when he finally settled. He looked exhausted. The burden of keeping the train going was starting to take its toll on him.

"So, what *is* going on exactly?" Dalton asked.

"I *really* don't want to tell you," Elizabeth admitted.

"Why not?"

"Because I'm not like you, Dalton. I don't trust people that easily."

"And why don't you trust me?"

Elizabeth pulled her legs close and hugged them tightly. "All my life, I've been surrounded by people who care about nothing but themselves. My mom taught me never to trust anyone–good advice in my opinion. "

"That's... really lonely."

"Which is why I was lucky to come across Clara. She and her mom showed me kindness. Apart from my adopted parents, it seemed like they were the only ones who weren't snakes. Clara is proud and honorable, unlike you."

"I'm proud and honorable!" Dalton retorted.

"Then why do you act so vain?"

Dalton didn't have much of a response to that. "I wouldn't call it entirely an act..."

"You're quite the hypocrite. You distrust your friends as much as I do."

"That's not true!"

"Then why do you feel the need to show off all the time?"

Dalton went to retort but couldn't find the words. Elizabeth answered for him.

"It's very clear from your story that even *you* can't completely trust if your friends will stay after what you experienced. So you show off and act all confident just to make sure they find you useful enough to keep you around."

Dalton frowned. He chuckled. "Yeah... I guess you're right." He racked his brain for a counterpoint. His frown switched to a smile when he found one. "But distrust isn't the whole picture with you, is it?"

"Huh?" Elizabeth looked at him as if he were crazy.

"If it were, you would have had Clara come with you on this secret mission of yours. You're scared of something. I never questioned it before because Chasm isn't fond of me either, but they were after you that night. You don't want to tell me or the others what's going on because you *do* care about them. And telling us would put us in danger, no? So I want to help you out!"

Elizabeth glared at him as he smirked back. "If you're just here to impress me and win my affection, I believe the risk is way greater than the reward."

"You're *still* saying that? I'm not here to make any moves on you or... or anything like that. It may be a hard concept for you to understand, but I consider you a friend–if you wanna be more than that, I'm all for it–and when I see my friends distraught and throwing themselves to face danger alone, thinking they're being selfless when they're *not*." Dalton took a deep breath to calm himself down. "I can't help but want to be there for them."

Elizabeth looked at Dalton and scanned his face for any sarcasm or sign of deception, but there was none. She finally gave in. "If I tell you, I'm putting you in danger," she sighed. "You were never supposed to come here in the first place."

"Well, now that I *am* here, there's no more harm to be done, right?" Dalton asked with a smile. "Besides, a little danger can be fun."

Elizabeth rolled her eyes and buried her face in her thighs. "You have to promise to keep this a secret from the others."

"I, Dalton Drake, shall not utter a word of this conversation," Dalton said in a regal tone.

The two sat in silence until Elizabeth finally caved. "My real last name isn't Baker. That was my adopted family's name. My true name is Elizabeth Asteria."

She let that sink in.

"W-wait. Like, as in the royal family? The one that rules Akerym right now?" Dalton asked, stunned.

Elizabeth nodded.

"Then what are you doing here?"

"Do you know a man by the name of Masamune Asteria?"

"Doesn't ring a bell, but he's obviously related to you somehow."

"Well, just a couple of days ago, he texted me, summoning me out here. If I didn't come, he threatened to hurt all of you."

"Well... is it a sibling rivalry going on between you two or something?"

"Something like that..." Elizabeth's fingers went to her beanie but froze upon touching it. "I showed Monty this already, but I never told him my origins..."

Elizabeth removed her beanie to reveal her cat ears and freed her tail from her pant leg. She looked at Dalton with a serious expression, expecting him to respond negatively.

"Oh..." Dalton said. "So *that's* why your hearing is so good! So, does being Wanari have something to do with why you're not in Akerym?"

"It has everything to do with it." She directed her gaze to the passing scenery once more and became lost in thought.

"Akerym is the worst place to be if you are one. My mother was a Wanari maid serving the royal family. She had an affair with the King himself and had me." She clenched her fists. "Of course, the royal family couldn't have a word of this; it would discredit them. So they made my mother keep quiet, saying they'd kill me if she didn't work for the crown her entire life."

"So, how'd you escape?" Dalton asked. But he could almost see the reflection of the frozen flames in her eyes.

"The Frostflame Massacre..." Elizabeth trailed off. "I was there and the only survivor." She took a deep breath, letting her legs dangle off the edge again, and relaxed. "What makes the Asteria so powerful isn't just their status, but their magic. They created a magic scroll to make passing down the family magic a certainty. They filled it with runes that give the reader the ability to learn all eleven Asteria Sword Techniques if they have Asterian blood in their veins."

Elizabeth pulled out the small golden case and examined it. "The whole point of that night was to pass down the Techniques to the Asteria next in line to receive them. However, amidst the chaos, my mother stole it and gave it to me. I flowed down a river next to the castle and made it back into town, where I passed off as the average Wanari orphan. The Asteria know I have it. Whether they know that I can learn them myself is a different matter. That Chasm officer was probably a family friend since they want to keep me a secret; only a select few know of my existence." Elizabeth looked at the Scroll longingly before tucking it away and putting her beanie back on. "Masamune is also here for the Scroll. I don't know how he found me though, or how he got my Chirp ID."

"I'm sure we can take him. You and me? C'mon, that's unfair," Dalton assured her.

"You don't know him, Dalton," Elizabeth snapped. "The Asteria has a branch family in Hinohana, and Masamune is from that lineage. No one ever thought he was going to succeed, he showed no promise, and since I had the Scroll, he can't even use the Sword Techniques. Magic is usually born out of necessity in a life-threatening situation. Masamune is the product of child abuse in the Asteria family. I don't know the specifics of what they did to him, but I know he was forced to get magic. He began training with Vega Cruz, and is currently the most powerful mage on Lokyer."

"Monty's dad?" Dalton asked.

"Huh?"

"Vega Cruz. That's Monty's dad, or I'm pretty sure that was his name."

"No way!" Elizabeth exclaimed. "What a class roster we have… Why doesn't Monty ever talk about him?"

"I'm not exactly sure. But he and his old man were never on good terms. He was always gone, so he never got to know him too well. Everyone on Prism has had their share of family troubles," Dalton sighed.

"Anyway, Masamune became a master photomancer. He earned himself a Prestige License and challenged three members of the royal family. He managed to defeat all three, and they had to acknowledge his power. However, he was never able to inherit the Scroll. Apparently, he had survived in the Barren Lands for three months."

"The icy region north of Hinohana?" Dalton asked.

Elizabeth nodded. "He's regarded as one of, if not the most powerful mage on Lokyer."

Dalton stared off into the distance. His muscles tensed up, and he could feel a rush of energy flow through his body. He couldn't help but get excited. "Well, I don't care how powerful people say this Masamune guy is, I plan to at least get one hit in."

Elizabeth scoffed, "Easier said than done."

"Hey, if we work together we'll be fine," Dalton said with a smile. "You're a princess in my eyes, and I'm your knight in shining armor." Dalton pointed at his chest with his thumb and had a great big smile on his face.

Elizabeth couldn't help but laugh. "Yeah, sure."

Elizabeth could tell Dalton was exhausted. Look past the glimmer in his eyes and smile and you could tell he was starting to peter out. He was trying his best to suppress how hard he was breathing, and she was sure his aura shield was paper-thin at this point.

He really is just here to help me, isn't he..? she thought.

"I guess it can't be helped," Elizabeth sighed. She scooched a little closer to Dalton and patted her thighs. "Come on, I know you're tired."

Dalton froze up. He looked at her suspiciously. "I'm not tired though? Also, why are you doing this so suddenly?"

So stubborn! Elizabeth cursed. She pulled out her pistol and pointed it at Dalton with a smile. "Is that how you thank someone for offering their lap pillow?"

"Okay, okay, chill," Dalton sighed.

Dalton started to lean toward Elizabeth until gravity did the rest and he plopped his head on her lap. Elizabeth put her pistol away and patted Dalton's head.

"You've worked hard. Get some rest."

"I could do more though," Dalton insisted.

Elizabeth smiled. "You're a good friend Dalton. Now get some sleep."

"Oh… well thank you…" Dalton chuckled nervously. He closed his eyes and he fell into a deep slumber. Eventually, Elizabeth's warm lap and the lull of the clacking tracks finally put him to sleep.

****

Dalton woke up when the sun's beams hit his face. He groaned, feeling restored, but groggy. The first things he noticed were that he was sleeping on the floor, the train was stopped, and Elizabeth was gone.

Oh, gods damn it, he cursed.

He ran out of the car and frantically searched the train for any traces of her. Nothing. He ran back to the car he slept in and noticed his sword was still there. He grabbed it and sprinted to the locomotive. He poured his aura into the cubby and the train creaked and groaned before it lurched forward and began to pick up speed.

I'm on my way!

****

Greedlake was a small mountain town next to a lake. All of the buildings were old and deteriorating. Some of the ceilings had caved in, leaving their interiors exposed to the forces of nature. The docks were destroyed and the small ships that were left there were scattered and broken. The quarries ran deep into the ground, and the excavation equipment that had been used to mine up the asterium ore were rusty and falling apart.

In the middle of the town was a stone church with part of its ceiling destroyed. Its gothic, stained glass windows were shattered and one of the walls had been reduced to rubble. It had one tower with a broken clock and Celestia's star atop the roof. Inside were rows of benches for prayer and at the end of the aisle was a four-meter statue of the Supreme Goddess Celestia, reaching down with an outstretched helping hand with a comforting smile. A tiara of flowers rested upon her head, and she wore an elegant white dress, but the paint of the statue had been worn off. A pile of rubble was at the base of the statue.

Elizabeth found Masamune at the top of the rubble, looking up at it with his arms crossed. The sun's beams shone upon him through the destroyed ceiling, basking him in light. It was odd, looking up at her ancestor. She took a step into the temple, making her movements as quietly as possible. She was able to take a few more steps before Masamune spoke up.

"Did you bring the Scroll?" he asked without turning, his voice echoing throughout the church.

Elizabeth gulped. "Yeah, I did." She pulled it out and gripped it tightly.

Masamune turned around and his gaze made Elizabeth tremble. He wasn't even trying to intimidate her. "You came here with no sword?

You were still with the main family when I last saw you. Surely you know what I'm capable of?"

How does he know I have Asteria blood? Elizabeth wondered.

"Yeah," she gulped.

"Yet a weakling such as yourself is still able to conceive an idea of beating me without one?"

"I—"

"Take that beanie off. It's an eyesore."

Elizabeth did as she was told and plopped it on the ground beside her. "I don't want to fight you."

"Oh, don't worry," Masamune chuckled. "If we did, it wouldn't be much of a fight."

"But I don't intend on handing you the Scroll."

Masamune's casual gaze turned into a glare. "You don't humor me. There's only one ending here: me leaving with the Scroll in hand."

"I understand I'm way out of my league, but I can't just sit by and let the Scroll fall into the wrong hands," Elizabeth explained calmly and drew her pistol.

"Pfft..." Masamune reared his head back with a laugh, "The wrong hands? I believe I'm much more deserving of the Scroll than you are."

"Even so, I can't break any more promises. Too many people know about this already. Sorry, I can't let you take the Scroll."

Masamune's smile vanished quickly. He turned his back to his opponent, his arms still crossed. "Such buffoonery!" Double-edge broadswords formed above his head one by one in an arc, aimed at her.

Elizabeth fired several shots from her pistol. The swords launched at blinding speed, obliterating past the scorch bolts toward their target. Elizabeth froze time for a second and jumped out of the way. The swords blasted through the wall behind her, sending debris scattering across the floor.

Masamune raised an eyebrow and looked over his shoulder. Another volley of golden swords and spears were created and once again launched at incredible speed toward Elizabeth.

I can't dodge these! Elizabeth cursed.

She stopped time for three seconds, trying to make her cooldowns as low as possible. She ran behind a bench and took cover. The swords and spears missed their target and destroyed the other part of the wall behind her.

Masamune finally turned around again. "Try dodging that again."

Another barrage of swords and spears flew at the bench she hid behind. She ran along behind it, the bench being blown apart behind her. She turned around and fired six shots in rapid succession. She immediately stopped time, and the bolts froze in the air. In a single motion: she unclipped a shock runestone from her belt, primed it with her aura, and threw it at Masamune. Attached to the runestone was a string, which she held onto, allowing it to move through frozen time. Once the runestone was between the bolts and her target, she let go. The runestone froze in place, and her four seconds were up.

Time resumed. A blinding flash, a thunderous *BOOM!* Elizabeth turned away from the ball of electricity that burst in front of Masamune. She started counting: *One, two, three, four…*

Elizabeth turned back around, and her eyes widened. There Masamune stood, with his arms still crossed. The attack left no signs of damage, even to his aura shield.

How? Elizabeth wondered. She gritted her teeth and glared, frustrated. *Keep calm. You know how strong he is. You can almost stop time again. Use it!*

Elizabeth started to move when suddenly *BANG!*

Dalton came flying through the broken wall at immense speed. He had constructed a cannon of ice and launched himself at Masamune with his leg extended. His foot plunged into Masamune's face, interrupting his concentration, and the swords of light dissipated.

"How does the bottom of my shoe taste, asshole?" Dalton snickered, breathing hard from running from the station across town to get there.

Masamune's cheek squished under Dalton's shoe, but he didn't flinch or get knocked off his feet. He turned his head, pushing against Dalton's decreasing momentum. He gave an irritated look.

Without saying a word, Masamune's shadow sprung to life in the form of a dragon. Its eyes were purple, and its lower body a wisp, like a ghost, tethered to his feet. Its arms were muscular, and its claws were in the shape of boxing gloves.

What?! Dalton exclaimed in his head, starting to bend his leg in an attempt to push off Masamune's face and escape.

The ghost wound back its arm, but Elizabeth stopped time. She sprinted over to him and grabbed Dalton's arm, resuming his time. She yanked him down just before time resumed, and the punch grazed Dalton's hair, sending a *whoosh* of wind past him. The two instantly booked it out of the church, dodging blades of light as they reached the main street.

Masamune's ghost snapped back to being a regular shadow on the ground as he formed eight swords of light that hovered above his head.

"See? Told you I'd get a hit in!" Dalton laughed.

"What were you thinking?!" Elizabeth asked as they kept running. A sword struck the ground next to her, nearly knocking her off her feet. "What goes on in that brain of yours that thinks it's okay to just leap in guns blazing like that?"

They ducked and bobbed and weaved as more swords and spears flew past, each one barely missing its target and tossing up pieces of the road upon impact.

"Because I trusted you would save me!" Dalton explained with a smile.

Elizabeth growled before shouting, "Idiot! Now is not the time to be worrying about my trust issues!"

"Now is the perfect time! Because…"

Dalton turned and twisted his foot into the ground, ushering forth a wall of ice. The oncoming volley tore apart the wall, and shards of ice and wind blew past them as they threw up their arms to protect their eyes.

"There's no way you're beating him alone!"

Elizabeth looked at Dalton, who was smiling like a child, and clicked her tongue. She quickly turned back to look in Masamune's direction and saw another volley of twelve swords and spears flying at them.

Dalton pivoted on his foot and created a wall of ice that stretched to the nearest alley. They ran toward it, using the wall as cover. They pressed their backs against the wall of the building they used as cover as they caught their breath.

"We can't beat him in a long-ranged or short-ranged battle. He can use his light magic to make swords and spears to hurl at us, as well as shields," Elizabeth thought aloud. "And if we get too close, he'll use shadow magic to keep us away. Dalton, can you see where he is?"

"Leave it to me!" He created a clone and formed a step with his hands. The clone stepped on it and Dalton threw him upward, higher than the roof. As soon as the clone was no longer behind cover, it was pierced by a pair of spears. "He's in front of the church," Dalton reported. "Bastard's still got his arms crossed…"

Elizabeth started formulating strategies, but none were viable enough to try. *Come on, think! Think!*

"Alright, I got a plan!" Dalton exclaimed confidently and lightly hammered his palm with a fist. "You distract him while I get close and beat him up!"

"No! I don't have that long of range, and unlike me, you can't stop time. His shadow would stop you."

"No, it wouldn't."

"Dalton!"

"Alright, ready? Break!" Dalton cheered and clapped his hands. "Oh, and uh, here." Dalton handed Elizabeth his sword. "You said your techniques had to be used with a sword, right?"

Elizabeth looked at the sword in her hands and frowned, tunnel visioning, so all she could see was the weapon. Her body urged her not to unsheathe it, as if a steel clasp kept the blade in its sheath.

"Dalton, wait!"

Dalton didn't listen and turned to run. Elizabeth growled and grabbed him by the arm.

"I said, wait! Your plan is stupid!"

"Hey, Elizabeth?" Dalton asked, placing a hand on her shoulder.

Elizabeth looked up and saw Dalton's close face, which usually would have been uncomfortable, but the warmth it emitted showed her only innocence and genuine worry.

"You don't seem to be ashamed of being a Wanari, which is good. But, you do seem to be ashamed to be an Asteria." Dalton broke eye contact. "Your family might not be the best people, they might be total assholes, but you're not your family."

Elizabeth was a little confused at where he got this assumption, but he was right—her widened eyes told him so.

Dalton smiled. His hands and voice trembled a tiny bit as he said, "It's your powers too. You have as much of a right to them as the douchebag throwing swords at us. But just because you got the same blood as them doesn't mean you're like the rest of them."

Elizabeth remembered when the Baker family first adopted her.

****

Elizabeth kept her eyes at her feet while Mrs. Bernardino held her hand and guided her out of a car. Clara remained inside the car with the driver.

They stopped, and Mrs. Bernardino knocked on a door. It opened shortly after.

"Clairise?" a woman's voice asked, surprised by her sudden visit.

"Hi, Denise. I just found this child, and I have an airship to catch. My husband wouldn't allow her to be adopted, but what about you and your husband?"

"Mmm… I don't know Clairise. This is so sudden!"

"I can't just let this child remain on the streets."

Of course, no family would want me, Elizabeth figured. *I'm just scum to most of these people.*

"We'll take her in," a man's voice said from inside.

Elizabeth's eyes widened, but she didn't look up.

"Really?" Mrs. Bernardino asked.

"Honey!" Denise exclaimed.

"What? We could use the extra pair of hands," the man insisted.

Elizabeth saw a shadow cast over her own, and she finally looked up. The tall figure was a burly man with black hair and a thick beard, someone you'd expect to be a lumberjack, not a baker. He bent down so that his eyes were level with hers.

"Whatt's your name, little one?" He asked, his accent thick.

Elizabeth didn't say a word. She was too scared to, scrunching her shoulders together and keeping her eyes on the ground.

The man watched her slight trembling and her attempt to shrivel into a ball by scrunching her shoulders and looking away, hoping to avoid any and all eye contact if possible. The man simply smiled and got up. "We'll take her in, Mrs. Bernardino. You're truly a kind person."

"As are you, sir. Thank you both."

Elizabeth was led inside and walked up a flight of wooden stairs to an attic. A bed was in the corner of the room, along with some bookshelves littered in dust and cobwebs.

"This is where you'll be bunking," the man said. "It's not much, but it's all we got."

Elizabeth was still trying to process everything. How had she suddenly found herself here? Wasn't she on the streets scavenging for food a couple of minutes ago?

"My name is Sam Baker. The woman downstairs is Denise, my wife. We'll be taking care of you for the time being. Dinner will be ready in an hour or so. You should walk around, get a good idea of your surroundings. It must be a lot to take in."

With that, he left her alone upstairs while he prepared dinner. Not knowing what to do or think, Elizabeth simply sat in the corner, hugging her legs to her chest. She eventually heard her name called and slowly made her way down, like a suspicious kitten to a new toy.

Steaming hot spaghetti with meatballs and parmesan cheese sat on the table. The sweet aroma filled Elizabeth's nostrils and made her stomach rumble. She tried to suppress it along with her temptation to drool. A divine scent filled the room as Denise came from the kitchen and placed garlic bread on the table.

Sam and Denise sat down at the table and started to eat when they noticed that Elizabeth hadn't joined them. Sam turned around in his chair and found her standing with her back to the wall some distance away. She trained her eyes on the floorboards, and she tried to make her existence as small as possible. Sam and Denise shared a saddened look before calling for her.

"Come on," Sam said.

Elizabeth's ears perked up, and she slowly tilted her head up to peek. All she saw was the warm couple smiling, waiting patiently for her.

"Let's eat, sweetie," Denise beckoned.

Elizabeth crept to the chair and sat in it. She noticed the order of the silverware wasn't in the proper order, and she began to rearrange her utensils and napkin, along with the two glasses. Denise and Sam watched on in surprise. After she was done, she put her hands in her lap and waited, keeping her head down.

"Alroight, let's get ta eatin."

The two started to eat but paused when they heard Elizabeth's sniffles. She was still sitting with her head down, and tears streamed down her face.

"What's wrong?" Denise asked a little nervously.

Elizabeth remembered when she and her mother would be fed sludge—and sparingly—while the human maids were served average meals cooked by chefs. Or the past few weeks of scavenging trash for scrap. She could picture the terrible food in front of her in a wooden bowl, and when she wiped her eyes with her arm, she saw reality.

"Nothing, it's just... I still couldn't tell if this was a dream or not," she sniffled, and smiled. She picked up the bowl and scooped some spaghetti onto her plate. "Elizabeth."

"Hm?" They both asked.

"My name is Elizabeth—" she stopped herself, remembering her mother's words about revealing her identity. "Elizabeth..."

"Elizabeth Baker," Sam finished. "This day forward, your name is Elizabeth Baker."

From that day on, she was put to work at the bakery—cleaning, cooking, waitressing, and earning money while she was at it. She wore a beanie over her head the entire time in order to hide her ears, a gift from her adopted father. All the while, Clara would come to learn how to bake and Elizabeth would often deliver pastries to the Bernardino Estate.

Eventually, her adopted father found the Scroll. "You wanna tell me what this is?"

Elizabeth averted her eyes and had her hands behind her back. "I can't say..."

"Why not? Do you not trust me?"

Elizabeth didn't reply.

"The way this scroll is ornamented, it's definitely expensive. Come on, tell me what it is."

Elizabeth finally caved. "My real name is Elizabeth Asteria, the illegitimate child of King Jackson. My real mother was killed at the Frostflame Massacre..."

"Holy shit..." Sam muttered. "Well, I was going to teach you how to fight anyway. You're a Wanari in Akerym, after all. You need to know how to defend yourself. And with that last name, more than just street thugs will be after you."

Elizabeth gulped and nodded.

"What's in the Scroll?" Sam asked again.

"The Asteria Sword Techniques. I heard people in my family say that all you need to do is read it, and you can do all of them. But..."

"You don't want to because you resent the family that abandoned you, right?"

Elizabeth nodded.

"Look, just read the Scroll, so you have the Techniques if you ever need them. I'm not going to force you, but I strongly suggest it," Sam said as he walked over to a locked drawer. He tapped his Omnicard to the lock, and it opened. "In the meantime, I'll be teaching you hand-to-hand combat and how to use one of these." He pulled from the drawer a pistol and loaded it. "This, I am forcing you to learn. Got it?"

Elizabeth nodded, and Sam handed her back the scroll. "Those are your powers too. It's your birthright. Don't let some other people with the same name as you identify who you are." Sam sat down in a chair and sighed. "It'd be nice if you had a training partner..."

"I could fill the part," Clara's voice chirped.

Elizabeth turned around and saw Clara standing at the door. Her hair was all frizzy, her right arm covered in burns, and her hand charred. Her breaths were weak and quick, and she looked to be in great pain.

"Clara? What are you doing here? What happened?" Sam asked worriedly.

She stared at her right hand and clenched her fist. Lightning began to surge beneath her skin. "I want to become a Prestige and bring honor back to the Bernardino name. For my mom..." she said solemnly. "I learned that you used to be a Chasm officer. I want you to teach me to fight."

Sam sighed, realizing what Clara had done to herself. "Then it's settled," Sam said. "I'll teach you everything I learned in my years with Chasm. Remember you two, what I'm about to teach you is for *self-defense only*. Got it? It's not to be used to seek violence but to prevent it. We start tomorrow."

****

"Family doesn't have to mean blood relations–Prism–we're your family now. We're here for you. *I'm* here for you, okay?" Dalton finished before turning to run again.

Elizabeth couldn't help but blush a little, and in her daze, Dalton ran out of range. She shook her head and snapped out of it. "Hold on, don't think you can just say some nice words and run!"

"Doing it right now!" Dalton shouted as he rounded the corner of the building they were behind. "I trust you!"

Elizabeth slumped her shoulders and facepalmed with a sigh. *Imbecile!*

Masamune clicked his tongue. "Such a waste of time." He created a mixture of sixty swords and spears and launched them everywhere, taking off chunks of buildings and causing some to crumble and collapse.

Elizabeth drew the sword from the sheath and pointed the tip toward the sky, letting the back of it rest on her forehead. She closed her eyes and prepared herself.

She ran out into the main street where Masamune was still waiting down by the church. He launched another twelve swords at Elizabeth.

Elizabeth quickly ran two fingers down the flat of the blade. "Asteria Sixth Sword Technique: Supernova." A white dome of energy flashed from her and shattered the swords of light.

"Oh? About time you actually started fighting!" Masamune shouted before sending another volley.

Elizabeth jumped to the side, dodging a handful of the blades. She deflected the remaining ones with Dalton's blade. "Asteria Fourth Sword Technique: Rupture!" She slashed the air in front of her five times, and five crescents of rippled space flew toward Masamune. She immediately dodged another spear and pulled her arm back. "Asteria Third Sword Technique: Ripple!" She stabbed the air five times, the space in front of her stretching like a rubber band before racing at her target.

Masamune stood his ground and put up a giant shield of light to block the attacks. "Oh-ho! Interesting!" Masamune put his shield down and one-by-one created forty swords and spears behind him. "But it's useless!"

I can't possibly dodge all of those! Elizabeth thought. *Think! What can I do? How can I block all of them? A supernova? No, that won't work! If I stop time and use Ripple and Rend, he'd just block them with his swords. The only option I have is...* Elizabeth started sprinting forward, spinning and slashing with her sword to generate energy. A silver cloud began to flow off her sword and surround her body. Silver clouds started to form and flow from Masamune's blades, and a few even dissipated. *I need to get close! Block these for me, Dalton! I'm trusting you!*

Masamune launched his attack, and as the storm of swords barreled toward Elizabeth, a wave of Dalton clones jumped from the rooftops and ran alongside her. Each had shields of ice at the ready and did everything they could to deflect and absorb the oncoming swords and spears. Elizabeth spun and slashed, getting lucky enough to deflect an oncoming sword with her blade. The cloud grew large and was in the shape of a spinning disc around her. As she approached Masamune, she stopped time. The swords in front of her froze in place, and she planted her sword in the ground.

"Asteria Fifth Sword Technique: Orbital Pull!"

Everything lurched toward her—the swords and spears, Dalton's clones, Masamune, everything. They were all still frozen in time as they flew toward her. She immediately pulled her sword out of the ground and spun once more, winding up to slash Masamune with her blade. The pressure and energy she was exerting from the continuous use of Techniques and stopping time cause her knees to nearly buckle.

This is it! Asteria Ninth Sword Technique: Protostar!

Right before she was about to slash Masamune with her sword, unleashing all of the energy that she sapped from him, which was now in the form of a disc around her, she froze. Her eyes widened and her gut sank. *What?! Why can't I move?! Even if four seconds are up, I should be moving!*

"I see you are no common Wanari thief. You really do have Asteria blood…" Masamune growled.

How can he..?!

"You've earned a little respect from me," Masamune said as he regained his balance and stepped out of the way of the strike. "Sometimes, if an Asteria undergoes an event of great stress they can unlock the secret of the Asteria family: Chrono Control, or the ability to stop time. If you have the ability and pay attention, you can tell when someone is using Chrono Control, and I could see during stopped time. However, it seems you can only stop it for four seconds. Such a shame. I can stop it for *nine*." Time resumed.

Elizabeth slashed the air in front of her, sending a shockwave of energy barreling forth, obliterating several of the blades and completely destroying the building next to her. But she couldn't dodge the other ones which found their mark. One went into her thigh but was stopped by her aura shield. Another slashed the side of her arm as it flew past, and another tore open her shoulder. She screamed in pain as she collapsed to her knees. "Fly!" he commanded and willed his shadow to life. It threw a single punch at Elizabeth and sent her soaring into the building next to her.

Dalton used the chance to sneak up behind Masamune, but Masamune knew he was coming. He decided he'd give Dalton a false sense of hope before dealing with him, and let him get closer than he should have.

Perfect! Dalton cheered. Dalton had an Aurora Ball prepared, and went to thrust it at Masamune's back.

Masamune's shadow sprung to life and slapped the Aurora Ball out of Dalton's hand. Dalton went wide-eyed. *Shiiit!*

Masamune's shadow unleashed a barrage of powerful punches into Dalton. But it was just a clone, and it turned into slush as the information was passed to the real Dalton.

The real Dalton ran to Elizabeth's side and helped her up. "You okay?" he whispered.

"He... He can stop time," Elizabeth was able to get out. Her aura shield was already on the verge of breaking. The swords of light already dissipated, leaving just the open wounds.

Dalton gritted his teeth and clicked his tongue. *Damn him!*

"Now..." Masamune said as he stepped closer. He looked down upon the two, his arms still crossed. "Give me the Scroll." His shadow shot forward, its arms reaching for Elizabeth.

Dalton felt a wave of frustration come over him and give him newfound strength. He turned and clapped his hands in front of him and unleashed a tsunami of ice that separated him and Elizabeth from their aggressor. Dalton put Elizabeth's arm over his shoulder and picked up his sword before running away into a different building down the street.

Masamune looked up at the enormous wall of ice and clicked his tongue. His shadow dashed at the wall, unleashing a flurry of punches at blinding speed. With each thunderous impact, the wall quaked and cracks slowly formed.

Dalton was able to find an old inn, and he laid Elizabeth down on a sofa in the lobby. He placed his sword on the floor next to it.

"So he can stop time?" Dalton asked, fog still coming from his mouth. "What's our plan now?"

Elizabeth held her head. "There is no plan. He can stop time for nine seconds. Our only window is his cooldowns. For as long as someone stops time, they can't use it again for however long they used it times four. But I thought I was the only one who could stop time. How foolish of me. I don't know if he somehow found a way to reduce the cooldown time."

"So basically, we have to make him stop time again, count how long he does it, then we have that amount of time multiplied by four to attack him?" Dalton repeated.

"But you can't count it! To you, it'd just look like he'd teleport."

"Got it," Dalton said and began to walk out. "So after he teleports is my window."

"Where are you going?" Elizabeth asked.

"To go beat that guy. If we don't, he gets the Scroll or hurts our friends, right?" Dalton replied matter of factly.

"No, we need to go together! I still have my aura shield, I'm fine!" She sat up and recoiled in pain, grabbing the side of her stomach where she had been punched.

"No, yours is paper thin. If it breaks, you might start bleeding more from your wound. Stay here." Dalton turned and started walking out the door.

Elizabeth grabbed his wrist. When he turned back around, he could see how frustrated she was. "Didn't what I said last night get through that thick skull of yours?!" She lowered her gaze to the ground. "It was your kindness, your patience, your willingness to be honest..." Elizabeth chuckled. "Even your stupid jokes and charm that convinced me to call you a friend." She looked at Dalton in the eyes with tears starting to build up in her own. "Don't die for a stupid reason like showing off to impress me."

Dalton's eyes were wide. He would've made a joke like, *this sounds like a confession to me!* But he blanked out on it. Memories of Monty and Paige never being impressed with what he did, no matter what it was flashed through his mind. *Were they... Am I that dense?*

"Dalton!" Elizabeth snapped.

"Thanks for the kind words Elizabeth, you're right," Dalton smiled. He pushed her away and surrounded the building in a case of ice. He turned his back to the prison he created and looked at the giant wall he made. He could hear Masamune's punches pound against it, causing it to rumble. "But I need to do it just one last time. Sorry."

Cracks sprouted across the wall, and with one more shockwave, it came tumbling down, crushing the roofs of the buildings beneath it. Masamune stood with his arms still crossed, infuriated, and bored. Dalton walked over so they were about fifty meters apart and tossed his sword away.

"You're just like my friend Simon," Dalton yelled across to him.

"Huh?"

"All you care about is power, that's how you measure someone's worth. For a while, I thought the same thing. I wanted to show everyone just how useful I am, but that's just a load of bullshit."

"Do I look like a counselor to you? I don't care," Masamune scoffed and prepared a volley of swords.

"Don't matter if you're the strongest asshole on Lokyer. If you're still an asshole, you're not gonna make any friends!"

A smile went across Dalton's face as his teeth transformed into fangs. He threw on his hood to hide his horns, which were starting to peek out of his hair, and his yellow eyes were cloaked in the shadow of his hood. He wrapped his tail around his leg, hidden underneath his pants. He created two daggers of ice in his hands and pointed one at his opponent. *Now that Liz's out of the picture, I can finally go all out.*

"I'm gonna make you uncross your arms."

"You'll do nothing," Masamune said boredly and sent forth his volley.

Dalton poured aura into his legs and zoomed forward. With his activated eyes, he could see the aura forming the swords and could track them as they flew toward him at blinding speed. He put up a dagger and used it to deflect the first sword. He was successful, but his weapon almost immediately shattered. He used his remaining dagger to block the next projectile, and it too, shattered. He immediately formed another dagger in his right hand and blocked the next sword.

Faster! he chanted. He kept racing forward, leaning from side to side, deflecting and forming new daggers along the way. *Faster!* He deflected another sword. *Faster!* He deflected a spear. *Faster!* Yet another.

"Come on man, just hit me already and be done with it! Stop wasting both of our time!" Dalton taunted.

Masamune snarled, "A bag of hot air is nothing to a hurricane!"

The next thing Dalton knew there were twenty swords only a meter away from him, threatening to turn his body into a pincushion. *He stopped time!* Dalton processed. Dalton put up a crossblock and the area around him became veiled in a cloud of dust and rubble. Dalton jumped out of it, a shield of ice covering both his arms. The only injuries he suffered were a couple of cuts on his arms and legs which had not been fully covered by the shield. *Now's my chance!*

Masamune's eyes widened with surprise before sharpening and filling with anger. "Don't get ahead of yourself!" Masamune created more spears and angled some of them downward at Dalton before firing away.

Dalton kept sprinting forward and did a baseball slide underneath the incoming projectiles. With the hand he had on the ground, he created a small wall of ice in front of him to block the spears coming straight on. He finally got in range. "Tranquil Snow!"

The blizzard whipped up around the two and Masamune found himself alone in the snowy twilight. He looked around him and scoffed.

"Cute spell, but this won't help you." Masamune summoned forth a plethora of swords and angled them in every possible direction. He launched them and used his shadow to deflect any that would hit him.

Dalton was able to see the swords form thanks to his eyes, and was able to sense the spot where the aura was least potent. He sprinted and dove for it, one sword found its mark and went through his calf where it stayed for a moment before dissipating. He screamed in pain, his voice resounding off the falling snowflakes.

Dalton quickly got up, and to his surprise the shadow dragon was already in his face. *How?!* With one punch, it sent Dalton flying out of Tranquil Snow's range and into a nearby building. His senses were thrown off and his head was dizzy.

"I sent my swords flying everywhere, even to my location, except for one spot. Either you blocked the swords, in which case, I could see they were getting blocked, or you try and dodge them," Masamune explained preemptively, figuring Dalton wanted to know.

An Aurora Ball shot from the building, but Masamune used his shadow to deflect it. "Enough," Masamune sighed. "I'll be taking that scroll now." He turned away from the building and started heading over to where Elizabeth was held.

"Not so fast," Dalton snarled as he climbed out of the rubble. "One punch isn't enough to do me in."

Masamune still didn't turn around.

Dalton clicked his tongue. "Hey, doofus! You won't find her in that building! She ran away with the Scroll. Only I know where she's hiding!"

Masamune didn't stop. "I'll level this entire place if I have to. It's no problem for me."

Dalton hurled an Aurora Ball and nailed Masamune in the back of his head.

"I'm giving you the chance to scurry away with your life intact. If you wish to continue, I *will* beat you senseless," Masamune warned as he turned.

Masamune gasped when he saw Dalton. His leg was bleeding and his right arm was bruised from having blocked the last punch. His hood was peeled back, revealing his yellow irises, his blue horns poking out from his hair, and the fangs in his smile.

"Bastard, you…" Masamune trailed off. He stopped time.

A little blip of light sparked in his palm. It was about the size of a firefly, a harmless-looking thing, but the result would be the opposite.

Masamune guided it to Dalton's stomach, where it hovered, frozen in time. Masamune put his hand in his pocket and got ready for the fireworks. Time resumed.

The firefly whined until it exploded, sending out a blast of golden light. Dalton's eyes stung from its brilliance and his whole body felt a wave of pain rush over it. His aura shield shattered and he was thrown backward with immense force. Pain welled up in his stomach and his chest and he vomited blood as he flew through a wall into a building, and into another, then finally through a third wall where he landed in a tailoring store. As he lay among the rubble and debris, he struggled to breath, a rib must've pierced his lung. The only thing keeping him alive was his demon form, which was desperately healing his wounds. He was in excruciating pain, so much so that he was on the verge of passing out. His mind started to drift off, and his breathing became sporadic.

Don't let your eyes close! Don't let your eyes close! Don't fall asleep! He chanted to himself.

But his eyelids had sandbags tied to them, and he couldn't help but close them.

****

"Why do you want to become a Prestige?" Sagittarius asked.

Dalton sheathed his blade and turned to face his teacher. "I'm a thrill seeker. I want to travel the world, go on crazy adventures, and when it's all said and done, get rich and live the sweet life."

"Hmph, is that so?" Sagittarius scoffed. He hopped down from the roof and began to walk away from his student. "I don't think that's true."

"Huh, you don't believe me?"

"No, that's not it. But, you're going to get that rush of adrenaline. You're going to get the adventure you speak of, and that's when you'll realize that's not what you really want." With those words, he walked away and jumped to another roof.

****

Dalton's eyes shot open and his body shivered in pain as he wheezed out a sigh of relief. His body had stabilized somewhat, at least, he was confident he wasn't going to die from his injuries. He looked up at the passing clouds that blocked parts of the sun.

Ah... So this is what he meant. What made this trip so enjoyable... Why I was even here in the first place... Images of Elizabeth flashed in front of him. He could hear Simon yelling at him, *"You won't survive in this world without any power!"*

Dalton couldn't help but wince, chuckle, and smile in response. "I lose!"

The sunlight overhead forced Dalton to close his eyes and the pounding of his heart against his chest was so loud in his ears that he couldn't hear Masamune walk up to him. But he could feel a burning sensation in his stomach as it shot up his throat and pooled in his mouth.

His eyes shot open and he coughed up blood like an erupting geyser. He looked down and saw a blade of light partly inside him. The burning wouldn't stop and he screamed out in pain, tears starting to stream from his eyes. He tried desperately to move, but couldn't do anything but grimace. His demon form kicked back in and his horns, tail, and fangs sprouted quickly and his eyes sparked yellow.

"That's funny, your blood is red?" Masamune chuckled. "I had come here not planning on killing anybody, but seeing you transform has changed my mind."

Masamune's sword slowly pushed further inside Dalton's stomach and he cried out in anguish. Masamune squatted and leaned in, his eyes menacing and filled with unadulterated hatred.

"You have thirty seconds to change it back..."

8: While They Were Gone Pt. 2

With a basket of blueberry muffins in one hand and a bouquet of Azaleas in the other, Monty walked through the hospital doors with Paige alongside him.

"Thanks for tagging along, Paige," Monty said.

"For sure," Paige replied. "Remember, after this, we're dunking you in an arcwater spring at my dad's temple."

"Yeah, yeah," Monty sighed. "You wanna muffin?"

Steam leaked out from the folds of the cloth wrapped around the pastries as Monty held up the basket at eye level with Paige.

Paige gave a defeated sigh, "How can I say no to your cooking?"

They walked to Melody's room and found it to be vacant. After a quick inspection, Monty spotted Melody in the garden. She swayed with her eyes closed as she played her violin. A calm breeze made her hair sway with her and the morning sunbeams from Plexis bathed her in a rose-gold light.

Monty placed down the azaleas and muffins on a nearby table and leaned on the window sill and watched her play. Paige was mesmerized by the tranquility of Monty's smile. His warm expression was finally in parallel with his power instead of the cold glares he usually gave.

He hated how he couldn't see more of it.

An alarm rang from the tv and an ominous broadcast played: "Signum have been detected within the city. Everyone is to seek shelter. Authorities have been called and will arrive shortly."

****

Back at the Prism dorm, Clara and Amy were in the kitchen when they saw the news. Within minutes they were dressed and out the door.

"Where are the others?" Clara asked.

"I don't know," Amy shrugged.

Clara called Elizabeth, but there was no response. Amy called Monty and was able to get through. "Did you see the news?" She put her Omnicard on speaker.

"Yeah, I did," Monty replied. "Me and Paige are already here. I've called Taro and he can come teleport you guys over here."

"Hey, you two!" Sagittarius' voice boomed.

The two turned around and saw him standing with his arms crossed on the roof of the dorm.

"You're not going anywhere! This could be an opportunity for Penumbra to attack. We still don't know where Dalton or Elizabeth are, and I'm not about to lose two more students."

Shit... Clara cursed and Amy hung up the call.

"Uh, actually..."

Sagittarius turned around and saw Taro's face surprisingly close to his. "Woah!" He swung in surprise and Taro sidestepped it.

"If you're just keeping an eye on them you can do it in Cysko!" Taro smiled cheerfully. His expression switched to a desperate one. "Seriously, we need help."

"Wha?!"

He put a hand on Sagittarius' shoulder and teleported to the two girls. "Group hug!" he shouted and in a white flash, he teleported them to the Port of Cysko. He groaned and clung to his stomach. "I've teleported one too many people today..."

"Ah, great. You've brought reinforcements," a man's voice said.

Behind them stood Monty and Paige, but also Miles Tovera. He had a goatee and very short, black stubbly hair on his head. He had light brown skin and stood tall—a whopping 193 cm. He wasn't the most built man, but he wasn't thin either.

He was equipped with two bandoliers with runestones and a belt containing different talismans. He had two pistols strapped: one in the holster beneath his armpit and one at his belt. A shotgun dangled behind his back, and in his hand was a Revolving Runestone Launcher, a.k.a. an RRL (pronounced "Rel").

"Miles, can I get a heal?" Taro whimpered.

"Sure thing buddy! But, you're not injured are you? A talisman will do!" he smiled and lobbed a talisman at Taro that stuck to his back like a magnet. White aura glowed dimly around Taro and he was invigorated with energy. Miles walked over to Clara. "I don't think we've met before. I'm Miles Tovera, Paige's dad."

Clara smiled and shook his hand. "I know who you are Mr. Tovera. Name's Clara, Clara Bernardino."

Miles smiled. "Well, well, We got an all-star over here!" Miles exclaimed. "Your mother and I kinda knew each other. She was wunna Vega's students. It's long overdue but, sorry that she passed..."

"Oh, no, it's okay..." Clara smiled solemnly.

"But enough introductions! We need to kill some signum, haha!" Miles laughed.

"Well, now that we're here Sagittarius..." Clara said with a smirk. "We might as well help out."

Sagittarius was stunned for a second before facepalming. "Ugh, just... don't die." His tattoo glowed and his bow appeared in his hand.

"My men are at the North Marina district," Miles explained. "We plan to create a pincer attack and hopefully push the signum back to the piers where Pisces will come in and help us finish them off. We already have police and the Runeseekers searching the outskirts of the Eastern Districts and so far they've found no signum. So we're left with the Central and Marina Districts."

"I'm going to go help my brother in South Central. See you all on the flip side," Taro saluted before teleporting away.

Paige hopped in the driver's seat of his pickup truck and they drove into the city. Stores had their windows broken in. Police officers were providing as much support as they could, building barricades with their cars and firing away with their rifles and pistols. People were evacuated and gathered into buildings that had their windows barricaded with wooden planks.

Hyenas covered in blight barked and yipped as they pranced about the street with their tongues out. Domestic dogs, cats, and other pets had been infected with it, their fresh bite marks little islands of pink flesh surrounded by a sea of black.

Amy riddled passing signum with feathers while Clara zapped everything with concentrated lightning. Miles fired off scorch runestones from his RRL. Sagittarius repeatedly let loose arrows of light.

They reached a police barricade and skidded to a halt. Clara and Amy hopped atop the barricade and saw the hordes of signum running rampant. Clara interlocked her fingers and stretched out her arms, cracking her knuckles. "Time to let off some steam..."

****

A child was being towed by his mother as they sprinted through the streets of Cysko, desperate for shelter. The laughter of hyenas, the hissing of cats, and the howling of wolves filled his ears to the beat of his heart.

"Don't worry," his mother assured. "We're almost there."

They bolted down an alley and a wolf pounced on them from the rooftop. His mother let go and was pulled to the ground. Two more jumped down and snarled. One of the wolves chomped down at the small of her back while the other bit her arm.

A woman's screams and a child's crying hit Monty's ears. Monty whirled his sword to life and raced towards it. He hacked and slashed his way through the signum that attacked him. He turned the corner and his eyes widened with horror. Two signum wolves were eating a woman who was barely alive while the other crept toward the paralyzed boy.

Maybe I can save her! Monty thought.

He stepped into the alley and one of the wolves turned and snarled. It ran at him and Monty sidestepped the lunge and ran his blade across its flank. Its claws skidded across the cement as it turned and immediately pounced again. Monty blocked with his sword and pushed against the beast, who was able to pin him to a wall. Its jaws snapped, desperately trying to get past his blade and tear off his face. Its black saliva flung onto his cheek and nearly got into his eye.

I'm going to have to use magic at this rate! Monty thought.

The hum of electricity filled the air. Clara hurled a spear of lightning at the signum munching on the mother. It pierced its heart and flew through its body to hit the other signum approaching the child.

"The hell are you *doing*?!" Clara snapped as she sprinted past.

Monty clicked his tongue. He turned his blade and pulled upward, wedging it in the signum's jaws. It chomped down on it and Monty pushed forward with a burst of force and sliced the top of its head off. He stabbed its heart and rushed to Clara's side.

Clara tackled the signum approaching the child and put it in a stranglehold. She concentrated her aura throughout her entire body and let loose an electrical discharge, frying the signum to death. Monty took care of the other signum lying atop the boy's mother.

Clara rushed to the boy's side while Monty watched, breathing hard. He did his best not to put his hand on his shoulder, which was aching with pain. He saw himself in the boy, his mother's corpse right before him. Clara also saw herself in him, and flashes of the crash flickered in her mind.

"Are you okay?" Clara asked.

The boy nodded his head as he sobbed. "But my mommy…"

Clara hugged him, almost squeezing the air out of him. "I'm sorry…" Tears were almost brought to her own eyes. "I'm sorry…"

"Clara!" Amy called. "Clara!"

She rounded the corner and came to a halt once she saw the scene. "Oh no…"

"We gotta go!" Miles called.

He joined them and saw the dead mother. A solemn look swept across his face as he knelt beside the corpse and put a hand to her heart and the other to her head and closed his eyes.

"Celestia, I pray you give off your heavenly radiance and lead yet another soul into your warm embrace. May they find happiness in your haven…" He rested his left wrist in his right palm with his fingers stretched to the sky. "*Pharos…*"

He walked over to the boy and put a hand on his head. "You'll be safe with us for now child. Please come with us. We can help you…" he had an alluring yet comforting voice.

The boy nodded and wiped his tears with the back of his sleeve. Clara finally let go of him and they headed back to the car. She bumped into Monty's shoulder hard as she walked past and it nearly made him collapse.

"You could've saved her," she growled. "You could've easily blown that signum to bits and saved her…"

Monty frowned at the ground silently, his fists clenched.

With the area clear, they moved their cars so Prism and the others can drive through in their truck. Miles could sense the melancholy among the team.

"It's hard, I know," Miles sighed. "But you can't save every life in this profession. You just need to be sure you can save those you can. Good job Clara."

Clara shook her head, her focus not in the present.

"We're going to be a little late," Kaze chuckled over the earpiece.

"What's that?" Miles asked, unmuting himself.

"Two poltergeists just sprouted in the South Eastern District," Kaze informed. "And the police captain told me there's four more in the North Eastern and East Central Districts."

"Two poltergeists showed up here as well," Jiro said over the call. "We took care of them quickly enough, but it also helped that they were specifically targeting us."

Strange… Miles thought. "That can work to our favor. Everyone evacuate your areas and lead all of the signum to Central Marina. "We'll be the bait. It's us they're after now? Well, that's what they're gonna get. Instead of us getting surrounded, we'll stick with the pincer attack except

Runeseekers will flank. We'll hold them off until you get here while the rest of my men focus on rescue and recovery in the areas with no signum. Plus, we should be in range for support from Pisces. Everyone got it?"

A unified "yeah!" was sounded in the call and everyone went mute.

Miles fired several scorch runestones in the air where they exploded. "We gotta get their attention of course."

Soon enough, they had a crowd of signum sprinting after their vehicle. Miles, Clara, Sagittarius, and Amy unloaded runestones, lightning, arrows, and feathers, slowing them down and killing a few over time.

They eventually saw their destination: green, small hills lined with palm trees before a golden beach. The truck zoomed through an intersection and was blindsided by a heap of police cars. They all tumbled across the pavement. The truck was sent into a roll and Sagittarius hugged onto the boy, protecting him from harm. The truck came to a halt, crumpled and beaten.

"Aw man, my truck…" Paige groaned as he got up.

"Is everyone okay?" Miles asked.

"Yeah, I'm good," Clara quickly replied.

"I'm fine too," Amy said shakily, holding in tears.

Miles looked and saw a large scrape across Amy's arm.

"Here, it'll be a quick fix," Miles chuckled and placed his hand on the wound. A white light glowed from his palm and began healing the wound.

"Thanks…" Amy mumbled. "I've never been healed with arc magic before." She hid her frustration with a smile.

"Pretty cool, huh?"

"Good luck fighting a human with it though," Clara scoffed as she blasted a signum with lightning. "You might as well be taking them to a hospital."

"Haha! I'm a Celestian Knight, my dear. I fight blight, not humans," Miles smiled.

They got up and ran back to the truck where the other men were getting out. Down the street was a twenty-five-meter-tall golem of crumpled cars, streetlights, shattered glass, and pieces of buildings. Blight-infected roots and vines wrapped around the parts, binding them all together.

"Do you guys know how to kill a poltergeist signum?" Miles asked.

"Its brain and heart are located in the same spot. But it can move it around in its body. Isolate the yellow glowing core and strike it," Clara said as she looked at the titan.

"Good job teacher!" Miles yelled over to Sagittarius.

"Stop messing around! We need to get to higher ground!" Sagittarius hollered back. He pointed to the hills and they began to run towards them.

A horde of signum chased after them, barking and yipping and laughing. Miles launched runestone after runestone, creating blasts behind them. Sagittarius let fly volley after volley, impeding their advance.

"Pisces, you there?" Miles asked.

After a moment of silence, a young man's voice came through: "This is Nimbus! You guys ready or what?"

"We're on the hills before the beach in Central Marina! We need immediate support or we're going to get surrounded. Make sure no signum gets on the sand!"

"Water bombardment on the way bratha!" Nimbus cheered. "I'll be joining you gents on the frontlines!"

"Huh, what?" Miles asked.

"Be there in a minute!"

He turned behind and saw a large canoe with a sail in the distance. A tiny shadow leapt from it and started surfing on a little wake with no board.

Okay, we just need to hold them off until the others get here, Miles thought.

Amy looked at the increasing horde of signum approaching them. She gulped and she could feel her palms starting to clam up. *Damn it! Be more like Clara! Don't be scared.*

Miles and Sagittarius wasted no time and opened fire upon the horde. Sagittarius used his arclight arrows while Miles fired away a variety of runestones, freezing, shocking, and scorching the rampaging beasts.

"They're gonna be on top of us pretty soon! A haven would be nice!" Sagittarius yelled.

Miles took a knee and pressed his palm to the ground. After a couple of seconds of channeling his aura, a white dome erupted around the group. Unlike Paige and other mages who require the help of an arc isotope runestone, Miles didn't need one and could create havens with ease. However, whereas a runestone would usually power a haven overnight, it cost a substantial aura for Miles to maintain them.

Miles threw out talismans and each stuck to the backs of everyone like a magnet. "Just keep firing away with everything you've got. Paige and I will keep your aura reservoirs from running out."

The signum charged the dome and parts of their bodies vaporized by just touching it. They yelped and leapt back, angrily snarling. Meanwhile, the mages eviscerated them with explosions and projectiles. Monty stood awkwardly, hoping no one noticed he couldn't use magic.

Miles looked over at Clara who zapped another group of signum. She breathed heavily and watched them crawl and snarl at the white dome, desperately trying to get in. Amy was getting tired too, as was Sagittarius. Without saying anything, Miles went around and placed aura talismans on everyone excluding himself.

"We're almost there guys," Miles encouraged. "Everyone's doing great."

In the distance, Taro and Jiro both teleported to a rooftop overlooking the park. The palm trees and grass were on fire, caging Miles and the group in their haven. Most of the remaining signum were evolved, and all though their numbers had drastically decreased, they were evolved nonetheless. Four poltergeists and that horde stood in the way between Taro and Jiro and the others.

They both were breathing heavily. *And surely the others too once they get here,* Jiro thought. *We're all bound to be getting tired.* He clenched his fists until his knuckles were white. *Just how did this happen? Where did they come from?!*

"Where is everyone?" Jiro asked with urgency in his voice. "I know the Prestiges that were with us are coming from the East. They'll get here soon."

"We're down the block!" Kaze replied. "There's a crowd of signum and two poltergeists in front of us though.

"I made it to the shore!" Nimbus' voice exclaimed in the call. "Sis is still on the canoe."

Miles turned around and saw Nimbus running toward the dome.

"Howzit?" he exclaimed with a big smile to the group.

"Is everyone ready to kill these things?" Jiro asked.

"Hoi, Miles!" Nimbus exclaimed. "Just give me a speed talisman, a defense talisman, an attack talisman, and an aura talisman and we good."

"Aight, gimme a sec."

Miles threw out four talisman and each stuck to their positions. The speed talisman went to Nimbus' calf and glowed blue, the defense and aura talisman stuck to his back, and both glowed orange, and finally, the attack talisman stuck to his arm and glowed red.

"Are we amplifying?" Miles asked.

"Of course! Just do your best not to destroy my city," Jiro affirmed.

"Shoots," Nimbus replied with a smile before he launched himself into the horde with a gust of wind.

He took off his necklace and spun. The hook extended with a lapiz glow and turned into a khopesh. He sliced apart the surrounding signum with his khopesh while pulverizing their skulls with his punches and kicks.

A three-meter, glowing orange ring made of tribal designs appeared next to him and an oblique pool of deep azure water formed where the ground used to be.

Nimbus shifted his grip to the string attached to the hilt of his khopesh and whirled it above his head. He cast it out and it went into the pool of little, rippling waves with a splash. A group of hyena signum pounced toward Nimbus from different angles. Nimbus quickly squatted and did a coffee grinder. An updraft kicked up and hurled the attacking signum into the air and held them there.

"Guppy! I got choke dinna for ya! Eat up!" Nimbus called.

From the portal of water, a humongous, eight-meter long shark with glowing orange eyes and made of clear seawater, volcanic rock, and coral leapt from the water. It opened its jaws wide and snatched the signum out of the air, plunging them into a different portal.

Nimbus guided Guppy with his hook in its mouth. Several more portals opened up, alternating from being right or left to Nimbus. Nimbus sped through between them, kicking up signum as he went and leading Guppy with his hook. It leapt from portal to portal, snatching up all of the signum in the air along the way.

A wolf was able to get its jaws around Nimbus' arm and the second he flinched, more wolves pounced on him. He threw them off but suffered several bites. Sagittarius fired an arclight arrow at Nimbus that healed his wounds slightly.

Sagittarius, Miles, Jiro, and Taro all amplified. Their hair glowed purple, white, aquamarine, and white respectively. Jiro unclipped his Goblet from his hip and thrust it into the air. Rain clouds swirled and billowed and soon enough, a gentle rain began to drizzle in a fifty-meter radius.

"We got ten minutes to let everything loose, guys!" Jiro exclaimed. "To those that don't know: this rain refills our aura and heals us while making the signum sluggish. Use it!"

Taro and Jiro teleported down and began slashing away at the horde. Sagittarius jumped around while firing an assortment of scatter, fire, ice, and shock arrows beneath him. Miles threw out talismans to all mages, boosting all of their attributes. In the distance, signum could be seen being flung up into the air and a wind blew through the area, indicating that Kaze had amplified himself. Small tremors could be felt which were undoubtedly being caused by Sol.

Amy created a large, bushy foxtail, and spun, batting away a line of signum. She looked over to her right and saw Monty hacking away at the oncoming signum with his sword. Amy turned and faced a poltergeist, the one that had blindsided their car. Thanks to her aura being constantly replenished, she could push herself further than usual. She sprouted her wings as well as two small scythes. She launched herself into the air and spun around the beast's arm. Her feathers and scythes sliced its body but did little to harm it.

The monster groaned and threw a punch where its fist detached itself and launched toward Amy.

"Oh my gods, it has rocket fists!" Amy quickly exclaimed as she dodged out of the way of the slow punch.

The vines retracted and the parts came back together.

If I could just blast it with a beam of light! Amy cursed. She put her hands together and concentrated. She could see tiny streaks of golden light start to accumulate in her hands. *Yes! Come on!* She looked up and saw the golem start to bring its hands down. A tiny bit of fear and uncertainty started to creep in. *Come on!* The light kept building, but if she released it now, it would amount to nothing. *I can make it!*

It brought its fists down and Amy shielded herself with her wings and arms. She braced herself for an impact but felt nothing. She opened her eyes and let down her guard and saw a giant sea turtle made of clear water, coral, and rock with orange eyes. It was upright, balancing on the end of its shell which was being used as a shield. Nimbus had his rope over his shoulder and the khopesh was in the turtle's mouth.

"Whew! That was close, eh?" Nimbus chuckled. The talisman lost their glow and fell off his body one by one.

"Thanks Pisces!" she thanked with a smile.

"Nah, don't thank me. Thank Crush," Nimbus said, nodding to the turtle behind him. "I'd stand back by the way."

She followed his instruction and he heaved Crush around his body until he was swinging it around him like he was doing a hammer throw. Crush contracted his head and flippers into his shell and Nimbus let go of the rope, letting Crush fly into the poltergeist's body. It groaned and lost balance, following down on its back. A portal opened back up and Crush fell through back into the watery abyss. Meanwhile, Nimbus' khopesh flew back to his hand.

Miles noticed something amidst the chaos. The vanquished signum's skulls began to tremble and shake and the blight that had turned into black vapor began to coagulate. *That's new…*

The mounds of the poison launched themselves to a new host, enveloping them in a black sludge. They were evolving. The skulls had been crushed and molded to form exoskeleton armor on their legs, head, and back. A tail sprouted with barbs at the end of it and finally, its eyes sparked yellow. A group of evolved signum komododillos stood in front of them.

Sagittarius pulled back a fire arrow and fired it at one. It snatched it up with its mouth and let out a burp. It cocked its head back and shot out a plume of flame from its mouth.

"Shit!" Sagittarius exclaimed.

More and more evolved komododillo signum emerged from the carnage and began spewing flames everywhere, setting the grass and the surrounding buildings on fire.

"What's happening?" Sol asked over the call. "We can see smoke from where you guys are."

"Evolved signum are being created from the dying blight," Miles informed.

"What? I thought blight self-destructs after its host dies!" Jiro exclaimed.

"I thought so too. But it looks like it's pooling up all of the aurae from the corpses and transferring it to a new host before it dies."

"Has that ever happened before?"

Miles gave a solemn sigh: "No…"

The golem got back up, but Nimbus was able to rip the back end of a sliced car away from its body. His muscles were toned, and yellow lightning was flickering across his arms.

"Nimbus!" Clara shouted. "Toss that car over here!"

"I don't get ya, but okay!" The lightning vanished from his arms and reappeared around his legs as he drop-kicked it over to Clara.

Clara bent her fingers like a claw and put her wrists together. She caught the car with an electric current. She groaned, pouring all of the aura she had into the attack. "Everybody, duck!"

A beam of light slashed through the sky as she fired her Railgun Blast. It eviscerated the poltergeist and went off into the atmosphere, breaking apart the clouds and letting in a beam of sunlight before it dissipated. Clara took a knee and breathed heavily. Even with the aura regeneration from the rain, she was still exhausted.

In her moment of weakness, a komododillo slapped her with its barbed tail and sent her flying. Amy rushed to her friend's side and caught her before she could hit the ground. Their talismans fell off their bodies.

"Clara, are you okay?" Amy asked.

Instead of responding, Clara threw Amy out of the way and took a tail whip to the gut. She caught it and surged electricity through it, frying its brain and heart. She dropped to a knee once again and blood seeped from her stomach for a short amount of time before the rain trickled into her wound and mended it closed.

"I'm fine," she muttered.

Amy scowled and turned around to hear a hiss. She quickly spread out her wings and blocked a spew of fire from an evolved signum. After the flames petered out, she responded with a flurry of feathers, but the signum rolled into a ball and came charging at her, deflecting them.

She formed giant claws of shadow and caught it. She saw a poltergeist golem coming toward them and hurled the komododillo at it. It caught its brethren and let it perch on its shoulder. Amy grew frustrated and dashed toward it.

It doesn't help that the clouds are making it so there's no shadows, Amy cursed. *I have to use a lot more aura than usual to keep my shadows as sharp and as large as they are!*

She quickly made her way to its legs and let her shadow wrap around its legs over and over. She pulled as hard as she could, trying to topple it over, but even with her shadows taught, it kept moving forward, dragging Amy along.

Are. You. Kidding. Me?! Amy cursed. She could feel her feet slipping and she created talons to anchor herself.

The komododillo let out a hiss and leapt from its perch, whipping its tail around. Amy let go of the poltergeist and put up her arms to shield herself. Thwack! The barbed tail sunk into her flesh and sent her flying across the pavement.

Amy backed up but was blindsided by a fireball. She was blown away and saw another komododillo approaching. Amy turned her shadow into a kusarigama as one lunged at her. She flung her chain and caught the creature, spinning around and slamming it into the wall of the building behind her.

Another appeared from the roof of the building and spewed hot flames. Amy shielded herself with her wings. The other two joined in and created a torrent of flame around her that ate away her feathers. She leapt into the air, but a poltergeist fist slammed into her and sent her crashing back down.

Clara turned to the sound of Amy's scream.

The three komododillos rolled over to Amy and continued their assault. Two more joined them and now a poltergeist was walking over to her. She took a step in Amy's direction, compelled to help her, but Henry's words echoed through her head. She froze.

Monty slashed through another signum. His breathing was heavy and Paige's talismans were all that were keeping him from being useless. *The rain doesn't heal fatigue, and it's not healing my blight,* Monty thought. *This sucks!* He turned around to face a pouncing signum, but Paige shot it out of the air. Monty plunged his blade into its head when he heard Amy's scream. He looked over and saw her being overwhelmed by signum. She was so far away...

Anyone?! Monty thought.

Everyone else was busy with their own waves of oncoming signum except for one: Clara. Hope filled Monty's heart until... Clara turned around. His heart was filled with confusion and frustration that made it sink to his stomach. He watched Clara run away toward a group of signum with his jaw dropped. He clicked his tongue.

"Paige!" he roared.

"I know!" Paige yelled. His hand quivered a little, knowing there was no choice. *Damn it!*

Paige flicked a speed talisman at Monty's legs and a blue glow wrapped around them before he took off. Monty dashed between Amy and the fires and channeled his aura into the oncoming flames. His paper-thin aura shield broke and he began to burn. He took control of the flames and pushed them away. Monty redirected them, making a spinning ring of fire. With a grunt and a pulse of aura, Monty made the ring expand and sliced the surrounding signum in half. An orange glow highlighted their wounds and as the top half of their bodies slid to the ground, embers fluttered off as they disintegrated.

The sensation of rusted daggers digging into his bones shot from his shoulder and Monty collapsed to the ground at Amy's feet. He could feel the blight crawling and throbbing in his flesh.

"Monty?!" Amy cried.

She hovered over her brother as a poltergeist loomed behind them. Paige chucked a scorch runestone that blasted a chunk off its arm. It groaned and looked over at him. Paige filled a handful of arctic talismans with his aura and sent them at its limbs. They slapped on like magnets and ice crawled over it, slowing it down.

A spread of red streaks soared overhead and peppered the poltergeist. The fire arrows set the vines holding the cars together ablaze and the orange orb had no place to go. Sagittarius drew back an arclight arrow and nailed his target.

Clara let out a sigh of relief. *Thank goodness she's safe,* she thought. *I have to do something! Otherwise, I'm nothing but a bystander.*

Clara ran over and surged an electric current into a poltergeist's body, taking control of it. She ripped it apart, and between the metal scrap was a glowing orb that zipped back and forth along the exposed vines.

Jiro opened two portals on the vines and closed them, slicing them until there was one vine left for the glowing orb to travel on. Taro teleported next to it and slashed it in half with his katana. The metal pieces fell to the ground and the vine went limp. Clara dropped to her knees breathing hard.

"Well done, Clara," Jiro said.

Clara waved her hand and shook her head, still catching her breath.

"Cloud… Cloud, are you there?" Jiro asked into his earbuds.

"Yeah, I'm still on the canoe!" she replied.

"Let loose a wave…" Jiro sighed.

That got everyone's attention.

"Uh… You sure?" Cloud asked nervously.

"Yeah, a big one. One that will wash all the signum out to sea and put out the fires. Kaze and Sol, help her out, everyone else too. Get as many signum into the water as possible. The rain is going to run out soon. I don't have enough aura to summon it again for a few minutes."

"Taro, find me on the beach and teleport me to Sol and Kaze. I'll give them the rest of my aura," Miles said.

"Got it!"

"Everybody else? Find high ground."

Taro teleported to Miles and teleported back to the rooftop and then over to Kaze and Sol. Miles poured his aura evenly between two talisman and placed them on their backs. "Go hard."

Taro began finding the others and teleporting them to safety while Kaze and Sol got into position.

Kaze hop-stepped forward and, with a heave, clapped his hands together. The air was pulled back and then rushed forward, pulling with it signum, sand, cars, and palm trees. Sol gripped the ground with his hand and shook it like a rug, causing a huge rolling earthquake in front of him, throwing signum into the air to be caught by Kaze's winds. They both fell over, deamplifying, completely and utterly exhausted from aura fatigue. The rain stopped.

"Your job isn't done yet Sol," Kaze panted.

"I'm aware," Sol replied. "I'm just taking a break while I can."

They all watched from a rooftop as the ocean's edge receded. A huge wave rose, taking the floating signum up with it. Nimbus whistled, impressed. The wave crested and with a *BOOM* the water hit the ground running.

Sol jumped down and leaned forward when he landed. The earth popped up behind him. He leaned back and the earth popped up in front. With a twist, he freed himself a large chunk of rock to surf on. He ushered the earth on the street upward and surfed along it, creating a wall of rock with a curved top. With the healing rain gone, Sol's body felt the full brunt of Amplification. His muscles ached and burned, and sweat dripped from his forehead. He finally couldn't take it anymore and fell, rolling across the ground with enough aura to maintain a shield to protect his body from the fall. Taro teleported over to him and teleported quickly back.

The water slammed against the rock walls and was corralled back toward the ocean. The water receded back out to sea, bringing all of the signum with it. Their cries could be heard across the water, being drowned and killed by water and sea creatures that Cloud had called to her aid. Everyone let out a breath of relief.

"I'll take the wall down later," Sol said between breaths.

"Don't worry about it," Jiro chuckled. "I'll commission you for helping with repairs." He turned toward everyone else. "Thank you all so much for your help! I really couldn't have done this without you guys. Seriously, Pisces and Sagittarius and Miles did all of the work."

"Ah don't mention it," Miles scoffed. "You can thank me by buying me some booze later haha!"

"Let's pau hana at a bar!" Nimbus cheered.

Jiro unmuted himself. "Cloud, great job!"

"No problem," she replied. "I'm spent though."

"Aquarius!" a policeman's voice came over the call.

"What's up?" Jiro asked.

"It's Bandit's Doldrum! The Wings are attacking it! We need immediate backup!"

"What?!" Jiro exclaimed. He clicked his tongue. "Taro we need–"

Cloud's voice came in. "Uh, guys... There's something weird happening with the blight. Look toward the ocean!"

They couldn't see anything from the shore at first. They couldn't see the blight sludge start to accumulate more and more into a surviving signum. The bones and flesh trembled and then sunk underwater. There was a moment of calm until the water's surface bubbled and frothed. What happened next, no one was ready for.

A huge hydra emerged from the water. Its seven heads let out an ear-piercing hiss. White bone armor was platted along its necks and head. Blight dripped from its gaping jaws and their yellow eyes looked upon Pisces' canoe with a hunger.

"Yo Sis, get outta there!" Nimbus shouted.

The hydra unleashed scalding water from its mouths at the canoe. The spray was stopped halfway, being pushed back by Cloud no doubt.

"Just what is that thing?" Taro wondered. He pulled out *Cat's Cradle* and put the hydra in its focus. "My *Cat's Cradle* isn't coming up with anything..."

"We need to get over there!" Nimbus shouted.

Jiro gritted his teeth. "Taro, you and me have somewhere else to be."

"What're you talking about?"

"It's Penumbra Wings. They're attacking Bandit's Doldrum."

"But that's all the way in Ayo!"

"I know."

Taro sighed. "I only have enough to take me and you there with the help of a talisman. Can't risk my aura running out and we teleport halfway to our destination and I pass out."

"That's fine, but–" Jiro looked over at the others and the hydra.

"Jiro, you got two Zodiacs and two members from Team Majestic here," Miles chuckled. "Go. We'll be fine."

Jiro nodded and gulped. "Right. Taro, let's go."

Miles placed an aura talisman on the brothers' shoulders before Taro teleported them away in a white sparkle.

"So," Miles sighed. "Nimbus, Sagi, Kaze, and I will go join up with Cloud. You guys look exhausted, take a rest."

"Roger," Sol said with a raised hand before letting it slap down.

"We can all hop on Crush's back," Nimbus suggested.

They went with that plan and the four students watched from the rooftop as the others went over to the canoe in the distance.

"Do you guys know what's going on?" Cloud asked. She held out a hand and Kaze took it as he got up.

"It seems blight is evolving," Miles said. "I've never seen this before in my life. When the non-evolved signum were dying in mass, the blight massed together to surviving signum and evolved them in what I can only guess is a last-ditch effort. And I guess when evolved signum die in mass… You get that thing."

"Same rules apply I suppose," Sagittarius sighed. "A combined attack should do the trick."

"Right," Miles said. "Kaze and I can focus on killing the brains. Sagittarius and Cloud can kill the heart or hearts underwater. If this thing has seven heads, let's play it safe and assume it has seven brains and seven hearts. Nimbus will protect the Canoe. Sound good?"

"Yeah, except for one thing," Nimbus said.

He took a deep breath. The air vibrated around him. His hair started to wave a little in the wind as if he were amplifying. Orange lightning sparked around his body. Orange, yellow, and dark blue aura glowed around him. The colors fought over each other until orange started overtaking the others. Orange embers jumped about his skin and his muscles bulked up.

"We'll just go straight to Twilight!" he muttered under his breath. He let out a shout and a rush of wind exploded from him, his aura finally reaching equilibrium. "Just give me a couple of seconds. Get 'dem attacks ready."

He vanished from view and a large splash of water pushed the canoe back a bit. Nimbus, within ten seconds, swam underneath the hydra and launched above it after kicking it high into the air. The hydra's lower half was built like a plesiosaur and it flapped its flippers in the air, trying desperately to get back to the water. The other mages immediately amplified.

"Alright! Let's kill it!" Sagittarius shouted as he drew back his purple arrow. "Go forth and devour!" He let loose his dragon that shredded through the beast's body. He took a knee and deamplified, his right arm sizzling.

The hydra shot out geysers of boiling water which Cloud redirected back at its body along with tentacles of water from the ocean that drilled into its hide and through its body. Kaze kicked crescents of wind that decapitated head after head. The regeneration was too fast to keep up with.

"Send me above it," Miles said to Kaze.

As if untying a bow, Kaze waved his hands and an updraft kicked up underneath Miles, sending him skyward.

Miles landed on the beast and grabbed onto its neck, wrapping his arms and locking his legs around it. He then poured all of his aura into the beast. His arc magic instantly started vaporizing its scales. White cracks opened up along the neck until it all burst. Miles put the rest of his aura into three talismans that would be usually used to heal humans. However, it had the reverse effect against blight. He threw them and they latched on to the back of the heads where they glowed and then in a blinding blast of light, vaporized them.

Miles' Amplification ran out, his body worn out for the day and his aura spent. Cloud caught him in a pillar of water that guided him back to the canoe, all the while healing him.

"Thanks. It's weird being the one healed haha," Miles chuckled.

"Don't sweat it," Cloud chuckled before it was her turn to deamplify.

Nimbus opened a large portal of water in the sky beneath him as he descended. "Come on out, JayJay!"

A humongous whale made of coral, water, and rock came out from the portal, about twice the size of the hydra. The portal closed behind it and JayJay let out a cheer before belly-flopping on top of the hydra, landing on it with a force to crush it flat like a pancake. The splash was as if a bomb went off underwater and sent out a huge wake.

The aura around Nimbus dissipated and Cloud caught him with a tentacle of water and guided him back to the canoe. His muscles were all sore and he breathed heavily. "Seriously though… I need a drink."

9: Debts and Remorse

The Fleck Forest was quiet that morning, the only noises being the echoes of the wind and the crackling of the campfire in front of Henry. A cool gust of wind blew past, carrying with it bits of dust, dried weeds, and grass. To Henry's left, in the not-so-far distance was Ayo, the city's skyline silhouetted against the rising sun. To Henry's right was the hill that Bandit's Doldrum sat upon. It was the prison that held criminals from Puakai's western cities: Atlas, Cysko, Lull, and of course, Ayo.

Behind Henry, the yellow hills with patches of green from the semi-arid climate stretched into the distance until it reached the sands of the Fleck Desert.

He sat atop a boulder, hugging his knees while wrapped in a wool flannel. The other Wings were gathered around the campfire beneath him. He thought about his call with the First the night before…

****

Henry sat in his apartment when the First called him.

"Henry," he spoke over the phone.

"Yes, boss," Henry replied.

"You are aware that your father is being moved to Coal Keep tomorrow, yes?"

"Yes, I am aware," Henry sighed. "I assume we are to break him out before that happens?"

"You are correct. Even with our connections, it will be impossible to save him once he's put in that dungeon in the depths of Central. Call the others, you'll be breaking him out tomorrow morning."

"Will you or the Second be joining us?"

The First scoffed, "Me? Of course not. The Second is still in Hinohana, so he won't be joining you. He's not needed though."

"Of course not," Henry chuckled. "I'm assuming I'm to lead this mission? Given the circumstances I mean."

"Yes, you'll take the lead for this one."

"Good to hear."

"Oh, and Henry…"

"Yes?"

"After your father is released, he will also be released from his debt. Of course, that debt will be transferred to you."

What? Henry thought, not entirely processing what was just said.

"His replacement will be joining you for this mission. Her name is Dakota Finch, I think you'll find her quite amusing."

"What? Wait, wait, wait! This is so sudden! Why is he being released?"

"Because while your father has helped the Mafia grow globally, he is obsolete in terms of fighting. Any remaining debt will be transferred to you. It doesn't just go away of course."

Henry was speechless. His mouth was agape, unsure of the emotion to convey. *Why, why, why, why?*

"Surely, he can fulfill it by just helping with Preston Company operations?"

"What are you on about, Henry? Of course, he can't return there, he's already been compromised! Why else do you think we had him fake selling off the company to a third party?"

"I-"

"We can't run from our debts Henry, but we can run out of time. And your father is past his sell-by date. We need new, younger talent. The Fourth and the Seventh should make that obvious!"

"O-of course, forgive my foolishness. I was just surprised," Henry chuckled.

"I taught you better than that, Henry. The only way we'll all be free of our debts is by working together. Call me once the job is finished." The First hung up.

Henry leaned back in his seat. He took a deep breath and sat in silence for a moment. His mind began to race.

This isn't fair! This isn't fair! Why? Why? WHY?! I was so close! Two years left and I would have gotten us out!

Envy was lounging on the couch across the room.

"I told you so," he said mockingly. "You still think your family bond is worth it?"

"Shut up!" Henry snapped.

He took a deep breath and calmed down. *It's not the old man's fault. It's Monterey's fault!*

It's not fair.

****

"Um, e-excuse me," a girl's voice peeped.

Henry turned to the source of the noise. She was about his age and had black hair that curled inwards and stopped around her chin. She had a pink hair clip on the left side of her head and covering her eyes were some large, white shutter glasses. She had on a Neapolitan-striped turtleneck sweater with black jeans and sneakers. Slung over her right shoulder was a rifle, which was nearly as tall as her. Her belt was a bandolier, and a pistol was in a holster at her hip.

"My name's Dakota Finch, it's nice t-to meet you. Sorry, I'm late, I got lost…"

He scowled. *Seriously? This is the person they're replacing father with?!*

"So you're the newbie, huh?" Henry asked. "What's up with the glasses? Paired with that sweater you look like a bookworm going to a rave!" Henry laughed.

Dakota chuckled nervously.

"Don't mind him, rookie," the Seventh said. "He's just having girl problems," she teased in a pouty voice. She was sharpening one of her knives next to the fire.

"Says you, Riley! I've talked to your boyfriend more in the past week than you have in the last seven years."

"First, he's not my boyfriend. Second, screw you," Riley, the Seventh, said before sticking her tongue out. "I'm *glad* there's another girl in the Wings."

"I'm surprised none of our numbers changed," the Fourth yawned. "Although, it would be a bother to remember the new numbers, so I guess I'm fine with it."

"That must mean the newbie's debt is pretty small, ey?" the Sixth guessed.

Henry dropped down from his perch. "That or she's just weak." He clapped the dust off his hands. "Just what *is* your debt?"

"Um…" she stammered.

"She and her brother are a part of Stella Lumine. He was caught by Chasm officers and was imprisoned. The First paid off his time and got him out," the Fifth said.

Everyone froze and Dakota was looking at him with her mouth agape. "H-how did you..?"

"Mark, if you would," Riley said.

"Yeah, I got it this time," Mark, the Sixth, said. His arm turned metallic and he extended it so that his fist was over his head. His fist turned into an anvil and he let gravity do the rest of the work.

"Ow!" the Fifth said.

"Don't mind Akio," the Fourth said. "He's a prick."

"Seriously, learn to read the room dude," Riley said.

"What? I thought you all wanted to know. We all know each other's debts anyway," Akio said as he rubbed his head.

"Because you did the same thing to everybody!" they all retorted in unison.

"So you're a Wanari?" Henry asked. "What are you, part monkey or something."

"I, uh…"

"I guess having a demon spawn on the team fits our description," Henry sighed.

"I'm not!"

"Oh?"

"We *aren't* demons!" she snapped.

"The Book of Celestia and our history would say otherwise," Henry chuckled.

"That Book is nothing but a bunch of lies!"

Henry got up into her face. "Got some bite to that bark little doggy?"

"I'm not a dog, I'm part owl butthead!" she cried and headbutted him.

Henry held his head and stumbled back. "Why you…" he groaned.

"Nice!" Riley applauded. "Give the racist a run for his money haha!"

"Awww," Akio said. "Poor little choir boy! It's sad you feel the need to look down on others to validate yourself."

"Akio, you read my mind!" Riley cackled.

"Actually, that time I wasn't," Akio said.

"Dude, I was joking. Also, how often are you in there? It's gross."

"Can we just start the mission already?" the Fourth groaned. "I'm getting tired. Who's the leader?"

"The First gave me the baton for this mission, so you all can suck it," Henry sneered.

The group all groaned in unison. Dakota jumped and looked around nervously. Riley motioned her to sit next to her and she took her up on the offer.

"What does that mean?" Dakota whispered to Riley.

"It means he's the leader until he passes the baton to someone else," Riley explained.

"As you know, there's a detective agency that's been annoying us lately called Runeseekers. Envy is currently unleashing a horde of my signum in Cysko to keep them occupied. That means I need more cannon fodder. So we're not just releasing my dad, but also *all* of the other prisoners," Henry said.

"That sounds like such a pain," the Fourth sighed. "Let's just save Gramps and get some drinks to send him off with—and to welcome our new member of course."

"Bandit Doldrum has six watchtowers," Henry continued. "Rookie…"

Dakota glared at him.

"You said you're part-owl, right? Given that and the fact you have a giant rifle, I assume you have good eyesight?"

Dakota was taken aback by his sudden professionalism, but it obviously didn't excuse him. "Yes, I have the eyesight of an owl."

"Good. You'll be taking out the guards in the towers as well as any guards roaming around the perimeter fence. Mark, you're in charge of cleaning up the bodies along the perimeter so no alarms are sound.

"Romeo, you'll lay out a fog which Riley can use to get into the prison with. Riley, once inside, go to the roof of the southwest building. You'll find two vents–use the one closest to the ocean to find the security room. Neutralize all of the cameras and play the recording I sent to you over the loudspeaker. After, find Pops.

"Romeo, Akio, and Mark after all the bodies are gathered up, you guys need to be prepared to rotate for any reinforcements that come. They're surely going to have some Archangels guarding this prison somewhere. Rookie, we're counting on you to keep us updated," Henry explained.

"Y-yes! You can count on me!" she stammered.

"Huh? Why did I get stuck with the hard job?" Riley pouted.

"C'mon Cloak, you're a pro at this type of stuff," Mark jested.

"Shut it, buddy."

"This is great and all, but Henry what will you be doing?" Romeo, the Fourth, asked.

"Oh, me? I can't show my face. As far as the media's concerned, I'm a poor boy who found out his dad is associated with the Mafia. If they figure out I'm a part of the Mafia, the Shipping Company is done for. So, I will be with Rookie up here as a lookout," Henry smiled.

Romeo clicked his tongue. "Slacker. Next time I have the baton I'll just slack off too."

"Okay! Go forth! Claim victory or whatever," Henry said, shooing them away.

A weak, collective cheer was given out except for Dakota who actually cheered, but shriveled up and was embarrassed after realizing she was the only one who did it seriously.

As she frantically looked among her new team, she and Romeo made eye contact. Romeo smiled softly and saluted by hovering two fingers over his temple and flipping them to face the sky as he swiped across the side of his head.

The Stella Lumine salute? Dakota thought.

They all went to their positions and Henry took a seat next to Dakota, who was laying on the ground. She took off her glasses, revealing large, intense eyes with bright orange irises. She looked down her iron sights and loaded a bullet into the chamber.

"So what's with the ancient technology?" Henry asked. "I haven't seen a bullet be used in my entire life."

"My magic lets me mark objects that I touch with a north or south rune. Then from that point, they act like strong magnets. So when I load a bullet in the chamber, I mark it. I can't really touch a scorch bolt."

"Ah, interesting, I see… Then why not have one of those uh…" Henry snapped his fingers a couple of times as he tried to remember. "Oh! Those magazine thingies?"

"Because I can only mark two objects at a time. Anymore takes too much aura."

"Oh, that's lame."

"But if something with my mark touches something else, that mark can be transferred to the new object."

"Interesting…"

Meanwhile, Mark and Romeo were hidden among the trees. Between them and the walls of the prison was a stretch of land with no cover.

"How intense are you going to make your poison this time?" Mark asked.

"If you're in it long enough you'll get dizzy and nauseous. Nothing lethal."

"Ah well," Mark sighed as he put on a gas mask. "Probably not good for my anemia either way."

"Probably not."

Romeo turned his palms to face in front of him and purple fumes shot out as if his hands were fog machines. Within a couple of minutes, a dense fog lingered over the open area.

"Okay, we're in position," Mark said over the earpiece.

"Ah, good! We can start then. Rookie, if you would?" Henry asked.

Dakota took a deep breath and focused down her sight at a guard in the guard tower. She slowly exhaled as she pulled the trigger. The rifle jerked back and let out a thunderous '*BOOM*.' Immediately, she emptied the chamber and put in a new bullet as the remaining guard scrambled for his Omnicard. She pulled the trigger again and down went the other guard.

"Both targets in southeast tower are down," Dakota said.

"It's showtime," Riley said with a smile.

She put on her mask and fixed her hat. She ran into the fog and merged with it. She felt her body get lighter and her stomach turned a little as it usually did, like being on a rollercoaster. She zoomed across the ground like a specter and easily went through the chain-linked fence.

A guard was roaming on the ground with a flashlight and a rifle. He stopped to inspect the fog, squinting at it. "What the hell?"

Riley suddenly appeared in front of him and cut open his throat with the flash of a dagger. Another guard was on their way and Riley tossed her dagger in the air and hurled it at them, lodging it in their skull.

While this was happening, two more sniper shots had been fired, and another watchtower had two more dead guards.

"Two more down. Sixth, you better hurry up," Riley said.

"On it."

Mark went into the fog and his arms turned metallic. They turned into linked chains and claws like you might see in a skill crane and went over the fence. He yanked back and carried the bodies with him to the cover of the forest where he laid them down side by side with their feet lined up.

As Riley approached the side of the southwest building, she pulled a smoke runestone from her jacket and primed it with her aura before tossing it up on the roof. A trail of smoke billowed from it as it ascended through the air, and like a koi going up a waterfall, she dove into it, merging with it, and swam up to the rooftop.

Riley amplified, her hair sparking pink. She held her breath and her body turned into a smoke cloud. She swam through the vents and into a hallway. She hovered close to the ground and underneath the door to the security room where six men were manning computers. She let out a gasp and put her hands on her knees, deamplifiying.

"Whew! New record!" she cheered.

The six men turned and she quickly drew her pistol and fired six scorch bolts from the hip, killing them all. She put the barrel near her mouth and blew at the neon blue trail of light, even though it didn't do anything to it. She gave her pistol a flip and holstered it.

"Okay, I'm in the security room."

"And all security guards in the towers and along the perimeter are dead," Dakota added.

"Good," Henry said. "Since I can barely see what's going on down there… Sixth! Congratulations, I'm passing the baton to you!"

"Eh? Why not me?" Romeo asked.

"Because you said you'd slack off next time you got the baton and I totally believe you."

"Tsk."

"See?"

Riley spun a chair and the corpse flopped to the ground. She cracked her fingers and scanned the screen. After a few clicks, she said: "Okay, cameras are off and I am playing the recording."

"As soon as you hit play, you have about ten minutes to find Pops before Chasm arrives with Instigators and Archangels," Henry guesstimated.

"And… here… we… go," Riley said and hit play on her Omnicard. She put her speaker right next to the intercom microphone.

"Hello, prisoners of Bandit's Doldrum!" Henry's voice said. "This is your pilot speaking, thank you for joining us on this express trip to literally anywhere but here! We are expecting foggy skies you can use as cover to escape to the southwest side of the prison! I'm letting you all free! The price for the ticket? Just say, with sincerity: 'Thank you, Mr. Third! I really owe you one. You are dashing and handsome!' Say that, and you're free to go!"

Riley rolled her eyes, "You make me cringe, you know that?"

"Bite me," Henry retorted.

"Thank you, Mr. Third! I really owe you one. You are dashing and handsome!" a couple of prisoners said. Riley opened their doors first.

Soon enough everyone was onboard and saying it. Riley opened them as fast as she could until she got over it and opened them all at once.

"You getting your cards?" Riley asked as she left the room. Alarms were blaring and there was fighting and wrestling everywhere.

"Yes! Dozens and dozens of them!" Henry said. He had his hands in a duffel bag as the cards kept appearing in his palm.

"It'll be faster if I go looking for Gramps too, no?" Akio asked.

"Sure, I'll cut you an opening," Mark said.

Akio had his half-mask pulled over his mouth and nose when he reached Mark and Romeo. Mark turned his arm into an enormous sword and cut the fence in front of him, making a rectangle. Mark clicked his tongue and went to try again, but Akio stopped him.

"I know you want to make a perfect square, but we really don't have the time." Akio sprinted ahead and into the prison.

After he left, Mark cut out a larger portion of the fence, making a perfect square. He gave a satisfied nod before heading to the front of the prison.

"Fourth, you're with me."

"Fine…"

"Rookie, you cover our backs. And remember to use our Wing numbers instead of our names in front of our enemies."

"I can do that literally!" Dakota said.

Another sniper shot rang out and Mark felt like he was kicked in the back. Another bang and Romeo nearly fell forward onto his face from the force of impact. They both began to feel aura surging through their body.

"I just shot capsules that contained aura talismans to you guys. Use them well."

"Hmph, not bad," Mark chuckled.

"Maybe this was worth staying up late for," Romeo smiled.

Meanwhile, inside the prison, Akio sped through the hallways, reading the minds of each prisoner or guard as he passed. He concentrated his aura into his legs, giving him bursts of speed as he bobbed and weaved between the swinging fists, batons, and shock bolts.

"He's not on the east or south side," Akio reported. "Seventh, how's the west?"

"I can't find him," she said, "Hey Third, didn't you send the weirdo of yours to get the blueprint?"

"He was only able to find the security room."

"Fantastic. Well Fifth, I guess I'll meet you in the north."

"Guys! I spotted an Instigator and three Archangels coming around from the front of the prison," Dakota said.

"Three Archangels?" Romeo said. "That's going to be troublesome..."

"Why didn't they bring the same number of everything?" Mark grumbled.

"You sure got your priorities straight," Romeo chuckled. "One slip-up and we're dead you know?"

"And how many times have we slipped up?"

They got up and stretched.

Romeo chuckled, "I guess us being alive answers that question. I'll put up a wall, you flank around," Romeo said.

"On it."

Romeo strained his hands and venom with the viscosity of lava oozed from his hands. He threw his arms up and the purple goo erupted into a giant wall. After a moment of waiting, the nine-meter tall Archangels leapt through the wall, the poison melting parts of their skeleton.

The three Archangel mechs were of the Paladin subclass, which meant they prioritized defense and durability over mobility. They had white armored plates around their bodies with a cylindrical torso that could rotate three-hundred and sixty degrees. Their limbs were bulky and their backs had extra armoring. The head was a dome with green glowing eyes like a spider.

In their hands, they carried a cannon with a bayonet so large and sharp it could cut a car clean in half. The cannons themselves acted like a Gatling gun. Unlike the rifles and pistols a normal person could have with only semi-automatic firing, these cannons were capable of automatic fire. They were able to achieve this by having each barrel have a primer, and as they passed the runestone the size of a highway divider in the back of the cannon, they fired a shot. By the time they looped back around, the primer would be ready to ignite again.

"Freeze!" the center Paladin commanded. All three pointed their cannons at Romeo, their fingers slightly pulling down on the trigger, causing the barrels to rotate but not fire.

Romeo gave a wicked smile. "Melt." He pushed his hands to the ground and let loose a thick cloud of poison.

The Paladins opened fire, eviscerating the area where he once stood with arcane bolts.

"Switch to thermal!" the center Paladin exclaimed.

Romeo clicked his tongue and amplified, his hair turned into a marble green and purple and his irises turned into a swirl of the same colors. Romeo launched at the left Paladin's feet and used its legs for cover. The mech shot at the ground below and its teammates didn't think twice about shooting at Romeo near its feet. Romeo danced around, continually pouring aura into his legs to run around the Paladin's legs for cover. All the while, he spewed walls of poison. Their melting armor sizzled like steak on a skillet. His muscles ached from being amplified for so long that they contracted and convulsed, begging for a break.

"Sixth! Are you done yet?" Romeo asked into his earpiece. "I'm running out of steam!"

"Yeah! I just got control of the Instigator! Feel free to drop down the wall!"

Romeo dropped the maze of poison. With one last blast of aura to his legs and feet, he rushed forward, sending out goo from his feet and using it as a slip n' slide underneath the three Paladins and into the cover of the forest. Arcane bolts followed him across and as he dove into the bushes, one hit his leg and one hit his back, shattering his aura shield and leaving a hole in the side of his torso. He scrambled behind a tree trunk before deamplifying. His body went limp for a second and he groaned.

"I've been hit and my aura shield is down…" Romeo got out between breaths.

"He's in the trees!"

Their cannons whined as they prepared to open fire, but they were interrupted by the sound of a large blast. One of the Paladins was blindsided by a ginormous arcane bolt. Thanks to Romeo's poison weakening their armor, the bolt went straight through, killing the pilot in the cockpit.

Mark fired another cannon shot from the Instigator, but the other pilot was ready and guarded with his left arm. The forearm split apart slightly and emitted a translucent shield that vaporized the arcane bolt as it hit. It was an anti-isotope shield.

The pilots fired back, their bolts easily finding their slow-moving target. One arm was used to aim and fire while the other held up its anti-isotope shield. The Instigator Mark was piloting blew up. He emerged from the purple fires, completely coated in metal. His clothes were torn and tattered, revealing his metallic skin. His jaw had grown in size and his teeth sharpened like a bear trap. His eyes were completely black and his fingers had turned to sharp claws.

Mark let out a roar, revealing his mouth full of razors and spinning blades. He sprinted forward, the arcane bolts from the Paladin's gunfire doing nothing more than making him flinch.

"Rookie! Hit me with an aura talisman as soon as you see me!" Romeo shouted.

"G-got it!"

The speed of Mark's advance was frightening, and the Paladins tried to move backward, but they couldn't move! Their feet were stuck to the ground from the ooze Romeo and let out earlier, which after hardening a little, had the viscosity and properties of a sticky and toxic gum.

"What the–?!" one of the pilots exclaimed.

Romeo waited until Mark was close and came out from his cover, he hobbled over to the open field again and felt a slap to his back and immediately his aura shield regenerated, stopping the bleeding from his wound. A wicked smile crawled across his face and he amplified. He focused all of his aura into his right hand as a green poison orb formed with a purple halo glowing inside of it.

He poured aura into his legs and launched himself above the closest Paladin.

Venom Bomb! Romeo exclaimed in his head and thrust his hand into the Paladin.

The poison around his hand melted through the armor, turning it into melted butter. He didn't even feel it when he reached the pilot inside, he could only tell he hit his mark when he heard the split-second scream from him before his chest disintegrated. Romeo clenched a fist and the slime unstuck from his hand. Romeo deamplified and pushed off the falling mech. The bomb detonated, letting loose a spray of slime within the mech, melting it from the inside.

Romeo didn't stick the landing and stumbled and fell forward onto the grassy plain. He looked over his shoulder and watched Mark launch himself at the other Paladin.

He began to literally eat through and tear apart its armor. The pilot tried to grab him off, but once Mark was grabbed, he spun, forming blades along his body, and tore apart the mech's hand before continuing his meal. The pilot screamed and spammed the eject button until the dome head launched itself from the body and rocketed away into the distance.

Mark hopped off the empty Paladin and reverted his skin to normal, revealing his silver hair and eyes for a second before he deamplified. His shirt was completely gone, revealing multiple bruises from the arcane bolts hitting him. He ran over and heaved Romeo over his shoulder and jogged over to the forest, out of range of Romeo's gas.

Both Wings were breathing hard and took a moment to catch their breath. Mark noticed one pant leg was now shorter than the other from being on fire, and he cut them so they were both equal in length. Romeo rolled his eyes.

"Status?" Mark asked through the earpiece. "We need to go before reinforcements show up."

Riley reached the north block of the prison, shooting and slashing any officer or prisoner that got in her way. She reached an intersection at the same time Akio did and they nodded at each other. They turned the corner and saw that all of the prisoners who used magic had all been defeated. They had all been kept in the same place and were now all unconscious on the floor, including the Eighth.

Standing over them were a tired Taro and Jiro, who had just taken care of them. They were bruised and had cuts along their clothing from their fight.

"Ah, Taro! What brings you here?" Riley asked.

"You know this guy?" Akio asked.

"Old friend of mine. Also, thanks for asking and not just doing your regular thing. That's brownie points from me."

"Sorry, Riley," Taro said between breaths. "The Eighth is not leaving."

"I'm assuming these two are Wings?" Jiro asked.

"Yep."

Taro silently clicked his tongue. *We're already tired from fighting the prisoners. Now we gotta deal with two Wings?*

Akio smiled underneath his mask after reading the thought.

"The girl can merge with smoke and is immune to physical attacks. I don't know what the guy does. Be careful." Taro amplified, his hair and eyes shining white.

Jiro did the same, his hair and eyes bursting aquamarine. "Ooo, so serious," Riley giggled. She took a deep breath and amplified, her hair and eyes turning pink. "But I can do that too now."

Akio followed suit, his hair and eyes glowing mint green. "Let's finish this quickly." His Amplification allowed him to read more than one mind at a time.

Taro teleported his swords *Twin Creeks* to his hands, but Akio read his mind and fired two scorch bolts at Taro's hands, causing him to drop his weapons.

"Seventh, the young one is opening a portal beneath your feet!" Akio exclaimed.

"Copy that!" Riley said and jumped to the wall, avoiding the attack.

"So I guess he can either see the future or read our minds!" Jiro shouted.

Riley threw a handful of knives at Jiro who used a pair of portals to redirect them back at her. She immediately took out two smoke grenades and threw them at the ground in front of her, filling the hallway with smoke.

A flash of white came out of the corner of his eye and he barely dodged Akio's sword. He summoned *Twin Creeks* to his hands again, successful this time. He blocked and parried, but refused to go on the offensive.

If he can really read my mind or tell the future, if I attack and leave myself open in any way or form I'm screwed! Taro thought.

He kept parrying and blocking until his wakizashi's blade glowed green. He slashed at the space in front of him and a strong gust of wind unfurled from the blade. The smoke was dispersed in time for Taro to see Riley striking from above Jiro's head. Taro teleported and tackled her while Jiro opened a portal to stop Akio's blade from reaching his older brother.

Riley turned into smoke and escaped Taro's grasp.

Well, that's new! Taro thought.

They were back to square one. A lightbulb lit up in Jiro's head.

No shit, he thought.

Akio read his mind and his eyes widened. *Quick! Make him choose!*

Akio threw his blade at Jiro and rushed at him. Riley didn't know what was happening, but she followed Akio's lead and focused on Jiro.

"Taro, quick! Teleport the Eighth out of here!"

Riley smiled. *Oh no, you don't!*

She anticipated the portal and rolled a smoke grenade across the ground. Jiro's portals didn't cover large enough space, and the smoke grenade rolled between his legs. Jiro kept the portals behind him and turned.

Right where we want him, Akio thought.

Akio knew Taro's next move and positioned himself to tackle Taro this time, shoving him away while Riley ran her blade up Jiro's back before he could turn to face her. She fired scorch bolts from her pistol until she saw his aura shield crack, but no further.

Taro teleported over to his brother, blood leaking out of his body. He snarled at them before teleporting to the hospital, where he passed out on the floor, completely out of energy. Riley and Akio deamplified, grabbed the Eighth, and ran down the hall.

"There's a Prestige here! A good one!" Riley shouted into her earpiece. "We need backup, Rookie!"

Akio hurled two scorch runestones from his belt and blew up the wall, exiting the hallway. They ran outdoors, carrying the Eighth between them. Riley had a saddened look in her eyes. Akio decided to take a peek: *I'm so sorry...*

****

Henry's mother was a Celestian Knight in the city of Aster. The lush meadows and golden rays of the sun were always present in his memories of her. His father was a simple delivery man and often spent his days traveling the countryside. Henry had been brought along once, but found it all quite stale. He didn't long for what was right in front of him, but rather, what he couldn't see with his own eyes.

His mother would take him to the creek, and under the shade of the tree, read him stories of ancient legends and prophecies. By just holding Henry's hand or tapping his head, she showed him all of Lokyer. From the shores of Hinohana to the sands of Azirion to the plains of Puakai.

"Mom, when I get older, I want to be a Celestian Knight like you!" he would say.

His mother would smile, a hesitant look always in her eye. "I believe you can someday Henry. You are the light of my life after all!" She hugged him tight and patted his head, her golden strands of hair falling onto his shoulders. "I'm sure you will be the light of other people's lives too. But I don't know if I could stand it! I don't want my little baby getting hurt!" she said as she pinched Henry's cheeks.

Henry didn't know what she was talking about. Every day, she would come back healthy. Every night, he was tucked into bed with a kiss... Until he wasn't. He was playing in the schoolyard with his friends until he was interrupted by his teacher: "Henry, your father is here to pick you up. Quickly, gather your things."

Henry did as he was told, and saw his father waiting outside the school gates with the car running. A distraught and drained look was draped across his face.

"Daddy? What's wrong?"

His father didn't reply for a long while. They just drove. And drove. And drove. After about twenty minutes, he finally mustered up the strength to say it: "Your mother is… not doing well," he sobbed, his tears hitting his steering wheel.

They arrived at the hospital and were greeted not so pleasantly by a fellow Celestian Knight. Henry recognized him immediately, having seen him at his mother's church before.

"I'm sorry Mr. Preston," he cried. He was young, and on his knees sobbing uncontrollably. "If only I had been stronger I could've…"

Henry could only watch, stunned. He was used to his bright expression, his snarky comments, but now… there was nothing there. His father just walked past, placing a sympathetic hand on his shoulder as he did so. At this point, his mind was blank, unsure of how to feel.

Henry tagged along, and soon anxiety began to fill the hollow void. The hallway seemed to extend, and the next minute felt like an hour. His heart pounded against his chest, fear choked his breath and made his body quake. He couldn't stand it anymore and rushed down the now shrinking hallway. He yanked the door open and there was his mother, laying in a bed with an oxygen mask on her face.

"Mummy!" Henry wailed and rushed to her side.

Even through the mask, she smiled, and with a wheeze said: "Hi, my shining light."

Henry could hear his father's footsteps behind him. "Kayla…"

"Honey…"

A doctor knocked on the door. "Mr. Preston? May I speak with you privately?"

"No… Henry, you need to hear this too…"

The doctor gave an apprehensive look. "As you wish." He gulped. "Your mother was dispatched to help defend a small village not far from here from a very powerful signum… By the time she was brought here, the blight was already in stage three. We were able to call a Celestian Knight from the Order with arc magic, but it's too late. He was only able to stop it from growing."

"Is she going to be able to live?"

"There's a chance..." the doctor sighed. "We can keep her on life support, but she'll never be able to walk–I mean... she'll barely be able to lift a fork to eat her food if she–"

"But she can live, right?"

"Yes, but I don't want to be the one to give you false hope sir."

Henry looked at his mother and saw only a weak smile. "Don't worry," she assured. "I'm going to pull through this okay? I promise." She placed her hand on his face and wiped away his tears.

Henry nodded, sniffling and gripping his mother's hand tightly. She grimaced and Henry instantly let go. They spent the rest of the day there, staying by her side until she fell asleep.

For the next three years, Henry's father knew being a mailman wouldn't pay the bills. He dedicated his time to his work, working his way up the corporate ladder until, eventually, he was able to become a manager. But it still wasn't good enough.

Henry came home from school one day to find an eviction notice taped to his door. He walked inside, flipping it back and forth. "Hey, dad?"

He looked up and saw his dad, smoking a cigar and drinking at the kitchen table. His eyes were sullen, and his skin pale. "Son... I may have done something terrible." He got up and knelt down to Henry, alcohol stemming from his breath. "But I want you to know, it's all for your mother."

What he had done was strike a deal with the Mafia. Soon, the Preston Shipping Co. was able to be the sole carrier of Bernardino goods and gained money fast. They could finally keep up with the bills.

Henry's mother died only a month after. This would be the biggest sorrow, the greatest remorse someone felt toward him. This would be the first bargain broken. This is when he got his magic. At the time of her death, a card had popped into his hand of a woman with white hair, nearly albino skin, and bright yellow eyes in a pitch-black cloak.

****

Henry and his father shared a look in awkward silence. The rest of the Wings were talking amongst themselves, not wanting any part of what was going on between them.

"Welcome to the Family of the Desperate!" They cheered for Dakota.

"Hey son..." the Eighth said, starting to grasp the situation. "My, my debt—"

"It's all fallen onto me," Henry interrupted, looking away.

His father walked up and embraced him. "I am so sorry my boy…"

Henry heaved a sigh. "It's okay, I'll take care of it. Anything for family, right?" Henry could no longer put his heart into those words.

Envy's words echoed throughout his head. *You're letting these obligations and expectations get in the way of what matters. What. Do. You. Want. To. Do?*

"Right," his father said. "If you need anything, I'll be there to help you."

"Welcome back, father…"

10: Finally, Time Marches On

Monty was looking at his Omnicard on an early Tran-Zip toward Cysko when he saw the news.

"During the sudden signum outbreak in Cysko, Penumbra Wings broke out the Eighth Wing Craig Powell, as well as hundreds of other prisoners from Bandit Doldrum. Ayo is in total lockdown and a request for Chasm's aide is in process as police and Prestiges are apprehending the escaped convicts..." he read from an article.

Monty didn't hear much past the fact about the Eighth. A quiet rumbling grew louder and louder in his ears until it was snuffed out by his arrival at Cysko Station. Monty put away his Omnicard and slung his backpack over his healthy shoulder. He took a deep breath and walked out of the car.

He knew the route very well. He walked it for two years of his life. The houses, the middle school, that beach. Memories of him and Dalton flashed behind him as he continued down the street and walked up the steps to a townhouse. Another deep breath and he knocked on the door.

Melody's mother answered the door and Monty looked at the ground instinctively.

"H-hi Mrs. Wallace, it's been a while..." Monty chuckled. He scratched the back of his head. The blight bit down on his shoulder and he quickly put his arm back down. "Uh, um..."

"Melody! Monterey's here!" she shouted back into the house. She turned to address her visitor. "It's nice to see you again, Monterey," she said.

Monty raised his head and saw the green eyes and blonde hair that Melody had inherited. She had a warm smile on her face.

"How's Amethyst and Monica?" she asked.

"Th-they're doing good..." Monty chuckled. "Thank you for asking."

"Have you been taking care of yourself?" she asked. "You're all pale and have these really dark circles around your eyes."

Monty smiled softly. "I cook for five people now, and with schoolwork and Prestige training I–"

Prestige training, Monty hung on those words.

"Take care of yourself, okay?" Mrs. Wallace insisted. "We know you blame yourself for what happened all those years ago, it's why you avoided us, right? We saw the azaleas and meals you always left, but never *you*... Even Mel told us that you only ever stay to say hi to her and leave most of the time."

"I... I'm sorry..."

"Monty..."

"I know, I know," Monty sighed. "Let me rephrase that: I'm trying to make up for lost time now."

"Well, I'm glad," she sighed. "And I know Mel is too."

Melody rushed down the stairs. "Hi Monbon!" she exclaimed.

She was dressed in the Constellation Academy spring uniform and did a twirl to show it off. "Whatcha think?"

Monty blushed a little. *You look cute.* He thought.

"You look healthy," he said instead.

Melody pouted, frustrated she didn't get the complement she was looking for. Monty laughed, pretending to be aloof. His heart squeezed a little.

We haven't walked to school together since that day... he thought.

They both said goodbye and walked to the Tran-Zip station.

"Ya know, you didn't need to go out of your way to walk me there," Melody chuckled.

Monty shrugged. "Well, you're going out of your way to help us with the play, so I wanted to show some gratitude."

"You're as silly as always," Melody sighed. "Ugh, I'm so excited to get back to my life!" Melody beamed.

Monty smiled and looked ahead of him. *I could care less about the Mafia at this point. What am I going to do about it anyway? I can't use magic. Screw it! I'm done being a Prestige!*

Monty and Melody talked all the way to school. Safe and unharmed.

****

The Atlas Public Library was enormous, as were the libraries in the other academy cities. It was six stories high with a dome, glass ceiling that let sunlight in to brighten the center of the library. Paige and the others got off the bus that let them off in front. The automated driver said, "We've arrived at the Atlas Public Library. Good luck with your studies!" As it opened its doors and let its passengers disembark.

Monty and Melody were a little early and were waiting at a nearby cafe. Once they saw the others, they ran up to each other.

"Melodyyyyyyy!" Amy squealed.

"Amyyyyyyy!" Melody reciprocated.

They embraced in a massive hug while the others watched on with warm smiles. Monty's thoughts transitioned to Clara and looked over at her. She was dozing off, staring into the distance. Wearing a yellow blouse with white jean shorts, a delicate and bright combo. Her hair was let down and swayed in the breeze.

Her hair, Monty repeated. His eyes widened as he finally realized that she was no longer wearing the hair tie he gave her. *Sure, I don't expect her to wear it every day but… come to think of it she hasn't worn it for a while now…*

Monty thought of her turning away from Amy. He clenched his fists. *I need to ask her about that.*

Clara was in her own head as well. Guilt crushed her heart, thinking about the attack on Cysko. Clara looked at Amy's smile and her heart ached. *I should just tell them,* she thought. But flashes of the werewolves on the roof, memories of their bone blades digging through her flesh made her shiver. *Could we really beat him and the Wings though?* She thought.

She looked to the side and caught Monty staring at her. Monty looked away and blushed. Clara turned away and frowned. *I'm so pathetic…*

"Hey, Clara!" Melody's voice broke through the static.

Clara wrapped a fake smile across her face in time to look at Melody. "Melody! So glad you're gonna be joining us soon."

"Me too!"

Wait, Melody isn't a part of the contract, maybe I could… Clara thought.

They began chatting while Paige went over to Monty and whispered, "Ay, how's that shoulder of yours?"

"It's fine," Monty sighed. "There's just no way I'll be able to use magic now."

Paige looked at Monty's pale complexion, his tired eyes, and his frown. *Liar,* he thought. *I could've done more…*

They finally walked into the library. Contrary to the outside world, the library was bustling with echoing footsteps and murmurs of conversations accumulated into a constant, low hum. The first floor had a large lobby and cafeteria, along with an enormous computer lab and a room filled with kiosks where users could search for a particular book and the navigation directions could be sent to their Omnicards. The bookcases were twelve meters tall and had cranes sliding up and down the shelves, which could be connected to a person's Omnicard wirelessly to retrieve a book they otherwise couldn't reach.

In the center of it all was a giant kinetic sculpture that dangled from the ceiling as the four moons of Lokyer: Cicus, Galilei, Grasse, and Vinci spun ever so slowly, orbiting around Lokyer, which was at the center of the sculpture. It was constructed so the beams of sunlight from the dome above represented Plexis, and as the moons orbit around Lokyer, the appropriate shadows would be cast upon it.

Henry was already waiting, sitting in a sofa chair in the lobby. "Ah, good morning! How are you all?" He got up and shook hands with everyone.

"We're fine," Amy smiled.

Henry paused and looked around. "There seems to be two of you missing… Where are Dalton and Elizabeth?"

Clara clenched her fists so hard that her knuckles turned white. She kept a close eye on the others, not wanting them to see her duress.

"We don't know actually," Paige said. "We called Sagittarius about it and they're trying their best to find them."

"Oh… I'm sorry to hear that," Henry replied. "I'm sure they're doing fine." He glanced over to Clara who was hiding her expression.

His eyes caught Melody. "Hi! My name is Henry. You are..?"

"Melody," she introduced herself. "Nice to meet you."

"Indeed. Well, I think it's best if we split into teams and gather information. Paige, you know a lot about history and religion, right?"

"I did grow up in a monastery," Paige chuckled.

"What topic do you know the least?"

Paige stroked his chin and looked at the ceiling as he thought. "I think I'll learn more about Syd himself."

"Okay then, you and someone else can work on that. Melody and I can focus on Celestia; Clara and Monty, you two can work on their companions on their journey Pre-Revival. Any problems with that?" He looked at Clara with an innocent smile.

"Just peachy," Clara growled. "C'mon Lava Brain! Let's go…" She grabbed Monty by the wrist and tugged him along.

"Oi, take it easy!" Monty exclaimed, nearly collapsing from the pain.

"Amy, you wanna help me out?" Paige asked.

"Yeah, sure," Amy smiled and everyone went their different directions.

****

Melody and Henry found themselves on the fourth floor. Henry was sifting through books, but wasn't really paying much attention to them. He already heard the stories of Syd and Celestia over and over again from his mother.

"Oooo, the Sinful Generals," Melody awed with eyes full of curiosity. "It looks like Envy can take appearances and techniques just from looking at someone, but to steal their magic he needs to be hit by it first. Syd chooses the Sins, however since he has been vanquished, there exists no more Sins."

Henry scoffed. *Well, that's not exactly correct. Envy was sealed away, not killed.*

Melody kept reading. "With Syd's arrival, came forth his Six generals, each with a power called their Authority. Syd himself was the Sin of Wrath, making him the seventh member. His ability was Blinding Fervor. In a surge of rage, Wrath takes damage that has been built up over time and unleashes it. Lust can put people under illusions by touching them, and Pride can refill his own aura reservoir as well as his fellow nearby comrades..."

Henry drowned out Melody's voice. He looked at her and remembered that day on the beach. *Well, I guess she didn't need to die,* Henry thought. *Had Monty not suffered from memory loss, that would've set back our operation and father would've gotten into more debt. I felt a little guilty at first, but seeing as she's alive I guess it all worked out for everybody.*

"Melody, we should be focusing on Celestia," Henry smiled.

"Oh, right," Melody giggled. "Sorry, I get a little carried away sometimes."

****

Meanwhile, Monty and Clara were in a different section of the library. Clara was hopping, reaching for a book on a shelf too high for her. Unfortunately, the claw didn't reach low enough to get it for her. She struggled and gritted her teeth, her fingertips feathered the book she tried to grab.

After snickering for a while, Monty walked over and grabbed the book for her. "Here," he said with a smile.

Clara didn't return the smile. "I didn't need your help."

Monty was taken aback a little. "You uh, you sure?"

"Yup!"

"So we're uh, back to this now?"

"Never left it."

Monty looked down at her, hoping his disappointment would ooze out of his body and make her feel sorry. "Fine shortstack, I won't help you anymore," he growled.

Monty put the book one shelf higher than where she found it and left Clara to fend for herself.

"Hey! That's not fair! You put it on a higher shelf!" Clara snapped in a hushed voice. "And who are you calling shortstack?!" Clara watched him leave with a frown. *I'm sorry...*

Monty rounded the corner and frowned. *Just ask her! Why didn't you save Amy?!*

****

Paige and Amy were still searching through books. "Chapters of a cult called, The Hand, began to form after Syd's second death from fighting the Twelve Zodiacs and the other Sins. They believe that Syd was a savior of sorts, someone the underrepresented and oppressed could seek asylum in," Paige read aloud.

"Why though? Syd was a traitor through and through. He betrayed Celestia, he betrayed his friends, and then he even betrayed the Sins he created! Like, what a jerk!" Amy exclaimed.

"Shh! Still in a library," Paige smiled.

"Sorry," Amy winced.

"They are fools, aren't they?" the Dean agreed.

Amy and Paige turned around and saw him smiling with a black pocketbook with a small chain attached to it in his hands.

Paige jumped in surprise. "Oh! Dean Mozaveen! What are you doing here?"

"Yes," the Dean chuckled. "The leader of the Hand's name was Sebastian Wolfe, a demon with very powerful magic. Your fathers were a part of the Prestige team that sealed him away."

"Interesting..." Paige mumbled.

"Are you having trouble finding primary sources? The Story of Syd interests me and I must say, I am excited for your play."

"A little bit," Paige said. "A lot of these books are all dating past 1 U. It's like everything before it didn't exist."

"What do we even call that time period?" Amy asked.

"AL," the Dean answered. "It stands for 'After Landing.' You are aware of the Time Capsule Culture that Dalton constantly references, yes? They all come from our distant ancestors who landed on this planet."

Paige shook his head. "Too bad a lot of books from that time were destroyed during Syd's rampage. The Time Capsules were one of the few things that survived."

"Yes, it is unfortunate," the Dean sighed. "But, I have something that may be of help to you."

The Dean handed the pocketbook to Paige. Paige opened it and flipped through it, realizing that the silky texture of the paper was of the same material as talismans and all of the pages were written in runes.

"What is this?" Paige asked.

"*That* is the *Magnum Codex,* the book that helped humans understand aura and magic," the Dean explained. "Celestia was only ever able to save a few pages from the original where we get our elemental talismans and speed and strength talisman runes, etc. But Syd destroyed the rest of it. So all copies across Lokyer are technically an abridged version of the original. A Prestige friend of mine found this in a sky castle and gave it to me, and it appears that it is the *genuine* thing." He gave a wink.

"Woah," Paige awed. "Thanks, Dean, I'll be sure to take a look at it."

"Of course! Just be sure to not blow yourself up in the process. Well, I shall get out of your hair. If you ever need anything, you know where to find me."

Paige watched him leave and examined the pocketbook some more. He noticed the creases of the cover and furrowed his brow. *This book is fairly new though…*

****

They gathered outside the library and said their goodbyes.

"Thanks for coming out today everyone," Henry said. "I'll see you all tomorrow at school."

"Later," Paige said and they all walked away.

"Hey, Melody," Clara said. "You into coffee?"

"Not really, but I'm into sweets!"

"Then you wanna go to a cafe together?"

"Sure! But what about the others?"

"Sorry guys," Clara apologized. "I wanna steal away with Melody for a night."

"Fine by me," Monty shrugged but silently pouted.

Henry watched Melody and Monty chat and couldn't help but be reminded of his mother. *It's not fair...* Henry thought. *Why is it that she comes back to you but my mom doesn't...* Henry glanced over at Clara, who had a frown of longing, looking towards Monty and Melody. *It's not fair, why do you get everything and I'm left with debt and dust?!*

Henry walked away with gritted teeth and eyes full of hate. *I can't wait to rip everything away from you!*

****

Kaze, Sol, and Saggitarius were at Runeseekers Headquarters going over all the information they had at their disposal. They were gathered around a table in one of the conference rooms with a touch-screen wall with images and videos.

"Sagittarius, you mentioned that the behavior of the signum was similar to those during the final exam in the Croconoas?" Sol asked.

"Yeah," Sagittarius said. "That's the strangest thing about this. Signum have the capability to coordinate, sure. But like, as a pack of wolves, not at this level. What other similarities have we spotted?"

Sol walked up to the wall and began sorting the videos, documents, and images by swiping across the wall. "The other similarity between the two events is that... Envy was spotted within the week of each attack."

"And of course, with Envy, Penumbra," Kaze added before taking a sip of tea. "Those are the easiest dots to connect, especially as the timing of the prison break with the attack is too coincidental to not be planned. Everything else starts to get foggy from here. There's a strong chance that a Wing is controlling all of the signum. This is evident from Clara and Amy's testimonies of numbers and letters being engraved on the evolved signum's bones."

"A mage controlling signum? What, do we have another Drakar on our hands?" Jiro scoffed.

The door swung open and Jiro walked into the room.

"Evening gentlemen," he said.

"Jiro! How are you doing? Where's Taro?" Sagittarius asked.

"Well, my back hurts like hell and I'm exhausted, otherwise I'm fine. As for my brother, he's on a field trip with Masamune."

"Masamune? Why?" Kaze asked.

"Apparently, Masamune challenged two of your students to a duel," Jiro sighed. "Then he left them there, thinking that they could call Taro, but haven't reached him yet. He didn't consider the fact that maybe their Omnicards were dead or got no service…"

Sagittarius leaned back in his chair. "That's a relief." He pulled out his Omnicard. "I'll alert the others right now."

"Anyway, I was just on a fountain call with the Zodiacs and we're treating the hydra as a fluke. They're confident that we can take care of any other threat like that," Jiro sighed. "Our main problem remains: Penumbra. They're currently selling Chasm-grade firearms and a drug called *foma* that makes you happy, influenceable, and nostalgic to Wanari neighborhoods. Currently, I believe it's an effort to destabilize the gangs in the areas and then take over."

"Okay, so we've pieced together that Penumbra are trying to expand their operations in the West and are stirring up more trouble than usual by involving Wanari gangs. But two questions we haven't yet answered completely: according to Dalton and Monty, they blew up their own HQ in Cysko. And what the heck were they doing in an abandoned Chasm facility in the Croconoas?" Sol went over.

"They blew up their own HQ to hide any evidence of them stealing rifles from Chasm which they stole from the abandoned Chasm facility in the Croconoas. After stealing Dalton's Omnicard, they probably leveraged some corrupt cops to find out information about the others. Baited them with the bottle Envy was found in, and then captured Paige and Elizabeth. Dalton and Amy followed them to some warehouses that they were using as a temporary HQ, where they found Envy. After that, they painted a target on their backs, and used Dalton's Omnicard or some information to sabotage their Sprawling Forest mission," Sol said. "Nearly a month of going over the evidence and that's the story we got. Obviously, we aren't one-hundred percent sure on some areas, but it's the best we got so far."

"Hmm…" Jiro scratched his head and slapped his face a little bit. He was visibly stressed and exhausted. "Well, it seems like their focus is off of them now. Most of their activity has been in Cysko and Ayo, not Atlas. I should know," Jiro chuckled. "I think moving them to Atlas helped move them out of Penumbra's crosshairs. Anyways, I got a long couple of days rounding up convicts."

Jiro walked back to the door. "So if you'll excuse me, I'm going to enjoy one last good night of sleep while I can."

****

Receiving the text from Sagittarius that Dalton and Elizabeth were fine wasn't enough to put Monty at ease. He woke up in a cold sweat and with a headache. He stumbled out of his room to the bathroom. He collapsed in front of a toilet, bent over, and heaved for several minutes. He took off his shirt and saw in the mirror that his blight had stretched from his shoulder down his arm to his elbow, across his right pectoral, and his shoulder blade. It throbbed with his heartbeat, waiting for its next opportunity to bury itself deeper inside his flesh. He threw back a couple of painkillers and guzzled a glass of water.

I can't let them see me like this… he thought. *I didn't make too much noise, so they're probably still asleep.*

He was somehow able to get dressed and hid the blight on his arm with a gauze bandage. He managed to walk downstairs without tripping and made breakfast for the others before heading to school early. He sat down at his seat in class and slumped over his desk. He was finally able to get some sleep, only to be woken up by a finger tapping his shoulder. Luckily, it wasn't his infected one.

"Monbon? Class is about to start," Melody said.

"Th-thanks," Monty chuckled.

"Are you okay? What happened to your arm?"

"I'm just feeling a little under the weather is all," Monty said. "As for the injury, I got hurt during the attack on Cysko, but it wasn't anything serious."

The bell didn't allow for any further talking. The rest of the day went as per usual, except now there was Melody. She introduced herself to the class and hung out with everyone at lunch. The painkillers had kicked in at this point, and so Monty was able to keep the act up. Classes finally ended and gears switched to preparing for the Azure Festival.

Monty and Clara were on opposite sides of the classroom; it was clear he was being avoided. Monty had the question burning in his chest and would glance over in Clara's direction once in a while. Melody took notice of this.

"Hey Paige," Melody whispered. "Does Monty have a thing for Clara?"

"Yeh," Paige whispered. "But things haven't been going well. She's been acting super distant lately."

"Hmmm."

"Are you okay with that?" Paige asked Melody.

"Yeah, it's totally fine," Melody giggled. "It's..." she heaved a sigh. "It's still hard even when you're expecting it..."

Paige frowned and wrapped an arm around Melody's shoulders.

"But! I'm happy just being able to spend time with you guys!" she beamed, stepping away from it. "It's like my life is finally moving forward again."

"Hey, Melody?" a classmate called. "Wanna help us out over here?"

"Sure!" she said and frisked over to that side of the class.

"Where's Dalton?" a girl whined. "We need to fit him for his costume today."

"He and Elizbeth are on Prestige business," Paige explained. "They're supposed to be coming back tonight or tomorrow."

"About time those two came back. We only got a month left before the Azure Festival. We need to get stuff done."

"Clara," Henry called out.

Clara turned around to see the scumbag at the front of the room, working on decorations. "We need more lights and a speaker from the supply room. It should be on the first floor–I think left to the library?"

"Yeah, sure thing," Clara smiled to the best of her ability and left the room.

Melody watched her leave and after a couple of seconds, said to Monty: "Hey Monty, the story committee actually needs something from the supply room as well. They asked me to go get it but, I don't really know my way around campus yet. Could you grab that Omniboard that's in there for me?"

"Yeah sure," he grumbled disheartenedly and left the room.

Melody watched him leave with a smile full of subtle longing.

Paige glanced over at Henry as discreetly as he could. Henry caught it anyway and simply smiled. He turned to his classmate and said, "I need to use the bathroom. I'll be back."

"Okay," his classmate said as they continued to take inventory.

Henry left the room, and his innocent smile turned sinister. *Oh Melody, you just made my job one-thousand times easier...*

****

The closet was dark and small, much to Clara's despair. She rummaged around the room, looking for the needed supplies. If she was actually focused on the task, she might have found them already. However, all she could think about was Henry. She was so deep in thought that she forgot just how cramped this room was.

How am I going to tackle this? Are the signum manifested from him directly or does he need to tame one? If the latter, how are they summoned? If he was here in Puakai before transferring, what is his real motive? Surely it can't just be about me, he even said so.

Her train of thought was broken by the door opening and closing behind her.

"You're sure taking your time," Monty sighed.

Clara's eyes widened as she snapped her head back to see Monty standing behind her with his hands in his pockets. He looked sullen and weary with even darker circles surrounding his eyes.

Damn it! I need to find the stuff and leave! Clara cursed.

She frantically searched for the items while Monty stood back and watched with a frown. He let this continue for some time until he couldn't stand it anymore. "I ask you if everything is okay, and every time you tell me it is. It's like, we keep going in circles. One day we make progress to becoming better friends. And then suddenly we're back to square one."

Not this time Monty. I'm sorry!

Monty's eyes had finally become accustomed to looking forward. But now… now they went back to looking at the ground in front of his feet.

"I see that you're not wearing your hair tie anymore…"

Clara froze. She took a breath before continuing with her task. *I'm sorry Monty, I don't want to hurt you…*

"I know you hate my guts, but I've been trying to become a better person. Revenge isn't my priority anymore. It's you guys. I want to become someone you can all be proud to call a friend…"

Clara wanted to reassure him that he was doing the right thing. That he had changed. But the fear of Henry held her tongue.

Monty started to grow frustrated. "I guess if you don't want to talk then you don't have to. I'll just take the board and get out of your way."

Monty snatched the board and turned to leave when he realized that the door was locked. He tried the knob again but to no avail. Clara's spatial awareness finally started to kick in and her breathing began to accelerate. Her chest tightened like the walls of the room seemed to.

Meanwhile, outside the room Henry walked away with a skip in his step, spinning the keys in his hand while whistling a merry little tune. Anyone who passed, he grazed with his hand and put them under an illusion so they didn't hear Monty's pounding much less see the door itself.

And now we wait, Henry cackled in his head.

"Well, great," Monty sighed. "Do you have your Omnicard?"

"N-No," Clara said. "I left it back in the class."

"Same here."

Monty just stared at the closed door. Clara's senses were being thrown into overload as the darkness of the cramped room suffocated her.

"Hey," Monty said. "If you're going to answer a single question I ask you, make it this one: I understand hating me, but what happened in Cysko? Why did you turn your back on A–?"

He was cut off by Clara snatching onto his back. She hugged him tight, her breath sporadic. Pain shot through his entire body from Clara's hand on his blighted shoulder and he fell to his knees. He still couldn't help but blush.

"Just what are you–?!"

"Shut up for a second!" Clara snapped.

Monty complied. He wanted to scream in pain and the room spun in circles around him. On Clara's end, her panic and anxiety finally leveled and started to decline. As her panic left, the calming warmth from Monty's body let deja vu sneak in.

"S-sorry, I'm claustrophobic," Clara stuttered. "I got stuck in a tight and dark place when I was younger and–"

"It was in a crevasse in the Croconoa Mountains," Monty interjected. "Thank goodness it was only a few meters deep."

Clara's mind began to clear. She slowly let go of him, shocked at the revelation. She stood up and her hands went to hide her mouth which was agape with shock. Her mind scrambled to put the rest of the pieces together.

"When you were asking about my scarf..." Clara muttered.

Suddenly, the door swung open, revealing Henry with a worried look on his face. "You guys okay? You were taking a while, so we all got worried."

The moment shattered like a home-run hit soaring through a window. The light from the hallway blinded Monty and he couldn't keep it up anymore. The painkillers wore off. He was close to vomiting again. Sweat glazed his pale skin. His breath was hoarse. His eyes rolled back, and everything faded to a murky black.

11: Broken Masks

All of the nurses got out of the way. Even Elizabeth watched in awe as Dalton was somehow able to hobble at the speed of a run. His face was in a twisted snarl like a mad dog. An added effect was his messy hair and the dried blood on his clothes. A hole was still in his shirt, revealing his torso which was wrapped in bandages with arc talismans weaved within to increase the healing speed. The same was with his left leg, which had a hole in his pants above his thigh where a piece of wood had punctured it.

They had been immediately taken to Miles by Taro, who was the one who gave them the talisman bandages. Dalton found out that they actually didn't do anything to him, most likely because of his demon-half.

Well, at least I can explain the fast healing, Dalton thought.

Elizabeth too, had rips, dried blood, and dirt on her clothing. Her body was bruised and covered in the same arc talisman bandages as Dalton.

"Uh, Dalton?" Elizabeth peeped.

"Where is he?!" Dalton snarled.

Dalton scanned the room numbers and as they approached the desired digits, he increased his speed until he found Monty's room. He yanked the door open and didn't even pay attention to Melody, who was in attendance. His eyes were tunneled on Monty, who was laying in bed.

Dalton launched his fist forward at max speed and slammed his knuckles into the side of Monty's face. Monty nearly fell out of his bed while Elizabeth hobbled over to Dalton.

"Dalton?!" Elizabeth exclaimed.

Dalton took a deep breath. He was on the verge of letting his eyes ignite yellow and calmed himself. "Sorry, Monty… But I made a promise to Amy that if you hid anything from us again, I'd sock you in the face."

Monty touched his cheek with his fingers and tasted for blood. After his analysis, he replied: "Long time, no see."

"How's wearing that fake smile serving you now, huh? When were you going to tell us you had blight?"

Monty just frowned. Dalton's glare was too overpowering and he dared not look back toward him. "Glad to see you're safe."

Dalton clicked his tongue. "Forget it." Dalton turned to leave but stopped at the door. "I love you to death. But stuff like this? It pisses me off *so much,*" he spat before leaving the room.

Elizabeth's attention turned to Monty. He looked like a withered beansprout; he was so pale and thin. He had black sandbags hanging from his eyes and it was obvious he was doing his best to hide the fact that he was in pain.

"How bad is it?" Elizabeth asked.

Monty didn't respond. He just sat there, frozen.

"Monty."

Monty sighed. "The doctor said if I use magic again, I'll die."

"When did it happen?"

"During the Sprawling Forest. When I was pushing back the avalanche, I was attacked by a signum," he muttered.

"So when I offered to help, you decided to do all of the work even though you should have been getting rest?"

"I couldn't sleep anyway. Too many nightmares." Monty wheezed a chuckle. "Might as well be useful."

"You know, I never understood why Dalton would get so mad about this type of stuff, but I think I get it now. You know trust goes both ways right? Do you just not trust us to help you with your burdens?"

Monty didn't have the energy to argue.

"This isn't friendship Monty. Friends help each other and you won't let us do that. This... I don't know what this is." Elizabeth turned to walk away.

"Clara is in the garden," Monty said.

"Thanks," Elizabeth muttered as she walked out the door.

****

Clara was hoping to be alone for a while, but near enough to where if Monty's condition became critical, she could rush over. She was laying down on a bench, looking up at the clouds. She remembered her and Monty's argument during their entrance exam.

"To think he'd grow up to be such a jerk..." she chuckled. "The exact opposite of what he inspired me to do. Although..." She reflected on how Monty's been acting the past month. "I guess he's been doing better."

Her fingers were drawn to the hair tie he had bought her, but she remembered she had taken it off. She heaved a sigh. "I have so many questions…"

Within those memories, she remembered how she called him a wimp, how she jested at him for not training or practicing, and all the times she jabbed or punched or elbowed him, even if lightly. She thought about how Monty didn't rush in to save the mother, and how she berated him after. She recalled her turning away from Amy and Monty needing to save her instead. Guilt flooded in the more she recalled.

Wait a minute… if he's had since the Sprawling Forest mission then, his blight got worse at that moment! Clara thought. *I'm such an idiot! This is all my fault!*

"Is everything okay?" Melody asked.

Clara snapped back to reality and turned her head to see Melody, standing, smiling.

"Can I sit next to you?"

"Sure."

Clara scooted over to make room for Melody who plopped down and stretched her arms to the sky. She let out a relaxed sigh, "I always went to my hospital's garden to pass the time." She let her head tilt back and looked up at the sky, which was filled with coral, light blue, and cream colors from the setting sun. "The sky's really pretty tonight. You like looking at it?"

Clara joined her and tilted her head back. "Yeah… I used to always watch the clouds pass by my window in my room. I was always so jealous of them. They were free to go as they please."

"I feel that so much! They look so fluffy and friendly too! I wanna take a nap on one."

"That would be ill-advised," Clara giggled.

"I know," Melody giggled. A moment's pause. "You and Monty are really similar, you know?"

"Huh?"

"You both want to help people. You both value your friends. And for some reason, you are both addicted to isolation."

"Pfft, I'm not addicted to being alone."

"Then why are you out here and not in Monty's room with everyone else?"

You don't understand… Clara thought. "It's complicated."

"See? That's totally something Monty would say," Melody giggled. "Is there something going on between you two? Did you get into another fight?"

"Y-yeah, I guess you could say that..."

"Did Monty screw up his second chance?"

"N-no he hasn't yet. He's actually changed a lot this past month or so. He's not so much of a jerk anymore."

"Yeah, I've noticed it too," Melody smiled. "Before, Monty almost never visited me. All he did was just drop off some azaleas once in a while. He couldn't face me or my parents, the guilt made him hurt so bad. No matter how many times I told him it wasn't his fault, he blamed himself."

"That guy... I don't know what goes on in that head of his."

"So if it isn't a fight and he hasn't messed up. How come you're not inside with the others?"

That question again, Clara cursed. "There's something... stopping me from going. Sorry, I can't say. Like I said, it's complicated."

Melody just smiled understandingly. She got up from the bench and looked at the sky once more before looking back at Clara. "Can I... share something personal with you?"

"Go ahead."

"I think you're really cool Clara. I'm actually jealous."

"Oh... well thank you?"

"Monty talks about you a lot. He told me how you ran to his side even though he tried to push you away. That's something... that's something I couldn't do. That day, Monty told me to run away. I listened to him and went to get help. I was so scared. I know I'm weak, but I can't help but feel like I abandoned him at that moment. Honestly, it's only right that I lost my legs..."

Clara watched as Melody's usually quiet smile contorted and twisted into a melancholic frown. Her eyes were glistening and her forehead was scrunched as she slid her hand across her thigh.

"But you're strong Clara. You ran to him because it doesn't matter what anyone told you, you did what you wanted to do. You don't seem like the person who would let others dictate your actions. Just follow your gut instinct, and I'm sure everything will work out."

"Thanks..." Clara muttered with a smile.

Melody smiled back. "Sorry I interrupted your cloud-gazing thing. I'm going to head home now, it's starting to get pretty late. I hope to see you more!"

"You too, Melody…"

Clara watched her leave before getting up from the bench herself. *Never faltered in the face of adversity before, huh?*

"My gut is telling me to find Elizabeth."

****

Amy couldn't bring herself to stay for very long. The hospital was only a ten to fifteen-minute walk away from the ocean, and Amy was walking atop the sea wall when Paige found her. A band of yellow sat above the sparkling ocean, and the sky above was painted with deep blues and indigos.

"Amy!" Paige called out.

Amy didn't respond, nor did she turn around to face him.

"I… I am so, so sorry," Paige said. "I've known about his blight problem for a while now. I-I didn't do enough to make sure he was getting rid of it! I shouldn't have listened to him! I should've brought it to everyone's attention. Sorry…"

"It's okay, Paige," Amy said. "It's my fault…"

"Huh?"

"He told you to keep quiet about it so that I wouldn't worry, right? So that I wouldn't think that I was a burden, right?" Amy whimpered.

She looked over her shoulder at Paige with an expression that sent shivers down his spine. A face so full of guilt and self-loathing that it wanted to make Paige cry. That face was usually filled with so much joy…

"What? Amy, no! It's not your fault. You're not a burden."

"Of course I am!" Amy snapped. "Monty got hurt saving me during the Sprawling Forest mission and got his blight marks. Then, he had to save me again during the attack on Cysko, which made it worse. He's done so much for me and the least I could do was just smile. Now I can't even do that anymore…"

Tears streamed down her face.

There's no way that smile is completely fake, Paige thought. *There's no way…*

"I'm nothing but useless *garbage*. Just a chore for Monty to take care of."

Paige's blood boiled against his skin. He could still picture looking at Dalton and Monty's backs, and Amy was up there with them, fearless and taking it in stride. He clenched his fists and seethed through his teeth. "Don't say that…"

"Huh?"

"Don't say *that*!" Paige looked at Amy desperately. "If you're a burden then what am I?" He planted his thumb into his chest. "If you're garbage, am I beneath that?"

"What're you talking about?" Amy sniffled as she wiped her eyes. "I'm always the one that needs saving. I can't fend off six evolved signum like Clara, or carry someone on my back while being chased across rooftops like Elizabeth!"

"You saved me during the Sprawling Forest mission!" Paige laughed. "I do *one* kick and I need help walking! I throw a *single* punch and I become monoplegic! I can't do anything on my own, I will always need to rely on you guys to succeed! I will always need *you*!"

Paige breathed heavily after finally venting out his frustration. He looked at Amy's expression, which was still confused–a ball of anguish for herself and compassion for Paige. He took a deep breath to calm himself.

You're an idiot Paige… he thought. *Amy needs you right now. Stop being selfish and turning the spotlight over to you.*

He walked over to Amy and gently embraced her. Her eyes went wide with surprise as his arms wrapped around her.

"Please don't say you're trash or worthless," Paige murmured. "Ever since we were little, I'd always be looking at Monty and Dalton's backs. I was always so cautious, so unsure of myself. I still am; it's why I didn't have the backbone to go against Monty's wishes. But on every adventure we went on, you were always up there with them, and made sure I wasn't falling behind. I admire you, Amethyst Violet. You are one of the bravest people I know."

Amy's eyes watered and her heart felt warm yet twisted. She buried her face into Paige's chest.

"But I'm not brave," she insisted. "I'm always so scared on our missions. I hate fighting."

"Then I respect you even more so for diving headfirst into danger even when you're scared. Having fear in the first place shows how courageous you are," Paige said.

He broke away from the hug and smiled.

"Go to your brother and ask him. I'm sure he'd deny that you're any burden on him. And it wouldn't be a lie either. You brighten everyone's day Amy."

Amy took a deep breath and gave one last sniffle before wiping away the last of her tears.

"Thanks, Paige…" Amy smiled.

"Of course."

They began walking back when Amy leaned into him.

"You too," she muttered.

"Wassup?"

"Don't say you're garbage or a burden either. You say you're always watching our backs, but it's comforting to know you're back there, watching over us."

Paige blushed and looked away before adjusting his glasses.

"Th-thanks…"

As the sunset behind them, creating streaks of coral pink along the blue sky, their hands tingled with anticipation. They wondered if it would be alright to take the other's hand, and hoped the other took theirs.

****

"Monica, I'm telling you, I'm fine," Monty groaned.

"You're obviously not!" Monica scoffed.

Monty had received a FaceCHIRP call from his older sister who was, understandably, worried sick.

"I keep telling you to not overwork yourself, don't I?" she asked.

"Yeah, but I also tell you the same thing and that never stopped you until I started helping out, right?" Monty retorted.

Monica's face turned pouty. "You're being stubborn…"

"It runs in the family," Monty sighed.

"So what now?" she asked. "Kaze's telling me you're finally done with your crusade, thank the gods."

Monty looked away for a second. He took a breath and looked at his Omnicard screen once more. "Yeah, I don't care about Penumbra anymore. Even after the Eighth broke out. With how I am now, I–"

The door opened and Amy walked in. "H-hey Monty."

Monty smiled. "Perfect timing."

****

Clara met Elizabeth back at the dorm. Amy was spending the night with Monica and Kaze at the Runeseekers Villas, Monty was in the hospital, and Dalton and Paige were back at the monastery. They sat in silence in Elizabeth's room, the cleaner of the two rooms. Like Clara's room, it had a small balcony that had its window open, letting in a small breeze and beams of light from Lokyer's moons.

Elizabeth was sitting cross-legged on her bed while Clara was becoming one with the large, green bean bag chair, which had been scooted from its original position in the corner across the room to the foot of the bed.

"I'm so glad to be sleeping in an actual bed again!" Elizabeth groaned as she fell back. A bit of hair fell upon her eyes and she blew it back with a small puff.

"I'm so glad you're back Lizzy!" Clara groaned. "Things have been so…"

Her eyes went wide and her brain did a hard restart. Her heart as well, almost as if the rivers of blood that filled her capillaries came to an abrupt halt.

That was close! I got too comfortable, Clara thought.

"...so lonely. It's not a full room unless it's with you after all," Clara finished. She adjusted her glasses.

"Me too! I thought I was gonna die with just Dalton around."

No seriously, we came close, Elizabeth chuckled.

"Tell me what happened! Why did you just randomly leave without saying anything?"

"Hmmm," Elizabeth hummed. "I wonder if I should. I mean, when I got back all I got was a hug? No tears?" she gasped.

"No, I was really worried," Clara insisted.

The tone of her voice was strong enough to make Elizabeth sit back up. Clara's expression was troubled, her face was long while her eyes conveyed aggravation.

"Everyone was. We were constantly wondering where you guys were and if you were safe," Clara said. Clara bit down on her lip and clenched her fists. "It's been so hard…"

"I'm sorry Clara."

"Why didn't you take me with you?"

"I–"

"I've known you for almost all my life Lizzy," Clara said. "I know all of your secrets, so why didn't you take me with you? Why *Dalton*?"

Elizabeth gave a sigh and explained how Masamune got in contact with her and how Dalton tagged along for the ride.

"I was obviously no match for him," Elizabeth said. "Dalton must have talked his way out of the situation. If not for him, I might have not made it back in one piece... As much as I make fun of him, that braggadocious prince really did help me out..."

"Lizzy, you should have asked me to come!" Clara exclaimed.

"I'm sorry, I didn't want you to get hurt."

Clara got suspicious. "Do you... *like* Dalton? Like you have a crush on him or something?"

"Huh? What? No, no," Elizabeth said, swatting the notion out of the air with the frantic wave of her hand. She blushed a little. "Although, my opinion of him has gotten better..."

"Better enough to tell him about your past, ask him to kiss you, and give him a lap pillow?"

"M-Monty already knows that I'm half-Wanari!" She exclaimed. "And as for the other stuff, I was testing to see what his motives were... And to make him fall asleep so I could ditch him in the morning, even though he caught up..."

Ah, Dalton is one of the types who's easily played huh? Clara thought before asking: "How does Monty know that?"

"He and I found each other after the avalanche during the final exam and he was able to figure it out. That weird, blue eye of his gives him really clear vision apparently."

"That thing always creeps me out..." Clara grumbled. "But how can you tell these people this stuff? We've only known them for half a year."

"Dalton was able to show me that he truly sees us like family. That he really does care about us, so does everyone in Prism. Monty even tried to convince me of that, in his own, brusque way of course. Don't you agree? That these are people we can trust?"

"I mean... yeah, but–"

"These people all have some sort of trauma from their past. They're the closest thing to siblings that we have, no?"

Clara was about to say something, but she was interrupted by her own thoughts. Times spent goofing around with Amy, the many times she's been asked "if she's okay" and told "we're here for you" in the past couple of months. Times in the forest, where the boy, Monty, had risked his life to save hers. How he gave her the strength to keep going after her mother died.

"I'm so sorry your mom died!" he shouted at her over the howling winds. His hands clasped around her shoulders and were gently shaking her. *"I am so sorry you don't have time to grieve or mourn! But you're still alive, right?! You still have something you need to do!"*

Clara grew frustrated with herself again. All of the memories of Team Prism offering support were accompanied by her moments of unwarranted harshness towards them. How she didn't help Amy.

How could I let myself turn into some self-pitying pushover?! Clara roared in her head.

"Your silence is an answer in itself," Elizabeth said.

"Even Dalton?"

"Huh?"

"You even see Dalton as a sibling?" Clara jeered.

"You know what I mean!" Elizabeth blushed.

Clara giggled and gave a sigh. She turned away, blushing a little. "Monty… is the boy from the forest…" She murmured.

"Huh?"

"Monty is the boy from the forest," Clara repeated.

Elizabeth's expression went wide with shock. "Then I suppose I have to thank him for keeping you safe. Has he changed since then?"

"Oh, quite a bit," Clara chuckled, recounting the times they've argued. "But at the same time… not at all."

"Then it seems we're in agreement," Elizabeth said with a nod. "I'm planning on telling them everything. Including what happened between me and Henry."

A nerve was pinched in Clara's spine like a pill being broken, and what came pouring out? Rage and worry.

"What *about* Henry?" Clara asked.

"It probably has something to do with his magic," Elizabeth sighed. "But screw it, I have faith that we, Sagittarius, and the Runeseekers can take him down. Henry is the Third Wing of Penumbra."

12: A Much Needed Talk

Miles Tovera sat on the steps that led to a courtyard within his temple. It was a beautiful zen garden with a large hot tub made to look like a mountain hot spring. It was in that tub where Paige had been taking Monty and plunging him in, as the pool was constantly mixed with arc magic, it helped with any blight someone might have.

"Morning dad…"

Miles turned around and saw his son standing behind him, his arms crossed and a long look on his face.

"Morning. You look down, what's up?" He patted the ground next to him.

Paige took a seat next to his father. "I really messed up… Monty had blight all this time, and he told me to keep it a secret from the others. I… I don't know why I went through with it."

Miles watched his son who was instead looking up at the starry sky. "Well, it's because he's your friend, right? When your friend pleads for you to do something, it's hard to say no. But sometimes you gotta be hard on people. People, when they get stressed or lost, won't be able to see themselves right. You gotta be their second set of eyes sometimes, let them see things in a different perspective."

"But I feel like nobody wants to hear what I have to say. I was appointed to captain, but I feel like I'm totally out of place. I don't even know how I was able to get accepted into the Prestige Program in the first place with no magic…"

"Don't worry about that now, Paige. You're in, just leave it at that."

"Right…"

"And you know the saying actions speak louder than words? Well, they really do. Some people can't be swayed by conversation, Paige. Some people can't be sat down and given a talking to, I mean, just look at Dalton."

"Hyeah…" Paige scoffed.

"Ay, as famous as I am, and as strong as I am, I wasn't the leader or the most influential one in the group."

"Who was?"

"Monty's dad of course."

"Really?"

"Yeah! I owe a lot to that guy. Hell, this property we're on, he sold to me so I could build my temple."

"They used to live here?"

"Yeah, they sold it to me after… well… after Monica, Amy, and Kaze came back from the Croconoas…" Miles shook his head. "Anyway, compared to those guys' talents? I was just about average."

"Well, that's because you're comparing yourself to others."

"And what are you basing your value on?"

"Uh…"

Miles placed a hand on Paige's shoulder and shook it gently. "Everyone has a role, Paige. You're the white mage, your job is keeping everybody above water. I had the same role on my team, I had to depend on my teammates countless times to protect me, and in return, I helped them do their jobs better. On top of that, you've been given the leadership role, but it's a role I'm certain you can play."

"I know you're my dad and everything but… why support me now? Before you hated the idea of me becoming a Prestige."

"I didn't think you were capable at the time, but I was convinced otherwise; I'm sure your teammates believe the same."

Paige just looked at the ground, uncertainty all over his face.

Miles got up and stretched. "If your team is anything like my team was, you're in a pack full of alphas. With those types of people, there are obviously times when you're going to need to be firm. However, with a young team like this? Someone like you who knows how important your teammates are to your success is the best thing for them."

"I'm the best thing for them, huh?" Paige muttered. He lost himself in thought for a second before getting up. "Thanks, dad."

They embraced and with a couple of pats on the back, Miles added, "Your potential is limitless, son. I'm so very proud of you. I'm sorry if I've ever made you think differently."

"Nah, it's fine."

"I love you."

"I love you too."

Paige watched his father leave for a second before pulling out his Omnicard and dialing Sagittarius. "Hey Teach, can we chill at your veranda this evening?"

"If you're all eating dinner I want some," Sagittarius replied.

****

That afternoon, Monty returned to the Prism dorm. He stood outside Clara's room, his heart racing. He took a deep breath and knocked.

"Clara?" he asked. "Are you there?"

Clara was sitting at her desk when he knocked. She didn't want to respond, guilt and anxiety holding her tongue.

"Yes," she was able to get out.

"I uh…" Monty trailed off. "Is everything okay? I know I've asked you already, but you don't seem like yourself. I can understand not liking me, I know I can be hopeless sometimes. However, I saw what happened that day…"

Clara's eyes went wide.

"If I offended you or hurt you in some way I'm truly sorry. Even though we've argued a lot, I have never once detested you," Monty said. He paused for a moment and looked at the closed door he was currently talking to. He blushed but tucked away his embarrassment for the serious topic ahead. "I want to know: why did you turn away from Amy that day?"

Monty paused once more to give Clara a chance to answer. He was met by silence. Clara's heart hurt, her eyes were watery. She couldn't forgive herself.

"It's so out of character for you that I can't be mad at you. Something must be wrong, right?" Monty asked.

More silence.

Monty took another deep breath and looked to the ceiling for solace before continuing.

"You know I was with you in the forest, right? It may not seem like it, but you saved me. I saw my mom die right in front of me, and I had no idea whether or not the others were still alive. I had to be strong in order for us to survive then, but I remember you being there for me when I broke down, thinking about my mom… I know you're a strong person, and that 99% of the time, you can stand on your own. However, even if it's just for that 1%, I want to be there for you!"

Clara's heart throbbed hearing his words through the door.

"Clara, I–" Monty began, his cheeks were boiling hot when he was interrupted by the door swinging open.

Clara rushed out and embraced Monty with such force that it was nearly a tackle. Monty was wide-eyed with surprise as Clara hugged him tightly. Monty gently put his arms around her.

"I'm so sorry," Clara said. "I'm sorry for being such a piece of shit. I'm sorry. I'm sorry!"

Monty let out a sigh of relief. *Oh, thank gods, she doesn't hate me.*

"It's okay," Monty reassured. "It's okay. What's wrong? What's on your mind?"

Clara stepped away and sniffled. She nudged her glasses out of the way as she wiped away the tears beginning to form in her eyes. She took a breath to calm down.

"I'm going to explain everything to everyone tonight at the meeting," she said with a determined expression. "Can you wait until then?"

****

Henry frowned at the two cards that just appeared in his pocket moments ago. One depicted a black knight in the Asteria's Cloak: dark blue with baby blue trim and a large yellow star of Celestia on the back. It had a patch depicting Cicus and its dust ring, Lokyer's largest moon, on the right shoulder. The other card showed a black coffin in a swirling vortex made of what appeared to be metal sand.

He thought about the night he joined Penumbra...

****

The days following his mother's death, Henry's father's will broke. Around Henry, he would act strong, he would be there for him, he would parent him. However, Henry knew his father would sneak away to drink his sorrows away behind closed doors.

One night, his father opened a bottle and told Henry to remove himself from the house. In the cold night air, Henry got on his bike and rode across the cobble roads back to the tree they would always rest at. He sat there for a while before Henry stared at the mysterious card that had appeared in his hand after his mother died. He found it creepy at first and threw it away only for it to return to his pocket. He stared at it, and stared at it, and stared at it until a spark went off in his brain.

She looks like mother... Henry waved it around, folded it, but couldn't figure out the point of it. *Why did it appear?*

Henry figured it was okay to go back home and returned to three cars parked outside. His eyes widened and his heartbeat quickened. He rushed over to the front door but stopped himself.

That's not smart, he thought.

Henry went around and climbed the trellis to the second story. Once inside he tiptoed to the top of the stairs and peeked through the railing. Downstairs were four men, two were lounging on the couch and one was standing with his back to the front door. Henry couldn't see the fourth one, but he could hear him from the kitchen.

"I was sure you had a son…" the voice said with crisp wickedness. "Is he going through a rebellious phase?"

"Sure, you could call it that," Henry's father chuckled.

"You and your company have been great assets," the man chuckled. "We gave you the money for all those months of medical bills to keep your wife alive. It's not *our* fault that she died anyway. We can't escape our debts. All we can do is work together to pay them back quickly. If you don't want to cooperate, I can force you instead."

Henry felt a rush of courage and adrenaline fill his body. Now was the time. *How can I be a Celestian Knight if I can't even save my own father?!*

Henry sprinted down the stairs and shouted, "I won't let you kill him!"

It was only a moment's notice, but he was able to process his surroundings. The two men on the couch were getting up, and he could see his father on the ground. Standing in front of him was a man in a black trench coat with long, silver hair and phantasmal green eyes that seemed to swirl with life that wasn't his.

Henry's pocket shined gold and the light leapt from his pocket to the ground in front of him. The light blinded him and when he opened his eyes, the sorceress from the card was levitating in front of him. It spread out its arms and black sludge began to drip from the folds of her cloak.

The sludge accumulated and molded into signum wolves that snarled and leapt toward the men on the couch and the man next to his father. Teeth sinking into their skin woke the grunts from their shock and they started to scream in surprise, unloading their pistols into the beast.

Henry was broken out of his paralysis when the man standing by the door apprehended him from behind in a nelson.

"Let go of me!" Henry shouted.

The sorceress heard Henry's voice and turned to help, but she suddenly vanished in a flash of gold that shrunk and leapt back into Henry's pocket. Where she once stood was the man with the green eyes with an outstretched hand. He turned to his two grunts who hadn't been so fortunate and were dead and bloody from their throats being ripped out. The wolves were snacking on their corpses when the man turned to them. They growled and pounced at him, but were blocked by some invisible wall. The wall turned and then squished them flat against the ground.

"I thought you checked upstairs," the man sighed.

"We did. There was nobody up there! He musta snuck in just a couple of seconds ago."

"Don't touch my son!" Henry's father said and scrambled to get up.

"Sit," the man commanded and his father was sent flying back by an invisible wall. "That's a very interesting power you have there, boy."

"Please, just leave us alone!" Henry cried.

"That's not how this works," the man chuckled. "Your father still owes me. People don't get to do as they please all the time."

"Please… I've already lost my mother," Henry said. "I don't want to lose my dad too…"

A warped smirk sprouted across the man's lips. "Tell you what, you could join me and help your father. I can teach you how to use your power and if you work hard, you can repay your father's debt a lot sooner than he could alone. What do you say?"

He held out a hand. Henry shook it.

"What's your name?" the man asked.

"Henry."

"My name is Viktor," the man replied. "I look forward to doing business with you Henry."

Not so long after, Henry became a part of the Mafia's Tax Collectors, a group of grunts in charge of retrieving overdue debts. He let the grunts do the dirty work and just collected the cards. One day, he stood next to the corpse of a Prestige, who had killed several of his men until he stepped in and eliminated him.

A memory flashed into his head: *I want to be a Celestian Knight when I grow up!*

Henry could do nothing but smile.

How ironic.

****

Henry was sitting in his car when Envy, disguised as a Constellation Academy student, returned.

"Why do you even have a car?" Envy asked. "It's not like there's paved roads or anything between the cities."

"I want a normal life," Henry said, ignoring Envy's question.

"Huh?"

"You asked me what I want to do. I want to live a normal life..."

Henry thought about Monty smiling with Melody and Clara. *I want his life...*

"Henry, you have failed to entertain me over the course of the past couple of months," Envy cackled. "You and I are very much alike."

Henry was willing to entertain the idea at this point. "How so?"

"Well, you must have a more burning question for me considering I was but a bottle of miasma when you found me."

"In that case, what are you?"

Envy broke out in laughter. "You know, it's funny: it's not often people ask me the 'whats' and 'hows.' They usually just ask me *why*..." Venom dripped off that last word as he spoke it. A chilling silence filled the air for a second before he continued. "There's a little secret magic trick that you can do if you have enough blight in your body and you know the right runes. You see, Syd Alyad incurred life-threatening amounts of blight after he was revived. Using runes he discovered, he was able to tie his blight to his shadow and his shadow *stood up* on its own. That shadow is me. Only reason why I can take the appearance of others is because I'm a Sin."

"Pray tell, how am I similar to a demon?"

"I wanted a normal life at one point. Immediately after my birth, Syd tried to eliminate me. Poor soul didn't have the strength to do it, granted I wasn't a Sin at the time so I couldn't really kill him. I explained my goals were the same as his and we agreed to a ceasefire. I was always there with him, through everything. I saw his friends as my friends, but they would barely look in my direction. All because they saw me as some *freak*, kept around to be used as a tool. All my life, just living in his *shadow*," Envy seethed. "Until he sealed me of course, and now he's long dead."

Henry listened intently, trying to pick apart what might be lies and what might be the truth.

"That's why, Henry, it's important to know what you want. Because you can love others, you can be loved... But once all is said and done, you only have yourself to rely on. Just like how you are now. So, Henry, you awoke me from my slumber. You've put on a good show so far. How are you going to end it?"

Henry racked his brain for ideas.

"There's no way you're going to let that brat go, right? If not for him your father's debt wouldn't have increased. If not for him, you wouldn't have taken on that increased debt. If not for him, you wouldn't have even been assigned this mission!" Envy egged.

"You're right..." Henry muttered. "I've decided: I'll stick with my original plan. I'll pay off my debt and enjoy *crushing* them in the process."

****

The last light of Plexis' rays retreated across the still water of the pond like orange fingers letting go of their grasp on Lokyer's surface. Clara and Elizabeth sat in chairs on Sagittarius' wooden veranda on the lake. The roof had cute little orange lights around the perimeter that illuminated the wooden deck.

"Yo! What's good you two?" Paige asked as he and Dalton stepped out of Sagittarius' kitchen.

"Nothing really," Clara sighed. "How about yourselves? You guys get any sleep?"

"Yeah, like a baby!" Dalton groaned.

"Hey everyone," Amy greeted as she walked in. "Sorry if I'm late."

"N-no, not at all," Paige chuckled. "How's uh, how's your brother?"

"He's alive," Amy sighed. "He's doing better than my other one at least."

"Oh..."

"There's a lot to unpack there..." Dalton chuckled.

"Sorry, sorry! I didn't mean to get dark like that," Amy chuckled.

"Glad you called us together Paige," Elizabeth sighed. "Clara and I have some urgent matters to discuss as well."

"That's great, we can get to it any second now..."

Paige and the others looked back and finally, there was Monty dressed in sweats and a hoodie. His skin looked a little less pale, and the circles around his eyes a tiny bit less dark.

Looks like he finally got some sleep at least, Amy thought.

Monty looked around with his usual, blank, innocent expression. He held up a bag from the supermarket in his left hand and his pair of tongs in the other. "I brought meat and veggies for barbecuing, haha!" He clicked his tongs together a couple of times to emphasize the point.

Aw, he looks like a happy crab! Elizabeth thought.

Monty fired up the grill and the others settled in with sodas in their hands. Chairs gathered around in a semi-tight circle with the brazier and their food in front of them. A pot of rice was being cooked nearby.

"Clara and Elizabeth, I know you said you had something to say, but let me go first," Paige said.

How can I be firm with these people who are better than me? How can I earn respect from these people who are stronger than me? Luckily, the thing that this team needs, I can do perfectly. Lead by example, Paige! What this team needs is… he thought with a gulp.

"We need to talk everything out," Paige continued. "We're a team, and we barely know anything about each other. I've observed we're all struggling with something. Clara, you've been distant ever since Henry showed up, meanwhile, Elizabeth and Dalton went on a field trip. Monty, well, his secret is out of the bag, and Amy… that's not my liberty to say."

Be firm, Paige thought.

Paige turned toward the rest of the team. "As your captain, I'm asking you to trust my call-outs, my suggestions. I understand you're all capable, but what we need more than anything right now is to open up to each other. Show a little weakness. I've been constantly wondering why Sagittarius chose me as captain, and how we screwed up in the team-bonding exercise. I think the reason why is because he knows that I know what it's like to need to depend on teammates to succeed. We all need some of that–we need to not just work together, but *understand* each other. If we don't open up, how can we support each other? How can we be there for one another?"

Paige looked over to Dalton and Monty. "I've constantly cursed my own weakness. For as long as I can remember, I've looked at nothing but your backs, hoping that, one day, I could stand beside you. Be honest with me, all of you, what can I do to be a better captain?"

Monty and Dalton looked at each other before laughing.

"Bro, are you for real?" Dalton laughed.

Monty was shoveling food into his mouth. "You stand beside us all the time, do you need new glasses?"

"What? No, I meant figuratively."

"Who always pulled us out of trouble when we were kids? Who was the one who came up with the plan to send Envy packing?" Dalton asked.

"I've also still never beat you in any board game or video game..." Monty muttered, eating even more food.

"Dude, Monty, slow down my guy," Dalton whispered.

"I finally have an appetite for once, shut up," Monty muttered as he continued to eat.

"Who was the one who saved me from falling into the river?" Amy giggled.

They all watched Paige's expression peel back into a confused and embarrassed smile, the pink in his cheeks almost starting to glow. "For real? But–"

"Paige, you said that you always look at our backs. Well, we rely on you to watch our backs," Monty said.

"Not to mention, but your grades have always been higher than mine," Dalton chuckled.

"You haven't caught up on your homework yet, huh?" Elizabeth asked.

"No, have you?"

"No, we're in the same boat for once."

"Oh, thank gods we can suffer together."

Monty swallowed another bite. "In all truth though, Paige, if I didn't respect you as a leader, if I didn't trust you, the Eighth would be dead by now."

His cold tone sent chills down everyone's spines and a silence wooshed into the area.

"So thank you, for stopping me then."

"Y-yeh, for sure..."

Paige looked over at Amy who smiled as if to say, "See? I told you so."

"Oh, gods, it's going to be this soapy all night isn't it?" Elizabeth sighed. "If that's the case, you want to go next, Popsicle Prince?" She looked over at Dalton and gave a smile.

"I like it when Elizabeth is sassy," Monty laughed.

"No, please, ladies first," Dalton chuckled. "I *insist.*"

Elizabeth smirked, but her expression softened to a gentle smile before she continued. "When I was on my way to Greedlake–"

"Uh, by the way..."

Everyone turned to Amy who had a hand shyly raised.

"I still have no idea why you and Dalton were gone..."

"Ah, me either!" Monty chuckled.

"Dalton didn't tell me crap," Paige chimed.

Elizabeth looked over at Dalton who shrugged. "It wasn't my story to tell."

She sighed. "Okay, I'll give you the short version."

She told the group of the events that happened with Dalton jumping in here and there to dramatize some things to make the story more exciting.

"Dalton can tell you about it later," Elizabeth said.

Dalton shot Monty a look of seriousness and he nodded.

Elizabeth continued. "When I saw Dalton had followed me, I was really irritated at first."

"Hyeah, you shot me after all," Dalton grumbled between bites.

"Like I said: I was irritated. But, as time went on, looking back I… I probably wouldn't have come back without his help. As for all of you, I also didn't really trust anyone except for Clara. When it came down to the wire, I didn't expect any of you to follow through." Elizabeth sighed and looked at Paige. "Earlier, you were talking about how you felt you weren't capable as a leader. Back at the Sprawling Forest mission, I honestly thought that, but no Paige, have faith in yourself."

"Th-thanks…"

"Of course," Elizabeth smiled. "And so continuing with trust, I'd like to reintroduce myself." Elizabeth took off her beanie and twirled it on her pointer finger. "I am Elizabeth Asteria, the illegitimate child of King Charles and Rebecca Swan, eighth in line to the throne, and adopted daughter of Sam and Denise Baker. Please, continue to call me Elizabeth Baker."

She wiggled her golden ears atop her head and gave a wink.

"OMG, your ears are so cute!" Amy squealed.

Elizabeth blushed and was instinctively about to put her beanie back on before she stopped herself.

"So, wait, Elizabeth, those Chasm guys that were chasing us…"

"That's right, they were after me. Sorry, Paige."

"Like I said, it's no big deal, I'm sorry to hear about what happened to your mom. I've been there, and so have Monty and Amy. You aren't alone in this Elizabeth, we're here for you like you said."

"Thank you…" Elizabeth sniffled. "Okay Dalton, it's your turn."

"Right! Monty, Amy, Paige, you know I used to be a homeless orphan in Yankee before I met you, but you don't know of my grand tale of action, despair, drama, and betrayal!"

"Get to the point."

Dalton re-lived his moments in Yankee once again, and unlike Elizabeth who decided to keep her story quick and concise with only the important information, Dalton was extraneous and like Charles Dickens, went into far too much detail. However, he kept his crowd entertained with small reenactments like a poor game of charades and lively voice acting. After his story ended, his bright deposition left him, and his shoulders drooped a little.

"Paige, Monty, you guys always told me you didn't care about my accomplishments or how strong I was. That was a foreign concept to me. I always thought it was my fault that the Cinema Club was broken up. All I was good for was running away… I couldn't save anything. So, I didn't want the same thing to repeat when I met you guys. I wanted to show how awesome I was, even despite how crap my personality can be, I could be useful, I could be fun."

"Bro, Monty's personality is worse than yours man," Paige laughed.

"By a metric ton, I'd say," Amy added.

"Okay, unnecessary," Monty mumbled.

"Yeah, I get that. Sorry, I didn't realize sooner. You guys were trying to show me that you didn't care how powerful I was, you were friends with me because of me. Thank you… You guys coulda just straight up told me though…"

Monty felt a tight pain in his chest that he didn't know what to do with. He didn't know where to put it and it ended up flooding into his cheeks in the form of a blush.

"Don't actions speak louder than words? D-Dumbass…" Monty muttered, trying to be his usual snarky self, but was too flustered to keep his composure.

"But we did tell you… a lot, it just didn't get into your skull," Paige insisted.

"I never had the best grades, okay?"

"Yeah, d-dumbass…"

He's cute when he's flustered, Clara thought. *Duly noted…*

"Okay, who's turn is it next? Monty! Thank you for volunteering!" Dalton smiled. "I want to hear what *you* have to say, you big fat liar! I'm still mad at you by the way!"

"I know, I know," Monty sighed. "I'm sorry for hiding my blight from you all. It's come to my attention that hiding my worries and injuries doesn't make people worry less, that's my bad. All my life, all I could think about was finding the people who hurt Melody, who killed my mom and big brother. The reason I wanted to become a Prestige was solely for revenge. However, after talking with Amy and my other sister Monica…"

Monty and Amy looked at each other and nodded.

"We've decided to quit the Prestige Program," Monty finished.

A moment's pause.

"Wait, what?" Dalton asked.

"Why?" Clara asked.

"I can't use magic anymore. If I do, I die," Monty explained. "Besides, even if I have lost family, I still have you guys. So long as you are all safe, I could care less about what Penumbra is doing…"

"As for me," Amy began. "I've always hated fighting. When Monty started training with our big brother and uncle, I always gave extra effort to stay motivated. Admittedly, during our fights with Penumbra, I was so scared… I can't do anything but slow you guys down. Being a Prestige and fighting things is just not for me, so I'm quitting and applying for art school. I enjoy drawing so… I'd like to pursue that passion."

The six fell silent for a second before Clara spoke up.

"Well, if that's your choice go for it. No one will blame you for leaving, and I doubt anyone sees it as running away. Fighting isn't for everyone, and that's nothing to be ashamed about."

"Thanks, Clara…"

"So I guess I'm last, huh?" Clara sighed. "My family, like Paige's, is a long line of Celestian Knights until my mother switched things up and became a Prestige instead. She started her own Asterium Company with no support from family, nothing. She had to convince people that a *woman* was capable of running such a company," Clara scoffed. "After my father took over… I always had the impression that I needed to do the same with taking it back. I still believe that I need to take my company back for myself, but until I'm strong enough to do that, I'll be relying on you guys to help me… I'll stop trying to do everything myself, and accept the fact that, as much as I hate to say it, I can't do everything myself. Which leads to what Elizabeth and I needed to talk about."

Clara addressed the whole group this time: "Paige, mentioned that I had been distant lately. Monty, Amy, you've shown the same concern for me and I thank you. The reason why I've been so distant is because Henry threatened me.

"What?" Dalton asked.

"Amy, I am so sorry I turned my back on you during the attack on Cysko. It's been eating away at me ever since," Clara apologized. "If I had just helped you out, Monty's blight wouldn't have gotten worse."

"Clara," Amy said. "It's fine. Monty having blight was my fault in the first place."

"Amy, we talked about this," Monty said. "I–"

"It's okay," Amy interrupted. "I don't feel guilty or a burden or sorry. I'm just taking responsibility."

Monty gave a frustrated frown and reluctantly accepted her position.

"Okay, real quick, dial that back," Paige said.

A creak of wooden planks drew everyone's attention to Sagittarius, who was leaning on the open sliding door with his arms crossed. "Tell me everything…"

"Henry also confronted me," Elizabeth said. "It was that night when I came home soaking from the pond. He told me he was the Third Wing of Penumbra."

The revelation whipped the four into a state of shock and confusion. They sat with mouths agape, trying to process what they just heard.

"And he told *me* that he was responsible for the evolved signum on the final exam," Clara added.

"Woah, woah, woah, hold up…" Paige said, putting up his hands. "Why are you telling us this just now?"

"He threatened both of us," Elizabeth said. "He put me in some weird illusion that felt way too real for comfort… It's like he took my memory of the Frostflame Massacre and manifested it somehow after manipulating it. He found out I was an Asteria that way and threatened that if I told anyone, he would send Chasm after me and you and bring the rest of the Wings."

"He didn't put me in an illusion, but he did threaten me in a similar manner. If I was nice to Monty or any of you in any way, he would attack us," Clara said apologetically, stealing a glance at Monty who was still wide-eyed.

Paige stroked his chin, trying to piece together the puzzle. "How would he know you broke your promise? Some sort of magic that lets him know if someone breaks a promise?"

"That's the conclusion we came to," Elizabeth said. "I decided to break my promise, betting on Dalton's word that we could get through it with the right amount of help…"

"If what you said is true," Sagittarius began. "Henry knows you told somebody and we can expect all the other Wings to be coming after you all now."

"Not exactly," Clara said.

"What do you mean?"

"Henry probably thinks that Lizzy and I just told each other. As much as I hate him, he knows that I'd be too stubborn to rely on anyone else other than her, at least, that's what he thought."

"No, we can't know that for sure. That's overestimating his underestimation of us, no? We're dealing with a guy that can put people in illusions and control signum..." Paige trailed off.

He turned to Monty, whose expression was so cold it could have made snow itself feel like a campfire. The sensation shot down Paige's spine like a rolling wave of chills, but the expression left Monty's face and Paige entered a state of uneasy relief.

"So Henry was the one that hurt Melody that day..." Monty muttered.

"Monty..." Paige started.

"I know, and I agree," Monty sighed. I think we should tell the people at Runeseekers and even get the other Zodiacs involved. I care more about making sure we're safe than some grudge at this point."

"Good," Sagittarius nodded. "I'll call up the Dean, the Runeseekers, all the Zodiacs. We can plan an ambush as soon as possible."

"Is there any other info that you can give us?" Paige asked. "Was there some common pattern or something similar between your experiences?"

"He had us seal the deal with a handshake," Clara said.

"Oh! He did that with me too after he drove me home!" Dalton added.

"Hmm, that might be related to his illusions? Like he has to make contact with you to put you in the illusion? But what about how he controls signum? And where does he get the signum from?" Paige wondered.

"Those are questions for the Runeseekers and the Zodiacs, Paige," Sagittarius said, his Omnicard pressed to his ear. "Until we give the go-ahead, I don't want you six leaving the dorm, got it?"

"No, the dorm has been compromised," Clara said. "Henry knew about some things that were said in the dorm. He must have some sort of surveillance equipment in there, it could scare him off if we started looking for it."

"Aight then, you six are to stay here tonight then. Sorry, but bear with sleeping on the floor, play rock-paper-scissors for who gets the bed and sofa or something. I'm proud of you six. Don't go anywhere until I give you the okay."

****

Later that night, Dalton and Monty stood beside the shore of the pond, skipping rocks. Everyone else was already in bed, the bed having been given to Clara and Elizabeth to share and the sofa to Amy. Paige was sprawled out on the floor with a blanket and a pillow.

"Elizabeth didn't give the whole story, did she?" Monty asked.

"No, she didn't. Masamune found out I was half-demon, and with some convincing, that information was kept hidden. I told you guys an edited version back there. Here's the full picture…"

****

Dalton still had his eyes closed. The sunlight overhead was stinging them and the pounding of his heart against his chest was so loud in his ears that he couldn't hear Masamune walking up to him. But he could feel the burning sensation in his stomach as it shot up his throat and pooled in his mouth.

His eyes shot open and he coughed up blood like an erupting geyser. He looked down and saw a blade of light partly inside him. The burning wouldn't stop and he screamed out in pain, tears starting to stream from his eyes. He tried desperately to move, but couldn't do anything but grimace. His demon form kicked back in and his horns, tail, and fangs sprouted quickly and his eyes sparked yellow.

"Oh, so your blood is red, huh?" Masamune chuckled. "Just what are you, demon?"

"I-I… I'm only… half…" Dalton rasped weakily, his strength leaving his body even more.

Masamune raised a brow and made the sword vanish. He sat down cross-legged next to Dalton and his gaze was shifted to the horizon. "Recover enough strength to talk. Then, tell me everything."

Dalton healed the hole in his stomach while he told Masamune everything. All the way from his time in Yankee to now.

Masamune laughed, his shoulders bouncing up and down a little. "You were that brat from Yankee? Oh, man!" He reared his head back. "Leo is going to love hearing this!"

Great... Dalton thought.

"So you know nothing about your father?" Masamune asked.

"Other than the fact that he killed Elizabeth's mom and that he's a lich? No, not really."

"Your father was actually a part of a Prestige team called Majestic. It's a team that bears an uncanny similarity to yours," Masamune grumbled. "Vega Cruz, Vayne Aimer, Miles Tovera, Kaze Amachi, Floyd Ford, and Xan Kahau. After the team broke up, Vega started training me, Damian Violet, and Clairise Bernardino." Masamune chuckled. "Although, I'm stronger than any of those people now."

"If you're so strong, why not just march into the Barren Lands and kill Vayne yourself?" Dalton asked.

Masamune broke out into laughter once more. "Don't get ahead of yourself, brat. I've been to that realm of ice. Vayne himself isn't the problem, it's his army. Take your clones and amplify them. Your clones share some of that necromancy your father possesses. However, whoever your father kills, he can take that person's battle experience and put it into his soldiers. When you're fighting against eight members of the Asteria family and several other Prestiges, it starts to get taxing."

"Oh..." Dalton muttered. *Is he that strong?*

"Does the girl know?"

Dalton sighed. "No, she doesn't know about it. Only me, you, the Dean, Taro, Sagittarius, and Monterey Cruz know about it. Oh, and Envy and Penumb–oh gods they can use that as leverage."

"Calm down," Masamune sighed. "The Magistracy and Celestian Order aren't going to believe in a Penumbra member." He got up and brushed the dirt off his pants. "I'll go get the stray cat. Stay here."

"Wait!"

Masamune stopped and gave him an impatient glare.

"I want to heal up some more before she comes. It'd be kinda awkward if she found out I broke all these bones and healed them in a couple of days."

"I hate lies and deception."

"That's something we can agree upon," Dalton groaned as he sat up. "But I'm not ready for her to find out just yet. Please, just a little longer."

Masamune growled and sat back down. "We'll just stay in place and let her find us..."

"Thank you."

"It's less work for me. I'll just take a little nap while we wait," Masamune yawned and laid down.

"Hey... if you could just one shot me like that, why not just take the Scroll right off the bat?"

"When my opponents are weaker than me, I like to play a game," Masamune explained. "I start at zero effort and see how much it takes to beat them."

"How much effort did we make you use?"

"I'd say about fifteen percent."

"That's so arbitrary," Dalton chuckled.

"The number is just for me to understand, not anyone else. Just get some sleep already," he yawned.

Dalton decided to do the same, and let his body focus on healing. After a couple of hours or so, Dalton was woken up by a kick to the face.

"Ow!" he exclaimed, nearly sitting up, but that hurt too, so now he was in double the pain and laid back down.

"She's down the street, it was time to wake up. Our story is that I ended you with one punch to the face and you blacked out," Masamune said.

"Not very glorifying."

"You're the one who wants to lie."

"Yeah..."

After another minute, Dalton heard hurried footsteps and the sliding of gravel as Elizabeth skidded to a halt and knelt beside him. Behind her worried expression, he could see that the sky had turned from bright blue from when they arrived to hues of orange and indigo.

"Are you okay?" Elizabeth asked worriedly. "I thought Masamune killed you."

He did a quick assessment of his body. *Everything is still really sore, but I think most of the broken bones have healed by now.*

"Yeah, well," Dalton rolled his eyes. "He almost did."

"We need to talk," Masamune said grumpily. "Take a seat next to your boyfriend."

"Wha-" Elizabeth blushed. "We aren't–"

He gave an irritated sigh. "Look, Elizabeth, you hate Vayne, right?"

"Of course I do."

"Well, I don't blame you," Masamune said. "But get rid of any notion of revenge that may be in your head."

"Why no–"

"Don't interrupt me!"

Elizabeth's ears went limp and she relaxed, slouching over a little bit.

"You're a long way away from being strong enough to hunt down Vayne," Masamune said. "If you could only take me on at fifteen percent of my power, there's no way you can stand up to Vayne."

"Then why are you going after him?"

"He has something I want," Masamune explained. A hint of melancholy washed across his face, only to leave in an instant. "Plus, I'm strong enough to not get myself killed." Masamune looked over to Dalton and smiled. "Besides, you have plenty of purpose elsewhere. Just enjoy your friends while you still have them."

"So you're saying I should just give up because I have friends? My only other goal in life is to keep the Scroll out of people's hands!"

"Speaking of the Scroll..." Masamune held out his hand. "Hand it over."

Elizabeth gulped and her body language gave off the feeling that she was ready to spring and attack or flee in a second's notice.

Masamune gave a tired sigh. "*Look.* I'm not like the rest of those idiots in the family. I won't let anyone have the Scroll that I don't find worthy of it."

Elizabeth gave a suspicious and frustrated look, looking back and forth between his hand and his eyes.

"Fine..." Elizabeth growled and tossed him the Scroll.

Masamune caught it and put it in his coat pocket.

"You finally get your wish. You finally get your Scroll."

Masamune paused, looking confused before bursting into laughter. "You pathetic little thing! I have no need for the family's Sword Techniques. I will continue to overpower them without them."

"Then why do you want the Scroll so badly?"

"To spite them. And hey, they're pissed at you for taking it, but now they'll draw their attention to me. You're welcome."

"You're just fine with me telling them that you have it?" Elizabeth asked.

"Of course!" Masamune scoffed. "What're *they* going to do?"

He started to walk away, but Dalton stopped him: "Wait, what even is Vayne?"

"I wasn't told the details. Vega was going on a mission to rescue him in the Barren Lands, and I begged for him to bring me along. He let me come, and we traveled for months before finally finding him as his natural self. He was currently chasing some demons, the ones from Alright Guys?"

Small world, Dalton thought.

"We got separated and I nearly died fighting off one of them. When I got back, I saw the demons were gone (they apparently escaped) and Vayne was plunging his sword into Vega's stomach. He transformed into that armored menace you saw that day and summoned the Knights of Asteria he acquired from the Massacre. Vega was encased in a pillar of ice, and I was pursued across the glacial wasteland, surviving on scraps and fighting off his minions until I finally escaped. Vayne's magic was being able to commune with spirits and absorb them temporarily to get their powers. I suppose he absorbed something foul and ended up betraying us."

Dalton frowned and everyone fell silent. Masamune grew impatient and sighed.

"If you don't have any more questions, I'm leaving." Masamune turned around and walked outside. "Also, you don't need to worry about the family learning about your presence when you use Chrono Control. Everyone who's had it, has decided to keep it a secret."

"I can only imagine why," Elizabeth said as she rolled her eyes. "Hey wait, how did you get my Chirp I.D.?"

"I don't have an Omnicard," Masamune said. "I heard about you from Kaze and a blonde brat told me to meet you here."

Elizabeth and Dalton looked at each other. "Blonde brat?"

Masamune's shadow leapt to life in the form of a dragon that licked its jaws and shook its head, as if it had been sleeping. He straddled it and it spread its wings.

"Anyway, give Taro a call. He'll teleport you back," Masamune said. "

And with that, the dragon launched into the sky in a black and pink flash. Elizabeth pulled her Omnicard out of her pocket and tried to turn it on. No good.

"Uh... Dalton..."

"Yeah?"

"Is your Omincard dead?"

"Yeah, it died last night. Why?"

"Welp mine is too. And I'm out of shock isotope."

"Oh... Well at least we have each other~"

"Dalton..."

"Yeah, okay this is bad..."

****

"So I guess your father is still M.I.A," Dalton said. "Sorry about that man."

"Well, he may as well have been dead to me anyway," Monty sighed. "You have it tougher than me when it comes to parents."

"Yeah, well, the harder part is keeping this demon crap a secret from everybody."

"Is there anything else to note?"

"Yeah, the Dean."

"What about the Dean?"

"Just who is he?"

"How should I know?"

"Our team is literally directly related to the nine people Masamune mentioned. And you remember how we saw that he looked different that one time?"

Monty recalled seeing the Dean as a tan young man with silver hair and eyes and pointy ears.

"Yeah... Well, he hasn't done anything bad yet. In fact, he made sure we didn't have any real consequences after taking down that casino."

"Yeah, you're right. Come on. Let's head back to the others."

13: Moving Pieces

The end of Henry's day was lovely. He was getting ready for bed when he heard the ringtone of his Omnicard. The Chirp I.D. was unknown.

"Hello?" Henry asked.

"It's me," the First said. His voice was cold and stern.

"How are you doing, boss?" Henry asked.

"There's been a change of plan. We need the one called Monterey Cruz alive. The rest you can go ahead and kill."

Henry's smile faded from his face. Even Envy, who was sitting in a nearby chair and reading a book, felt a chill go down his spine.

"Why do we suddenly need him alive–*if* you don't mind me asking?"

"Our allies need him alive. He might have some valuable information that they want to interrogate him for. They didn't fill me in on the details either."

Henry puffed his cheeks and clenched his free hand before pacing in a circle. "What could he possibly have that they would care for?" His voice trembled, his composure threatening to break loose at any second.

"Know your place, Henry. It is not your job to question me, but to follow my orders. You've had your fun, now it's time to get the job done."

"But I *am* getting it done!"

"You're clearly not. None of the six, now five, targets are dead. Which, I suppose I should be thanking you for your incompetence this time."

"But–"

"I'm having the rest of the Wings stay to make sure the target is captured. They've stressed his importance to me and I have an obligation to comply."

"I can handle it myself!"

"Watch your tongue! You're lucky I'm not giving your baton to someone else for this mission!"

Henry closed his mouth and nearly bit his tongue. After a moment's pause, he spoke: "I understand. I'll get it done at the Azure Festival in accordance with our ongoing operation."

"Good. After this, I want you back in Yankee. I still think you're ready for bigger and better things Henry. Don't make me wrong."

The First hung up.

Henry ground his teeth together. *Damn it! Damn it! Damn it! All they do is take! Take! Take! Take! TAKE!!! Screw your plans for me!*

Henry looked at the two cards that had appeared in his hand yesterday. He gave a little chuckle that grew louder and louder until he was laughing with tears running down his face. He squeezed the cards in his hand to make a fist and pounded the mirror in front of him. Over, and over, and over. Finally, he slammed his head into it and pulled away. Blood began to slowly trickle down his face.

He looked at himself in the mirror, his face so contorted with fury that it almost tired him out to keep the expression. But internally, he was in an odd state of clarity, as if the pieces of a jigsaw puzzle fell into place.

"They don't fear me, do they? Well, I'll show them… I'll make them *suffer!*" Henry spat. *That girl, the one I attacked that day… she was alive and well at that hospital!* Henry couldn't help but think of his mother. *Why? Why does Monty's friend live and my mother dies?! Why is his love reciprocated while mine is thrown in the garbage?! He doesn't deserve a happy ending! HE PUT FATHER IN PRISON! HE MADE HIM USELESS! IF HE DIDN'T EXIST, I'D BE OUT BY NOW!!!*

"Envy…" Henry murmured.

"Yes?" Envy asked, deeply intrigued by Henry's actions.

Henry whipped his hair back and wiped the blood off his face. "I am going to make Monty and Clara suffer as much as I have. I'm going to make their friends suffer at their feet as they helplessly watch. Then, it'll be their turn."

"I love it!" Envy cackled. "You're betraying Penumbra?"

Henry nodded with a twisted smirk. "That's right. I'll take them all on! It's impossible to run away from them anyway!"

Envy wrapped his arm over Henry's shoulders. "That's it! That's what I'm talking about! You're already too late for saving! If you're going to suffer anyway, might as well spread the wealth. *Do what you want to do.*"

"If I don't get to have a happy ending, they don't get one either…"

****

Henry received a call from the Dean's office the next morning just as Plexis itself was breaking over the horizon. He took the first bus of the day to the Space Tower whose peak still pierced the clouds like a plow through snow. Henry hurried through the shroud of drizzle that surrounded the building and brushed off the droplets as he went inside.

If you ask me, that's a design flaw, he thought.

The center lobby was surprisingly bland in comparison to the building's exterior. Across the open space was a corridor that led to offices found on the bottom floor as well as conference rooms and a cafeteria. A waiting area with a tv playing the news with couches facing it.

"If you are just joining us, several nights ago, Penumbra Wings successfully broke out hundreds of prisoners from Bandit Doldrum, including the Eighth Wing Craig Powell. Two Chasm legions have been deployed in Ayo to help in finding the escapees," a news anchor reported.

B-roll of Archangels helping rebuild the prison and foot soldiers on the ground with anti-magic exosuits were going through the city streets. Even Slipstream hovercraft were hovering around the outskirts of the city. They were medium-sized attack hovercraft with two wings. Each wing had a large hole in it with a ring that could rotate three-hundred and sixty degrees. The rings were powered by gale isotope and shot forth large blasts of wind that let the vehicle hover, turn, and ascend or descend. Each was equipped with a searchlight, two arcane cannons like what the Archangels had, and a stock of missiles on each wing.

Inside there could be a pilot and a co-pilot in the canopy with enough space to store some equipment like ammunition. On the sides of the body were two large sliding doors with four seats inside for soldiers.

Heh, that's right morons. You go after the nobody criminals and let me have my fun, Henry chuckled.

It switched to the Archon of Ayo: Cameron Sala, a tan man with black hair. "This is inexcusable and we urge our people to remain indoors while Chasm does their job. While we didn't exactly ask for reinforcements, we welcome them with open arms."

It switched to Jiro, who was visibly shaken and worn out. "I have failed you as a Zodiac Guardian and I will do everything in my power to get these guys back behind bars. If you have any concerns or reports, my door is always open. Pisces will also be helping me with containing this catastrophe, and I thank them from the bottom of my heart."

"Mr. Preston?" a woman's voice asked.

Henry turned and smiled. "Yes?"

"The Dean is ready to see you now."

Henry followed her to the elevator and took it to the top floor. An intricate hallway led to a small lobby and from there you could go to the

Dean's private quarters which were guarded by a door with a passcode, or his office, where he was waiting.

"May I come in?" Henry asked, knocking on the open door.

"Ah, yes! Take a seat!" the Dean said, clearing his desk before getting up and getting some tea. "Would you like some tea?"

"Sure, thank you very much."

The Dean poured Henry his cup before pouring his own. Henry paid close attention to his movements, to every minute detail. *He's not letting his hands get close to mine...*

"So why the sudden summons, Mr. Mozaveen?" Henry asked.

The Dean sighed and leaned back in his chair. He held his mug in his hands and firmly placed his feet on his desk, making the papers and monitors bounce. Even Henry was surprised at the aggressive action. The Dean gave a twisted smile and said: "You messed up." He took a sip.

"Excuse me?" Henry asked.

"I said: you messed up Henry Preston, Third Wing of Penumbra."

****

At the Runeseekers office, Kaze, Taro, Miles, Sol, Sagittarius, and Jiro sat at a table, frustrated.

"Damn it!" Jiro cursed, slamming his fist on the table. "Were we seriously not sneaky enough?! Is Runeseekers bugged too? Or is someone here a traitor?"

"Take it easy," Sol said. "Chasm officers will be looking all over the west coast for him now that we've identified him as a Wing. We'll find him in due time."

"Just more stuff on my plate," Jiro groaned.

"No, I got him," Sagittarius said. "If he wishes to do harm to my students, the responsibility is mine."

A loud crash sent all of their attention to the front door, and Masamune barged in. "The Dean can't be trusted..."

****

Henry sat stunned while the Dean kept smiling. *How does he know? Did Elizabeth tell them? Did Clara? There's no way, right? Those two only trust themselves!*

"Whatever are you talking about Mr. Mozaveen? I'm not–"

The Dean ignored him. "Now, you must be scratching your brain, wondering how I know," the Dean chuckled. "And the most obvious conclusion to reach would be that you underestimated them and Elizabeth and Clara told the rest of Prism who told Sagittarius who told me. Which, then, you'd only be half right."

Henry was still stunned. He didn't know what to do. *My cover is already blown, do I just do it now? But nothing is in place yet! We'd be a month ahead of schedule!*

"Oh come now Mr. Preston," the Dean sighed. "Relax, no need to keep appearances up. Let loose. It's only you and me up here and there's no cameras or microphones."

Henry's expression slowly turned into one of suspicion. His hand slowly started going to his pocket and he leaned back, ready to run at a moment's notice.

"What do you mean I'm only half right?"

"Well, because I've already known for some time now," the Dean laughed. "How peculiar that you transferred into the same homeroom as my students *on the same day* as they did. I've followed your every action since you got here."

"What's your game then?" Henry chuckled. He gulped and he could feel sweat start to drip like an insect crawling across his skin.

"That's actually my question to you! Because you see, Chasm officers are raiding your apartment as we speak! As well as the Runeseekers and two Zodiacs. You've been here for over a month now and only really started to make moves a little over a week ago with the whole field trip to Greedlake. Now, you'd be behind bars and the Wings would be *really* pissed that you got caught if not for me summoning you here."

"Wait, so you called me out this early–"

"Precisely," the Dean smiled. "Does that convince you enough that I'm here to negotiate?"

"What do you want?" Henry gulped.

"You see, my students love to get themselves into trouble. So, inevitably, they attracted the wrong type of attention, especially if they're sending all of the Wings to the west coast, to my knowledge at least, as made evident by that prison break. I brought them to Atlas so I could keep watch over them, but just like how they told me that you were a Wing, they told me their plans for the future, and now two of my students are planning on quitting." The Dean got up and leaned over the table with a menacing glare that nearly made Henry shiver. "And that is not in my best interest." The Dean stepped back and straightened his tie. "It seems telling them to live a normal life so they wouldn't get into trouble has backfired slightly. I need someone to give them a little... motivation. Perhaps some more family members dying would do the trick."

"If you know so much, then surely you know I mean to kill them?" Henry chuckled.

"I do. And I'm fine with that. If they can't overcome an obstacle like you, then they weren't the kind of caliber I was looking for in the first place." The Dean swished his tea around before taking another sip. "Oh, I don't doubt your strength. Surely some sacrifices will need to be made on their side which will hopefully relight their vigor, so here's my proposition to you Mr. Preston."

The Dean turned his back to Henry and looked out across Atlas. "I'm giving you a second life. You will be able to seek asylum in my quarters and remain hidden here for however long you need to conduct whatever plan you want to do. I will be your little minion and make all the preparations you need while my students act like little chickens and stuff themselves with peaceful living and drop their guards. Then, you will execute your plan and try to kill my students. Of course, if it comes down to it, I *will* stop you and save their lives, but I'm at least giving you a shot at it. Sound like a deal?"

"Yeah, sure," Henry gulped. "That's perfect actually."

"Now, before we seal it, I want to clarify: if you backstab me before you execute your master plan, I will not hesitate to do the same to you. Okay?"

"Right."

"Good! And given the info I have on your ability, you can tell if I break my end of the bargain, and I'm smart enough to know if you break yours. So go ahead and take the guest room, the passcode is five, seven, zero, six, five, zero, one. Get comfy because you're not leaving that room for a while. I have some errands to run, and when I get back you'll tell me exactly what you need. Toodles!"

Henry found himself alone in a deafening silence. It was too humorous, he couldn't help but smirk. *Let the games begin then...*

The Dean stepped outside and looked at the cloudy skies. A smirk went across his face before he hummed a happy tune and walked into the city.

You've had your fun my students, but now… now, it's time to take leaps and strides towards your destinies… You six are meant for so much more…

To be continued in Prism, Vol. 3!

Afterword

Hey, Brandon here!

You may have noticed that the style has changed from the first volume (or maybe you didn't and will only now see it that I pointed it out). That's because the first volume is actually the most recently written. By the time I finished volume 3, I looked back and saw that volume 1 was not up to par, so I ended up rewriting it.

Funnily enough, I find myself wanting to rewrite this volume again too, but alas, I am satisfied with where it is at. I hope it was just as enjoyable as the first volume.

I feel like the world of Lokyer also begins to open up a bit more in this volume as you meet the other characters of the Runeseekers, like Masamune. I hope they were good additions to the story!

As always, thank you to my family and friends for keeping me going and supporting me on my author journey.

Volume 3 is a wild rollercoaster ride. I seriously can't wait to share it with you all. I hope you can wait until then. Talk to you again soon.

www.ingramcontent.com/pod-product-compliance
Lightning Source LLC
LaVergne TN
LVHW041925090826
845145LV00015B/687

* 9 7 8 1 7 3 3 1 3 6 2 5 9 *